'Mark Blayney explores with an audacious imagination and stylistic brio the uncertain border between reality and illusion, identity and its dissolution, and the fragility of love. Full of surprises, this is a fine collection.'

D. M. THOMAS

'Absolutely brilliant stories… a fascinating style, and a cunning way of manipulating us into believing one thing which in reality is something quite different. Short stories are not easy to tell; they need a patient, well-trained mind to leave us always wanting to know what comes after – I was gripped.'

VICTOR PEMBERTON

'Fluently contriving to intrigue, amuse, surprise and unsettle all at once, these highly entertaining stories address the reader in a sharp, kinetic prose which is wide-awake to the ironies of life and the radical uncertainty of things, and they pull it off with a confidence and verve that make this collection a cracking good read.'

LINDSAY CLARKE

Mark Blayney won the Somerset Maugham Prize for *Two Kinds of Silence*. His story 'The Murder of Dylan Thomas' was a Seren Short Story of the Month and he's published poems and stories in *Agenda*, *Poetry Wales*, *The Interpreter's House*, *The London Magazine* and *the delinquent*. His second book *Conversations with Magic Stones* was described by John Bayley as 'remarkable... as good as some of the best of Elizabeth Bowen's, and praise does not go higher than that.' Mark performs comedy as well as MCing regularly and his new one-man show *Be your own life-coach... with ABBA* tours this year.

DOPPELGANGERS

Mark Blayney

PARTHIAN

Parthian
The Old Surgery
Napier Street
Cardigan
SA43 1ED

www.parthianbooks.com

Published with the financial support of the Welsh Books Council.

First published in 2015

ISBN 978-1-910409-68-8

Edited by Claire Houguez
Cover Design by Robert Harries
Typeset by Claire Houguez
Printed and bound by Gomer Press, Llandysul

British Library Cataloguing in Publication Data

A cataloguing record for this book is available from the British
Library.

For Tom

Contents

The Murder of Dylan Thomas

This is a memoir of a strange town, and of how my first attempts to become a journalist were shaped and eroded there. I was sent to cover a minor scandal, in the last days of newspapers, when the oldies fretted about how news was going to survive when everyone expected to read everything for free on the net. It didn't occur to us how it would actually go: that within a few years there would be two or three publishers and everything would be syndicated. The three guys at the top own everything, the national papers run the local papers; and the locals are essentially county papers, with a tailored front page for the town or village.

Now I'm old it's strange to look back. I certainly didn't realise then, as a gauche eighteen year old, how influential that weekend would be or how much I would think about it over the following decades of my life. These days there's no monetary value in a memoir like this. I'm writing it for my own pleasure, and that's what writing should be.

I was sent as a cub reporter; how quaint, centuries-old, that expression sounds now. The scandal wasn't very interesting. Man buys restaurant and everything goes tits up; nothing more. The only reason it was in the papers was that the man happened to be a celebrity. I covered the story in the space of an afternoon, because everyone in the town seemed to know every detail and it wasn't hard to email back a competent report by evening. But I was there for the weekend, and the editor told me to stay and enjoy myself. My hotel was paid for and the train was booked for Monday. At the time I thought this exceptionally generous, and it's only later I realised it would have cost a lot of money to change the train ticket all the way back to London, so it was easier to leave me where I was.

So I stayed and was glad I did, because what I discovered was far more interesting. The first draft of anything is shit, Ernest Hemingway once wrote, and that's why I've written and re-written these pages until I no longer have any recollection of which parts are true, and which are the inventions that now seem real because I've reworked them so many times. (You know what journalists are like.) I appreciate this is of little benefit to you as the reader – you want to know the truth, as long as I cut out the boring bits. But that's how it is, so at least in saying this much I'm being as truthful as I can be.

My hotel, Seaview, had once been the home of Dylan Thomas. I didn't know who he was because we didn't get taught him at school, and I quickly became embarrassed at my lack of knowledge, as everyone in the town seemed to be talking about him. The flashes of conversation as I walked by the castle, along the estuary and beside the grand Georgian houses, were almost always about the same thing. *Have you been down to the boathouse yet?* And, *This was the pub where he would drink, and write.*

It was, as hotels were in those days, simply furnished and spacious. Dark wood, I remember. Or was it light? I should have taken pictures. I remember the outside, anyway: canary yellow, and although it had been renovated only a couple of years before, damp was discolouring the facade, breaking through as if insistent that the rough and ready of the house had to be on display, despite all attempts to paper it over.

Pictures of Dylan and his wife leaning in to each other, eyes closed, clinging on to the other's frayed clothing. They possessed nothing, said the owner at breakfast as I looked at the photos. He had one suit, which was covered with ink. He only owned what he needed – a roof over his head, paper, pen. His only real possession was a bicycle.

They were always drunk, my bearded friend added, nodding towards the pictures. They look drunk, don't they?

They did, they looked very drunk. I ate breakfast, which was huge. The eggs were mesmerisingly glossy. I looked at the estuary and marvelled at the silence. Yes, you could write here. My room was in the attic, tiny but immaculate. I remember the wooden struts holding it all together in elegant triangles.

The boathouse where Thomas lived for the last few years of his life propagated the legend. Everything was boxed behind glass, preserved, stuffed, the way it is in museums. A set of cufflinks – the only ones he ever had, and true to form he gave them away. A video on a loop described in rhythmic, bassooned Welsh vowels how, on the night he died at thirty-nine he'd declared, *I've just had eighteen straight whiskies, I think that's the record*. An elderly woman in front of me gasped.

Later I saw her with the rest of her party, boarding a yellow coach. How much do you have to drink, I wondered, to collapse into a coma and die so young? The coach chugged to itself like an impatient cat as it waited to be off.

According to the iPad, he spent so much time in Browns pub that he gave their phone number as his own. I was surprised to see it open for business, as the iPad said it was closed. I realised as I stepped through the door that it may have just re-opened; the marble tiles on the floor were brand new and it smelled of paint.

Pushing the door to the left, the room was covered in dustsheets. Maybe it's still closed after all. But the owner, sat behind a curvy desk imported from a sci-fi film, jumped up and assured me that the bar on the right was serving; they were just making the final preparations for the hotel. You can never get a meal in this town if you haven't booked, she said, so we're pretty excited about it.

The bar was, I remember, dusty and dark and full of old men. Or maybe it was light and airy, full of cushions and bold, colourful pictures. There was someone smoking a pipe, but that must have been someone outside, or perhaps he didn't have any tobacco in the pipe, as this was several years after the smoking ban.

My only real recollection of people smoking in pubs is my dad, lighting one of his last cigarettes and looking gloomily at the door, saying, I'm not going to be allowed to do this next week. I was about twelve at the time. It was the greatest affront he could think of. That faraway people, who knew nothing about him, could decide that he, who just wanted to sit by a window and smoke and watch the world go by with his pint, could no longer do so.

This distant act compressed all his fury about government, society, employment and capitalism into one angry red light, flaring and crackling, stubbed hard into a ceramic bowl that would soon be whisked away and piled up with others in a skip. It didn't matter, he died a few weeks later.

An attractive young man behind the bar served me a shy coffee, blushing as he spilt the milk. Some men at the side table looked at me. Japanese tourists in colourful, see-through macs, even though it wasn't raining, appeared in the doorway. They wanted to know where he wrote, where he drank.

He sat by the window, the young barman piped up. There was now a curved seat, which didn't look the best place to write. Click. The tourists took souvenirs. Click. Against the light their macs made them transparent like sweet wrappers; purple, pink, green.

A man took pictures of me; he said my hair looked good against the wood and would I mind sitting by the window. His English was excellent, and when I told him so he looked embarrassed. You are very kind.

I took my cup and saucer to the bar. There was a swirl like a question mark at the bottom of the cup. Do you want to come to a party? the barman asked. I nodded. It's tomorrow, he said, there's a big wedding going on. Everyone's going. I can't go to a wedding, I said. He said don't worry about it, it's the evening, not the wedding itself. You can be my plus one. He poured me a glass of ale, which I couldn't drink.

Dressing, I watched a steady stream of people make their way down to the chapel. Fuchsia pinks, lemon yellows, sunset oranges; it was as if they had been painted against the blobby green marsh of the estuary. Above it all loomed the wood, dark and impenetrable, and heavy clouds lying across the trees, though it did not rain. I ran down the stairs and through the heavy door and the owner came down the steps after me, asking didn't I want breakfast. I shook my head and smiled and he rubbed his hands on a teatowel. The air was fresh, I had never known air like it. I combed it through my fingers.

Down the narrow alley, past the bright blue house and imagining leaping from bench to bench. The tide was out and mudbanks lay exposed like naked shins. There were torpedo sounds; birds breaking the water and diving underneath for fish maybe. Staying to watch, I saw the sound was actually formed by slabs of sand dropping into the water.

I felt my energy ebb as I considered this happening every day. The tide washes in and smoothes the sand like silk. It drains and the sandbanks are perfect, vast wedges of caramel chocolate. Over the rest of the day, the sand falls into the water, kilo by kilo. Birds pick around it curiously, startled when a block drops. At the end of the day, the whole process starts again. The pointlessness of it, and its scale, made me queasy.

More wedding guests processed. Most were smartly dressed but some were raffish. Top hats and tails found in mouldering attics; long coats with buttons on the back; thick tweeds and heavy fabrics that we don't make nowadays, and even then the inhabitants seemed out of place, moving slowly, pretending to be in a film. Some in bowler hats, flexing the wings of their long coats like cormorants. In my jeans and t-shirt I didn't think I would fit in, but Richard assured me the evening would be very laid-back.

Bells rang. I sat outside the chapel and the wild flowers nodded, confirming their approval in the wind. They did not find just cause or impediment, and expressed a leaf-shrugging acceptance that you can do what you like, if you're not troubling anyone else. I liked their philosophy.

Someone on the bench opposite me read a newspaper; there was nothing on the front about my story, which I found a good sign. Robert emerged from the chapel and put his arms round me. I turned but he put a finger over his lips. I've crept out, he said, I don't do churches. We walked back into town. All that ceremonial stuff, he said, and have you ever noticed how weddings go on about death?

I shook my head. It's all, till you shuffle off the coil, joining everyone else, the majority of people are dead, you're just the current few who happen to be alive at the moment but it won't be for long. It's bizarre, he said, stopping on the path and sticking his hands in his pockets. You'd think a wedding would be about life, about celebrating living. But it really isn't. You keep being given this reminder, smacking you round the head every five minutes just as you think the church is finally giving you permission to be happy.

The streets were empty. We ate our own sandwiches in the pub and stole the wine glasses when we had finished. Come on, he said. Richard, not Robert. We sat by the castle and watched the waves lapping the edge of the car park. The tide comes in quickly, the path floods at neap tides, he said. The posts marking the lane where cars could pass were half-submerged.

The reception was in a pink Georgian house by the river. It's very impressive, I said as we went in. I felt like an impostor.

Yes it is, an old man with a gigantic moustache declared, leaping from behind a pot plant. The houses aren't Welsh, he told me, as if convinced I was about to argue with him. No, no, no, they aren't Welsh. This town isn't Welsh, he concluded victoriously. I looked confusedly towards Robert for help but he shrugged. It's in the depths of west Wales, I thought, how can it not be Welsh?

As if guessing what I was thinking, moustache man squared up in front of me. It's surrounded by Wales, but it isn't Wales.

Okay, I said nervously. First law of journalism: agree with whatever the other person is saying.

You go to the castle, he said.

Right.

Lots of signs saying that the Welsh took the town, but then they lost it again.

I see…

So who were they taking it from, hmm? He looked at me, expecting an answer. When I said nothing he continued. And think about the use of the word they. It's not written from a Welsh point of view. This town is a republic. We quite like them really, but no one speaks Welsh, do they? He didn't pause long enough for a reply. No one has a Welsh accent, hmm?

I haven't been here long enough to—

We have our own Parliament. Like the Isle of Man.

Really?

The Portreeve runs this town, I'll introduce you if you like. We set our own rules. Nothing to do with anyone else. It's pretty remote, he said, leaning into me and revealing some cracked, blackish teeth. His moustache twitched. Don't often get people up from London.

I'm not from—

And if we do, they don't do well.

We don't want to be late, said Robert, taking my arm and leading me gently away. Don't mind him.

Is he the only person in the town not invited? I asked.

Everyone's invited, he said, affronted. I slipped my arm into his and he did not resist. Mind you, he added as we slipped through arched doorways, he's the only one who probably won't come.

Cake. Some miniature houses, perfect as models, made of iced sugar and planted in paper cups. I was given a glass of champagne and welcomed enthusiastically. The wine made me dizzy and the welcome seemed unreal. Dancing couples.

Music travelled along wires and through speakers

planted in unlikely places. A child under a table, in an enormous white silk skirt which ballooned up in front of her. A smaller child crawled out from beneath it. A marble statue in the corner; a woman with no top on. One of the boys, about nine he was, stood behind it and snaked a hand up and a cupped a breast. The statue ignored him poshly, a glazed look on her face.

I was introduced to a relative but had yet to see the bride or groom amongst the bustle. Adam, he said, shaking my hand briskly. There were small black hairs gnawing their way over his hands, over the knuckles, the backs of the fingers even. He had very square, very white fingernails. First law of journalism: notice the details. He looked at a picture of Dylan on the wall, young and uncertain, mouth slightly open. Terrible man, he said. The way he treated his wife. Women left right and centre. And Caitlin at home, bringing up three children, and not a bean to live on, because he drank every penny.

Why is he so famous? I asked. Adam looked at me as if I'd asked why his trousers had two legs. I mean, poets don't become famous, I continued. Pop stars, yes, but not poets. Yet everyone here seems to know who he is – was, he's been dead sixty years.

He was a visionary, said Adam, glancing at the picture and Dylan raised his eyebrows in mute recognition. He was like Blake; you know Blake?

I shook my head.

Don't know what they teach kids these days.

They teach us skills, I said. Useful things, for the real world.

Oh, *that*.

Dylan's portrait nodded to Adam, encouraged him to continue, fill the void. He saw through things, Adam said. He saw what was underneath.

I heard he was a sex-mad alcoholic, I replied, just to provoke. First law of journalism, generate an interesting answer.

Adam shrugged. He was a writer, of course he was a sex-mad alcoholic.

Underneath, I wondered. What is underneath?

But Adam was off, as a waiter gleamed past with a tray full of shining glasses, the wine green and sparkly, and I never found him to get my answer.

Tight t-shirt, he said, I can see your breasts. I breathed and said nothing. Slim-hipped, he said, pink jeans like rosehips. I watched, waited for more. She laps it up, she licks words like swallows. As he spoke birds swooped past. I think, I said, that I would like to walk down to the water with you. He nodded seriously, put a hand out and I took it.

The river flooded, the water swirling in and around the bridge. You could see it rise as you watched. It lapped at the stone, it climbed up the poles like ivy. The wheels of cars in the car park were already submerged. They won't float away, Robert said. There may be a little tide damage in the morning, that's all.

A couple stood uncertainly at the edge of the rolling water, conferring with their heads tipped like wading birds about to take off. The man shrugged and the woman glanced at her wrist and out to the horizon. Eventually he stepped forward and walked carefully through the water, placing each foot down hesitantly before continuing, reaching the car as water and mud kept his ankles submerged.

The locals know about it, Richard said. There's usually a sign.

The car backed away magically, floating on an opaque sheen that spun circles like record grooves. The woman applauded and we joined in. They wheeled to the side of the car park, a little mud and seaweed trailing from what I recognised for the first time as literal mudguards – flaps of rubber valiantly, like soldiers, warding away mud.

We returned to the party. Towards the end young men lolled like dozing dogs. In the morning the wreckage of them will still be there, Robert told me. He led me through a small door and we were in the garden. It was night; I hadn't realised. The castle hovered above us, black against the purple sky, jagged.

Do you want to go in, he asked.

I looked at him oddly. This is a strange town I know, but not one where the castles are open at midnight.

He grinned. We have a gate, a secret entrance. He fumbled with the key, turning it this way and that. There was a moon, but it was behind the castle and its diagonals did not fall on the doorway. Eventually we were through. I stumbled but he knew the way and guided me. We sat in a crook of stone, hollowed out in ways that were familiar to him, so he could nestle his back into the right shape and I, tucked up next to him, was uncomfortable. He took his jacket off and rolled it to create a cushion.

Far below, the estuary snaked, a black slick, to the edge of the stone. The flood surrounded us now on three sides. The benches were submerged and nothing could be seen of the stone bridge. The car park was wet to the gate and one car remained in the centre: a Mercedes, its logo proud on its bonnet like a CND symbol, wheels underwater.

As Richard leaned in towards me and slipped a hand into my top, a white cone swept across the edge of the water: the bride, and less visible behind her, the groom. She floated like a beacon, illuminating him in the wake she left behind. Robert kissed my ear, my neck, and I raised my head to let him, which gave me a clearer view of what was happening below. Oona – I had seen her name in wobbly black icing on the cake – seemed to glide, then billow, towards the car. As she descended into the water, Simon – his icing was even wobblier – followed, reaching a hand out.

I stayed Richard's hand as it reached into the hem of my jeans; three buttons down, two to go. He moved closer. Too cold? he asked. Shall we go to my room?

Look, I said, and to begin with he thought I was changing my mind, and then he did look.

They were at the car now. Are they drunk? he said.

Is it theirs? I asked.

He shook his head, and anyway, he said, why would they drive on their wedding day? He drew a line on my thigh.

They're crazy. Or they're stealing the car – a wedding prank. Or they've decided, in their elation, that they need to rescue it for whoever it belongs to.

Oona dropped onto the water and her dress cascaded behind her. Come on, Robert said, jumping down from the stone. We need to go the long way round, he called over his shoulder. I heard lapping water. We ran through the arch and he showed me a shortcut through hedges.

Simon stood by the edge, legs slightly apart, dripping wet but tall and serene, James Bond newly emerged from an underwater adventure.

Oona stood near him, her hair occasionally tossing dolphins of water.

Between them was a small child, bedraggled, holding on to Oona's dress like a magic, satin blanket.

We lay in the wet grass by the stone and rolled together, and I looked at the moon, which, from behind a thin cloud, became luminously whole. Much later, bells woke us.

We walked in silence to the house and slept deeply, for those hours of summer when it's light but no one's fully awake. I got up earlier than Richard and pretended to have a hangover. I poured pint glasses of water for us both and waited for him. I sat by the bed and watched him sleep, his face blueish in the light. He snored and rolled over. I got dressed, not particularly quietly, and eventually walked down the stairs and through the door.

The town slept and the water had returned to normal. Seeing it now, there was no evidence that last night had happened. The tables were not damp and the posts were undamaged, and there was no sign of the wedding.

The town was dead apart from one gaping door. Inside I breathed musty books. In those days there were still one or two second-hand bookshops left; it seems strange to us now, all that space, covered with virtually worthless stock, but at the time people still liked flicking through old volumes and paying a pound or so for them. (A pound then was about six times what it is now).

I bought a biography and some poems. The owner was a happy soul, burrowed in the corner, a literate vole. He paused from wrapping a slim first edition in brown paper and stacked my pound coins in front of him.

On the trail are we, he asked mildly.

Just curious to find out more.

He nodded. You know nothing anyone says about anything to do with Dylan is true, don't you?

Oh?

But he had returned to his careful wrapping, a man for whom every day is Christmas. I blinked in the sunlight.

I wrote this much last night and now it's the morning and I'm looking down to the sea. Five o'clock and no one is up but the light is strong and the day marches. The older you get, the less you sleep. I know you know that, but it's what old people say, so I'm saying it. It keeps you awake. The clot in the leg or the brain can carry you off in a moment: awareness of this means that when you come to consciousness early in the day, you get up. My legs are stiff, my body feels tired though I am not. It's is a strange sensation you get when you're elderly. Strange too, being young. I'm a different person now, although I suppose it must have been me.

I walked up to the castle and, with a few hours still to kill before my train, paid my £3 and went through the gates. It didn't seem right to knock on the pink house just to get in for free. The till was so loud that I didn't hear what the boy handing me the ticket said, and by the time I opened my mouth to ask him to repeat it, he'd gone back to his visitor satisfaction checklist, which he ticked diligently.

Through the gatehouse, and the familiar shudder when you enter an ancient place. How many people have walked these exact steps and seen these exact things, over so many centuries. Before electricity, nylon, radio, saxophones, three-pronged forks, plastic, elastic, railway timetables, Saturn's discovery, penicillin, aeroplanes, branded goods and chocolate, piano keys and mirrors, people touched these stones and contemplated this estuary.

How does a fridge work? How do we get through life knowing so little? I stood at the top and looked down on the glistening water and did not see the signs that said, do not climb up here, it is dangerous.

There was a summerhouse: a round mussel stuck to the side of the stone where Dylan wrote stories and Richard Hughes wrote *A High Wind in Jamaica*.

Now I am old and interested, I read somewhere that Hughes owned Seaview and let Dylan live in it; Dylan never had the money for a house. The first he borrowed, the second he was given. But it's Dylan's name on a plaque outside the grand yellow Georgian exterior where I'm staying. The ghost of Richard Hughes might be pretty annoyed, should he come walking up the street and see what the house looks like now.

The young me was interested in none of this, she was walking along the stone balustrade and seeing gulls fight and spat with each other along the ledges below. I slipped off the wall and knocked my head sharply against the stone: a ringing sensation that made me momentarily think, is this how I go, a blow to the head and an early death? Yet here I am now, ninety-one and remembering this; so we know I came to no harm.

Richard Hughes wrote the world's first radio play; where's his blue plaque? And we must not be like Vernon Watkins, poor Vernon Watkins who spent all day droning in a bank, refusing promotion, staying lowly, so he could work breakfasts, lunchtimes, evenings on his poetry. He stayed in each night to write after work. Dylan, according to the long-suffering Caitlin, went out every single night of their marriage. Why did she stay with him? He earned no money, he womanised, he drank.

We don't forgive him the women, although as I saw him heading towards me, brow lowered, fat cigarette shoved in his mouth like a spoon, I could understand it. Were I a lover, I would love him. Were I a wife, I would stay. He paused then continued towards me, curly hair high on a balding head, yellowy fingers. Crossing the forecourt was the same man, older, fatter, face bloated.

On a stone, the same man scribbling in a notebook. By the entrance he argued with a woman. I watched all these versions of Dylan and tried to think of the killer question. First law of: always be ready with a question.

One in a bow tie said, *never believe that you cannot change the past*.

Another read a poem that I rather liked, but as he turned and read it differently, it sounded terrible.

The older one, although he cannot have been as old as he seemed, looked me up and down and said, *be quick. Be quick*.

Am I really ninety-one and remembering this, or is it actually the next morning and I'm in a hospital bed, dreaming that I'm old, because I'm disorientated? We'll never know, certainly not now we are on the last page of the story.

I looked across the stone walls and saw Robert in the garden, naked. He held a sheaf of papers and recited from them.

Dylan liked to sit with his arm on her neck, he said, *his finger hooked in her bra*. He dropped the page and read from another one. *Bed me now*, she said, *come, bed me now, now*.

He turned and walked towards the house, and did not see me.

'There is no turning place: go back', a slate sign with white, horror-film paint reads.

The narrow dogleg road is hemmed with double yellow lines, stitchings for a boot. At a fence two gatekeeper butterflies bordered me, one with darker colouring. Later, on the train I remembered this and looked it up on the iPad; turns out it was actually the Saldany Moth. Sometimes it is out in the daytime, disguising itself as a gatekeeper. The Saldany Moth; I had never heard of it before, although it sounds familiar. Lepidoptery is not something I'm up to speed with. First law of: do your research diligently.

At the Boathouse I admired the vastness of the view and smallness of the rooms. There was an outside café, its terrace cleared of chairs and parasols because the flood had only just gone down.

It even floods here? an elderly lady asked as she picked over the crumbled cliff of her scones. Yes, replied the owner, also elderly. Two more elderly ladies sat at the tables, studying the sea. One more behind me, nodding slowly. It was amok with elderly ladies. I was in an elderlylady of elderly ladies.

I opened my book on Dylan and the old spine cracked.

Nothing in that is true. A bony, blue finger jabbed the pages.

Really? How do you know? First law of.

Because I knew him. She settled opposite me and winced at the hard wood.

Elderly ladies have pale blue eyes; they bore at you, waiting to peck you like a worm. When do old ladies become old? There is no age you can fix it at. (I know now, but I was thinking this then.)

He wasn't the boozer everyone claims he was, she says, her voice surprisingly soft after you've had the eyes at you. He couldn't afford booze, he never had any money.

I must have looked questioning because she continued. It wasn't that he was drunk, it was that he couldn't take his drink. She sat back. *Quite* a different problem, of course. So he appeared heavily drunk when he'd only had a few.

People still said *of course* in those days, like the previous generation said *you see*, and to us it sounds imperious and to them it was normal. A vast pot of tea appeared. I wondered if it was somehow for both of us, but there was one cup, one saucer.

He liked living here because he could have a couple of drinks quietly in the pub – did you go to Browns? – I nodded – and watch the people going by, and write.

She pursed her lips and rattled the teapot. Old ladies like their tea strong.

I knew his wife too. They were kind, gentle people. It's all been exaggerated. Even the video they have on upstairs – she nodded to the house – has that line about the whiskies, the eighteen whiskies. It isn't real.

I thought he… everyone says… well known that…

She sipped her tea between each part of the list.

He spoke fiction. Everything he said was made up.

I nodded. Be patient, let her talk.

Look at the letters, you soon see that. He spins yarns, he boasts, he invents personalities.

So… why did he die so young, if he wasn't drinking that much?

One of her clones took the tray away. Would you like cake too? she asked. I shook my head. There was a ringing sensation that buzzed around my ears.

When he was in the States, he was ill. He was always ill. Pleurisy, asthma, bronchitis, you name it.

Dylan sits on the wall, swinging his little legs. *I was a sickly child*, he says, as he puffs on the stub of a cigarette.

The elderly lady examined the remains of her cake. A doctor there thought he was drunk. Sedated him. Gave him cortisone, and morphine. Together!

Dylan stands beside me, looking out to the estuary. He turns and glowers at me. And, he says, forehead a granite mountain, benzedrine. *Benzedrine*!

The old woman leant forward. Can you believe it?

I suppose… that's what they did in those days.

By the end table, Dylan shakes his head and points at me. I follow him and we go through the low-beamed door, Dylan waddling ahead, me ducking to fit inside. Past the corridor is a white-walled room, pipes running at shoulder height, ancient electricity sockets like boles on branches. Dylan lies in a rickety bed, motionless, and as I stare at him a woman breaks away from two white-coated juniors, their horn-rimmed glasses jiggling comically on their heads. Rushes over to Dylan and glares at him.

Is the bloody man dead yet she says, before she's bundled away again – or doesn't say, because I'm not quite sure I heard her right. The more I think about it, the less sure I am that it's what she said, but I can't remember now to report differently. It's all chaos and movement – photographers are there now, leaning over the railed balcony, flashlights illuminating Dylan's face and making him alive, his lips and eyebrows twitching in the changing beams of light.

We wait for him to say something, pause dutifully to hear what he might come up with. We've done all we can, explains the doctor, his voice gravelly and American. As much as we possibly could.

He is a special patient, you can see the doctor thinking; we have taken far more care over him than we normally would. We thought of everything we could and gave it to him, because the eyes of the world's press are on us; what would it say if we were accused of neglecting him?

I'm pushed out along with the other journalists and glimpse Caitlin's face, the disbelief, the wail of certainty. Outside, the calm of the estuary washed over me. The elderly lady was demolishing the last of her cake. For some reason, she said, this particular doctor decided to overdo it massively.

I see.

That's what sent him into the coma.

So how, why...? How could they make a mistake like that?

She looked this way and that, over my head to a temporary logjam of elderly ladies, back to the cottage, and down to the dog house. The blue eyes bored in all kinds of directions then homed back in on me. Well, who knows? I don't want to invent things after the event. Possibly, he was an undiagnosed diabetic. That would explain a lot. Anyway. One way or the other, all the wrong stuff to give him.

Yes.

Tragic doesn't cover it. All those years he didn't have, the poetry he didn't write.

Indeed.

He'd be a hundred now.

As must you be, I thought, touching the back of my head, where a bruise had formed.

It would be wrong to use the word murder, she said, touching the tips of her teeth as if they might crack and shatter at any moment.

?

That's the kind of word journalists would use.

Uh-huh…

But I would use the word manslaughter. Yes. *The Manslaughter of Dylan Thomas*. Would that be a good title for a story? She drained her tea and grimaced, a brown skull in the making.

Probably not, she concluded, in this day and age.

Back in the city on a Friday night I made my way home past laughing teenagers falling drunk from pubs and clubs and nearly getting hit by buses.

I suppose it makes sense. Even if he was knocking them back at an extreme rate, you don't fall into a coma and die at thirty-nine. What the old woman said about the doctor has more of the ring of truth about it.

First law of, question everything. We read something

and we take it as fact. Why would we not?

The story about the local scandal, for which I was paid and which was printed, is long forgotten. And with Dylan, what I found by talking to people was inconsistent, unverifiable, not reported – so less real.

Nowadays, whenever I say the word 'net' and the screen lights up, it makes me dizzy. The information, the text. The stream of it, the endless content. It is real because it is written down.

So that's my version. The official version is still what it says on Wikipedia – look it up. After you've read this, you may go there and update it and things will be different. Or, they might have been re-updated back to where they were before. Truths get rounded up to tell a story.

Anyway, we like our heroes dramatic and exciting. We want our stories neat and strong like those eighteen whiskies, and we want to know the beginning and the end. Our icons die young and stay compelling, they do not go gently into old age and wear a cardigan.

I saw a new drama about Dylan Thomas. It trotted out the same old things. The drinking, the coma. Perhaps I am wrong. I am ninety I'm losing track of it now.

There was no train station but I came from London on the train. I must have got a bus from the village to the next town; I just don't remember it. I did see a stream, its sides deep and narrow, and in front of it a terrace with names like Cutting House and Rail Cottage.

Perhaps this was the ghost of the train line, that once connected Carmarthen to Laugharne and opened the town up to the Georgians, who built their proud, colourful houses there. Now it is remote again, as it was centuries before, before it was Welsh, before it was French.

Oh yes! Who cares about celebrity front pages when there's so much embedded in old stone walls like milk teeth to be slowly, satisfyingly, dislodged? What news is there anyway, apart from climate change – we need to fix it, and fix it urgently…?

It is a republic, and it has its own currency.

Probably time I ate something. I walk into a pub and sit down, and someone asks me if I'm all right. There is no menu. I say I'll have whatever they've got.

Notes. I am ninety-three today, or is it ninety-two. Richard Hughes did not live in Seaview. There is no such thing as the Saldany Moth.

Four Tales from Seville

1: Fiesta

We were splitting up, and meeting to discuss division of possessions. I went to the agreed place at eleven but Miguel wasn't there. I sipped a drink and watched Eduardo take deliveries. Late morning light beneath flamboyant posters.

Boxes of chocolate ice cream landed on the counter, Eduardo ticked them off on his invoice and said, 'no, two chocolate and three strawberry', and the man apologised and went back to his van as Eduardo rotated towards the kitchen. Above, the ballet, a svelte woman dressed as a toreador held the observer's knowing eye.

A few regulars came and went. Miguel didn't respond to my text. Eventually I felt foolish on my own and went for a walk along the river. I tried to ignore the anxiety of the coming week of work, and the knowledge that we needed to get things sorted today, or I'd be living with boxes of his stuff for another week.

If I had any doubts, the unreliability of the man made me certain it was the right decision. I need someone who can at least turn up when he's supposed to. The river murmured to itself in half-hearted agreement.

They were preparing to knock José's dancehall down. The workmen nodded at me as I paused to watch. I like being forty. You feel appreciated, without being leered at.

The scaffolding has been up for ages, the cheerful ceramic name above the door now grimy and veiled in green gauze. The 'J' of 'José's' curled sadly in on itself, knowing its time was up. Gaping jawbone of door. Holes of windows. The interior walls, which as long as I'd known the place were blue, had been ripped back and different coloured wallpapers appeared: yellow, pink, and lastly blue again.

Miguel and I had one of our first dates in that place. It must be five years since it closed. It's good they're doing something with it. I moved on when the youngest of the workmen smiled at me. I had to squeeze against the wall to get past a truck as it tipped sand from its back.

Twelve-ish. Shade in the Murillo gardens, satisfying as lemonade. Scruffy dogs chasing pigeons. In the heat, just for a moment, Miguel stood in front of me. The old Miguel, not the one we've got now. The fuzzy image held its hand out and led me to the old Arab wall.

When we were first married, we tried to climb it in the middle of the night. A celebration. 'This wall's been here hundreds of years,' Miguel said. 'If we can conquer that, we can conquer anything.' I believed him. We almost got to the top, but were laughing so much that we kept sliding back down.

I open my eyes and he's gone. Too hot now to stay outside. No message on my phone. I went to ring him, then decided not to bother. On the far side of the park gates I slipped into a café and had a lemon shandy. The bliss of the courtyard: not really outside, not really inside. The sense of freedom, of potential.

Still too hot to go anywhere and my phone stares at me blankly, damn the thing. This is typical of the man. Remember the days he was supposed to pick me up from work and forgot, or left me stranded when mum was alive and I was supposed to be getting her to the clinic, or said he was working late when I knew full well he wasn't. 'I don't care who she is,' I used to say, 'just be here when I need you.' He'd look at me quizzically and pretend not to understand.

A glass of wine, please. This seems to be a cue for single men to approach. Each accepts my shake of the head with grace, because it is early in the day.

The wall stretched in both directions. I looked for a section that had plenty of gaps between the stones and crumbly bits, and licked my hands. They knew what they were doing, those Arabs. Who would have thought it would still be here all these centuries later. No one about; the depths of siesta time. Palace bells rang distantly and lazily.

I scrambled up the first half of the wall easily. The second was smoother and more difficult. Tears formed in my trousers. I slipped back down, but this was just lack of practice. I could see how to get to the top if I zig zagged across when I was two thirds up. From the bottom you can assess it, like a map; you just need to visualise that map when you're on the way.

Next time I got four-fifths up and my heart raced. It's like a computer game; this last stretch is the bit that counts. How many lives have I got left? I dug my fists and swung my legs across. Unyielding stone bit into my fingers. A scramble to slide across the curved top. You're there! Fanfare. Bonus life. Admire the view.

'Hey! Get down from there!'

I felt my shoe fall to a faraway clunk. Miguel was with me for a moment and we grinned.

A local policeman appeared at the bottom of the wall on the side I'd catapulted over the top from. My hair dragged and caught but I was over; I clung on and breathed deeply for a minute, then slithered to the bottom on the other side.

An old lady looked at me in astonishment, false teeth clicking. I brushed my hands together, like you'd see in a film, stood up and tried to look dignified. Hobbling away on one naked foot, I wondered what to do. Then my shoe came sailing over the top. Miguel materialised in front of me, knelt down and gently replaced it.

I was covered in grime and my knees bled; little dark spots appeared on the bits of my trousers that weren't torn. I wiped the dirt off my face; this was a mistake, as mascara ran everywhere and it looked like I'd been crying.

Serene river. Five hundred years ago this was the most important port in the world. From here people would sail round the world for the first time, or find gold, or discover America. You wouldn't detect it now from the sleepy pastel houses and empty jetty. I have a photo somewhere at home (I hope it isn't in a Miguel box) of this view from the 1920s. The neat river fades into the mud and gipsy children skip on the banks with sticks for fishing rods. Houses crumble away and the old single-storey slums appear. I shake my head and walk on.

He's not having the photos.

Short cut past the street they're excavating. Black snake-like tubes draped from house to house, smaller snakes forking off for each resident's makeshift water supply. They think they're going to find Roman ruins or something. It's been like this for about two years, a temporariness becoming permanent. Cars parked bumper to bumper on the adjacent road by the church, covered in dents, mourning their absent owners.

An old man looks down on me from a balcony, hands behind his back. 'When will it end?' his slapping hands ask. '*Seville: Building a Dream*' says the important glossy sign at the end of the road. It's a long dream. One of those where you know you're asleep, but can't wake up.

A huge ball swung into the side of José's and the earth beneath me shook.

We went there again for our third anniversary. I was in a turquoise dress which seemed the height of fashion at the time, and Miguel got his job at the post depot. Everything was coming together at last, and we were going to have a baby too. This was before mum got ill and we had to look after her. Two girls clambered up and danced on a table; I didn't have the confidence to do that. Miguel looked at them admiringly, until they were shouted at to get down by the owner. Recently I threw the dress out. There's no point keeping stuff and I was never going to wear it again.

Another boom went through the building and I stepped forward, hoping to get a souvenir perhaps; then I thought better of it and carried on.

Eduardo took the chalk from behind his ear and wrote 2.25 on the bar between us.

Miguel's still not here, the bastard. I don't know why I imagined he would be. I haven't seen him, Eduardo said apologetically, hands raised like a statue. On the far side a dreamy teenager, mooning about future loves if the expression on his face was anything to go by. I envied him.

I could see mum's face in the aluminium of the bar. The last time I saw her in the home she looked like grandmother; and now, I realise, I am beginning to look like her.

Eduardo jumped into the edge of my view and looked me up and down. He smiled and said nothing.

'How are you?' I said eventually.

'Stupendous.'

He looked at the slits in my shirt and the orange dust in my hair. When I didn't react he leant forward and studied my trousers, putting his head on one side like a dog who doesn't understand what you're telling him.

He held up a long finger. 'Wait a minute.' He brought me an amontillado in a glass so large I couldn't guess the size of the measure. He placed in on the aluminium and indicated it with an open palm. He looked like one of his posters.

I took a sip and nodded. At the end of his shift Eduardo offered me a cigarette. I went outside and we smoked, two feet apart. Above the river a full moon gracefully rose, taking it's time, looking at one point like it might not actually bother.

Eduardo cautiously asked if I had any plans for the evening. I wondered whether to shake my head, or nod. In the end I did both.

2: The lover

Aldo taught me some basic Cuban salsa steps because he said it would help me meet women. I find it hard to talk to people. I don't have an interesting job and I'm no good at chit-chat. Aldo has a friendly face, a belly like a shelf and tiny, nimble feet. He's been single as long as I have but has a more optimistic expression than me, and somehow that makes his condition less permanent.

It doesn't matter here anyway. Women will dance with me because their much better looking boyfriends are always clinging to the bar like cockles, too fearful to dance. They don't mind me dancing with their girlfriends as it takes the pressure off, and I don't mind when they go back because there's usually someone else to dance with.

In a break I stood at the bar and the unsmiling waitress poured red wine with ice without asking me what I wanted. When I moved up here I thought it was crazy that people put ice and water in red wine. What are you doing, I thought, watching Eduardo in Eduardo's, spinning the top from the bottle, splashing it in the glass, throwing in ice, topping it up with water. Sometimes he even sticks lemon juice in there. What are you doing, and what else is in that fridge that you might put into red wine if I hang around long enough?

Yet like many strange things, soon it becomes normal and after it becomes normal, before you know it you're asking for it yourself.

I danced a couple of times with a girl called Lia and pretended not to notice Aldo's enthusiastic eyebrow raisings and encouraging winks. The man has a face like a lighthouse sometimes, it's surprising I could concentrate enough on the steps. Lia was pretty; she had large round eyes and a curviness made all the more alluring because she wasn't very tall; she looked up at me as we danced and I held her waist and couldn't help getting to know her figure. Aldo was practically red in the face and whistling like a kettle as he watched and for the first time since I met him, I wanted to thump his fat face and tell him to move his little nimble feet outside and take up smoking or something.

I steered Lia over to the bar and the waitress, her face now like a piece of rock because the lights had gone blue, spun the lid from the red wine.

Lia and I talked and drank, and she looked up at me with those huge brown eyes, and Aldo danced over and we all introduced each other. Aldo and I work at the car factory, spraying the doors. Lia nodded with a convincing attempt at looking interested.

Aldo danced away, the lights flashing red and green on his big bald head, and Lia and I smiled at cards on the counter and I touched her back as we spoke. She leant into my arm and we stood with our arms round each other for a while, rotating the glass and pretending to complain to Miss Stony-Face that it was too warm. She pretended not to understand, and we all had good fun pretending to be annoyed with each other. I asked Lia what she did, and she leant forward to whisper something in my ear. 'I do this,' she said, and kissed me.

I must have looked disappointed when we eventually broke away from each other because she kissed me again, this time more sensuously, and my hand slipped and slid along the back of her dress and for about a year and a half the music and the flashing lights vanished. The big brown eyes were close to me now, framed by a glossy fringe of hair, and I looked down and tried to change my expression.

'It's okay,' she said, squeezing my hand. 'I like you. So it's free.'

I didn't believe her and shook my head. Thinking I couldn't hear, she took a napkin from the bar and stole the waitress's pencil. 'Lia and Paulo, €O,' she wrote, the 'O' as big and as round and as friendly as her eyes.

'Let's have another dance,' I said, and put the warm drink down. Lia nodded and pulled me to the dance floor. The band moved up a gear and a trumpet appeared for one of the tracks. A couple had an argument, and danced more sensuously afterwards as a result.

Lia told me she was from Guatemala and couldn't go anywhere in Europe but Spain, and that this made her sad, but it was okay, because she liked dancing. She looked for a moment like she might get tearful, and this gave me an opportunity to kiss her head and smell her hair.

She held her head against my chest and nuzzled my shirt absently as the music slowed down a fraction and the band played their last couple of songs. When they stopped, there were good-natured boos from the crowd and cries of 'one more!' as we formed, without noticing we were doing it, a semi-circle around the band. Just one more fast song, and then just one more faster song, and then the band stopped and this time it was definitely over, and the musicians smiled wide white smiles and packed their instruments away and tried to shuffle past the applause.

'Why not?' said Lia, her mouth small and moist and brushing my cheek, and I shook my head and she repeated the question, and I couldn't think of a good reason why not, so I said yes. My ears rang with the music, I could still hear it although it was long-finished, and it seemed hard not to dance out of the room to its invisible rhythm.

Outside we were about to walk home when Lia saw some friends across the road, and waved. While she chatted away and her friends looked me up and down, I asked one of them quietly if Lia was all right.

'Yes, she will go with you,' she said.

'No I meant, can I trust her?'

The friend tugged Lia's arm. 'He's asking if he can trust you.'

She tipped her bag out on the table and made funny breathing noises as she turned over coins, combs and make-up until she found her phone. She sent a brief message that she didn't give any thought to, then examined a small envelope stuffed with notes. When I came back from the bathroom she had disappeared. I found her in the bedroom, naked and standing by the wardrobe. She smiled at me. 'Beautiful,' she said, and I guessed she was talking to her reflection.

She pulled away from me before time, and slid down and kissed me, taking hair from her eyes, and squeezed on me until I came and the room flashed red as it shot hot as a poker across me. She licked and massaged me and snuggled into my side and fell asleep with a deep snore.

Later I lay in the dark and heard her move. Something about the friend we had met by the river struck me as wrong. I saw Lia standing by the wardrobe and wondered what she had been looking for. Without waking her I reached on the floor for my trousers, took my credit card and put it in my pants. I left the wallet where it was; if she wanted to take some cash, I didn't mind. I knew she would be gone by morning.

Falling asleep like descending stairs two at a time, I had

strange dreams about her being on the roof, climbing across the tiles, slipping down them and looking up at the moon for guidance. The moon raced through clouds, halving and waning and becoming full again like a wine goblet emptying and filling with milk. Waking around four she was still beside me, breathing shallowly, an arm across my back. 'I wish you were real,' I found myself whispering to her skin; all that red wine had made me sentimental.

In the morning she kissed me. She tipped her bag out. 'Ah, me me. Women.' She jumped up and down, naked. 'There you are.' She took her phone, held it suspiciously, then dropped it on the bed. 'Wait a minute,' she said, as I was tying the cord on my trousers. She made me untie them, rubbed a hand up and down me and laughed; a high-pitched, joyous snort.

She sang in the shower; a song about a horse and carriage, and the horse went on strike, and the driver had to pull the carriage and the horse sat in the back, its hooves resting on the window. When she emerged she took her dress from the floor and pulled it over her head.

'Lunch?' I asked, and the word felt large and unwieldy as it came from my mouth; she smiled and shook her head, and said she had to go. The root around in her bag again; it was like stirring stew. A long slinky dress emerged, magically appearing from a bag that didn't look large enough to contain it. She held it up against herself and asked me what I thought. She pulled out a white flower, and put it in her hair and danced with me, then looked under the bed for her shoes. She wrote her number on a piece of paper.

She looked sad as she kissed my shirt. 'I am nothing,' she said.

'No you're not. You're – '

But she was gone. I watched her go down the street,

swinging her bag, my wallet still sitting inconspicuously on the table beside me.

I made some breakfast and talked to myself. The cat came in, wondering what the noise was, and demanded food and stalked out with a contemptuous arch when I didn't move from my seat.

'There's something not right,' I said to the bread. 'There's no such thing as free. Is there? There has to be a price. Doesn't there?' The bread looked back at me blankly.

I felt guilty when I rifled through my wallet and checked she hadn't taken anything. This act, not what happened last night, but this fingering of banknotes, counting them, made me feel dirty.

I remembered, with a piece of ham halfway to my mouth, that she'd said she was Guatemalan and could not move round Europe. Dropping the food to the returned cat, who leapt out of the way as I ran upstairs, I tipped the drawers out. My passport was there, with paper clips and staples still stuck to it.

Not the passport then. And my credit card lay in the bed, looking at home in the crumpled sheets. I looked up and caught my reflection in the mirror, rifling through my possessions, caught in the act of stealing them. For a moment I saw her naked reflection in the dusty surface. 'Beautiful,' she said. 'Beautiful.'

I walked in the shade of the white canopies slung across the roofs of the narrow streets, all now with a discreet Coca-Cola logo at the bottom of each panel. From a high window, someone slaughtered a violin. In Triana, past the ceramics workshops, a van reversed up the street until some boxes fell out and crushed themselves satisfyingly under the wheels.

Some half-hearted swearing; you're supposed to swear at something like that, but the man who got out of the cab with a cigarette hanging from his mouth couldn't make the effort. A girl skipped along the street in a bright pink t-shirt that read 'Independent Republic of Triana' in assertive, cocky lettering. She grinned at me and hopped and jumped away. I went into Eduardo's and sat by the door.

I ate too much, thinking about her, and sent her a text. Eduardo sensed there was something up and gave me some of his special sherry. I'd never tried it before. The label read 'Eduardo's'.

I looked up at him and he smiled. 'You make this too?'

He shook his head. 'I get it in, because it's called Eduardo's. It's funny, isn't it?'

'It is. It must be nice to own a restaurant that's named after you.'

'It's not named after me. It's named after my grandfather, who was called Eduardo.'

'Ah '

He raised a finger. 'I tell you something else that's funny. When I was a little boy growing up, I thought it was named after my father.'

'Who was called – '

'Eduardo. There's a picture of him up there.'

He pointed up, above the toreador photos, above the glossy black-and-white snaps of famous patrons in the 50s and 60s, to a line of dusty family photos. Wide lapels, thick fabrics, handkerchiefs with large spots.

Later in the day, I texted Lia again. Something still told me that there had to be a price, but it didn't look like there was.

'I have experienced a miracle today,' I said. Eduardo was covered in end-of-day sweat now and wanted to go home. 'I think I am in love.'

He nodded. 'Me too. One day. Yes, one day.'

I drank more sherry and waited. I waited, and waited, and texted again. I went back to work. Aldo and I hammered our car doors into shape. Eventually, I worked out what the price was.

3: The thief

Palaces are the best places for thieving. People are off their guard; jaws drop, bags swing. Today, however, all the palaces were closed and I was at a loss as to how to spend my time. It was the day of the strike and it seemed somehow immoral to take advantage of the crowds that formed as a result. Especially when they all had smiles on their faces. It was a fiesta, a day off, and I decided (as thieves don't have unions) not to join in.

Instead I went to the gardens. Past the statue's strange alabaster dress and fan, as 11.30 approached I found a shady spot to avoid that flare of day when the sun switches on fully and it becomes like standing next to a radiator. By the fountain, a beautiful girl hunched over her phone. She looked cross, her body folded into a cedilla. She was so intent on messaging I had plenty of time to idly watch her. Eventually she looked up and studied me as if judging a specimen, then went back to her phone.

I must have dozed because I was woken by the sound of bells and marching. A few stragglers from the procession walked past; perhaps they had lost their way, or just felt like having their particular version of the strike march past statues. The gardens are nowhere near the route, but it's a strike; sticking to the rules isn't the prime concern.

When they saw us – the girl was still there, and still on her phone – they shouted, *huelga, huelga*! She raised her arm to her heart, then high in the air. *Huelga*!

'What's the strike for?' I asked.

She looked at me as if I were an idiot. 'It's a general strike. No one is working today.'

I nodded. 'I mean, what's it for? More money?'

She paused, crossed her legs, went back to her phone. I dozed again. A fly buzzed me awake. Now she had crossed her legs in the opposite direction so that she faced me. 'You can ask my dad,' she said sourly. She stood and her bag swung across her dress. 'I'm going to try to find him.'

She looked at me, with a slight lift in her head that said, 'Coming?' I got up and followed her. 'Marina,' she said. I nodded and introduced myself.

'What does your dad do?' I asked as we walked along the dust and out on to the street alongside the university.

She didn't answer. We were swept up by energetic strikers pushing and pulling us towards the plaza, the red and white t-shirts and flags making it seem like match day. Two children, caught up in events and distraught because they had no flags to wave. Their father climbed up on the railings outside one of the embassies and pulled down plastic banners. The children laughed and waved their flags as the man jumped down and the cordons of police affected not to notice.

'I don't think he's here.' Marina pulled me through the crowd and we pressed on towards the cathedral. The day got hotter and the noise got louder. Someone slapped a sticker on my back; it felt like a punch, and I wanted to punch back. We wriggled through the mass of bodies, occasionally pushed back by someone's sweat or an intruding back, and she smiled, if briefly, for the first time. 'He's not here either. He can be a bit – difficult to pin down.'

I kissed her arm as she dragged me through the streets. She smelled of sun cream and her dress, see-through in parts, gave tantalising glimpses of stomach and thigh, and the line of her figure showed in silhouette when we crossed from the shadows and into the fierce light. There was nothing to steal from her, the dress would not have concealed anything; and I was glad at least that that particular temptation was denied me.

The sticker on my back made me belong, and we found banners that had been dropped, that we held proudly. Not only were all the main tourist sites closed but, to the distress of many, even the Starbucks were all shut. These are my main hunting grounds. I only steal from tourists; a thief needs to have principles.

Surprisingly however, an occasional bus still made its way through the crowd. No one tried to stop the bus's progress or make signs to the driver; it was just ignored, and rumbled slowly along on its route. Also working were the bright yellow carriages, the horses plodding on indifferently, not letting the joy of the fiesta affect their outlook on life. The drivers were freelancers, I supposed. Wouldn't they come out in support?

She shrugged. 'What about you?'

'I'm still at school,' I said.

She didn't look like she believed me. At a street corner where lines of the march crossed, jostling each other in mock annoyance, she pretended to bump into me and put her tongue briefly in my mouth. She still looked cross though.

'Let's go this way.' People pointed at a post box; its mouth steamed from a firework someone had dropped inside. We waited and eventually heard a muffled bang. Smoke billowed from the blackened mouth and we sensed a low rumble, as of bad indigestion.

The palace bells rang – who's ringing the bells, I wondered – and the surge of people thickened and became more riotous. Someone had a drum and the beat became faster until it was hypnotic and dizzying. The cathedral loomed above us bearishly. We sat at the side of the road, its dustiness drugging us, wondering where we would get something to drink.

I lost her at the edge of the old town. For the rest of the day I looked for her floaty dress, the dirty pink band in her hair, and for her angry green eyes. The procession fizzled out not long into the afternoon and again was reminiscent of a football match; the anti-climax of it being over, the sense of disappointment even if the game had been won. People dropped the banners which were soon trodden into the dust. A flag fluttered diagonally from an abandoned beer bottle.

As the last stragglers went home I crossed the bridge to Triana. More bright red lines of whistling, shouting, bell-ringing strikers marched alongside the river bars and down to the old fisherman's houses. I sat at the tapas bar in Eduardo's.

Several times I thought I saw her come in. Several times I thought I saw her walk past. Eduardo, noting my expression, put more beers on the counter and chalked the prices up in front of me, and after a while the blue dress fluttering in front of my vision became orange and blurry. More beer, and I day-dreamed she was sending me texts, one after another, the messages getting impatient as she waited for my reply. I looked up at the posters and tried to find her face in one of them.

The next day everything was open again and life returned to normal. Marina and the strike had been a dream, and people carried on as if the day had never happened.

In the north palace I had a purse and a phone and it wasn't even ten o'clock. I sat in the courtyard and closed my eyes and listened to the fountain trickle. A buzz in the air as the day warmed, pale light on stone yellowed, shadows moved rapidly downwards.

'Please make sure you stay on the green carpet,' the guide said. 'Here we are in the long gallery.'

Those at the end of the narrow room shuffled up together as if on an overloaded bus. The strip of ragged carpet held us pinned between its invisible walls.

'Here we have a very special painting, because this is by Goya.' We all craned forward to see the tiny picture at the far end of the room. I could make out a rock and some sky. More urgent than Goya's special painting was the sweaty smell of the man in front of me. His wallet made my pocket sag.

Next room. 'This is the main bedroom, and here you can see a wash basin that was first used in the seventeenth century.'

We tried to look impressed. I studied a painting above it; a woman dressed in silks, with a gigantic oval hat and a faraway, distant smile. Glossy hair fell in ringlets and despite being young she held a long stick, as if suffering with consumption or some other antique condition. One hand on her hip, she looked at me sardonically from long-dead centuries.

'Here we have a writing cabinet believed to have been used by Ferdinand and Isabella.'

One of us trod accidentally on the exquisite tiles, and stepped back in alarm as though they might be mined. Her friend's watch was in my shirt pocket, and I could feel it ticking.

I don't think it can have been the same woman in the portrait in the next room, because she wore clothes of a different period; but perhaps she was a descendant as she had exactly the same expression in her eyes. She wore high-necked frills of lace and riding gloves, ready and waiting for a film.

Or maybe it was the same person, dressed up in historical fancy dress? And now it's all historical, and we can't tell the difference. Will future generations think we look dressed up for something, as our photos parade through streets in dark suits with lime ties, flouncy white dresses, baggy jeans and caps turned back to front?

For a moment I drowned in her huge blue eyes. It was 11.30 and getting hotter; my neck burned when we stood in a diagonal blade of light. The windows had lead frames and diamond shaped panels. There was a squeak, and the guide was on the case. 'Please, remain on the green carpet. The floor is very precious.'

The last room was too small for us all to get in and we squashed ourselves near an antique clock that, as the guide spoke, chimed sonorously to ask him to stop droning on and let an old clock get some rest.

Something clutched my legs. The fear, the heart-burning sensation that I had been discovered. It had to happen one day. I had the watch, the purse and the phone. I felt like a bomb that might go off at any moment.

I stayed calm and looked down. A child of two or three, dark curly hair, clung to my knees. A woman gently tugged him away and apologised. The boy looked up sleepily; caught in another blade of light he closed his eyes, bored. He turned and held the legs of the man next to me. 'Sorry,' said the woman again.

Down the ornate staircase, covered from ceiling to floor in tiles. Three hundred years ago I suppose it was the latest in chic, but today it bears an uncanny resemblance to a fried fish shop. The tiles were badly cracked and damaged; the impact, we were told, of the Lisbon earthquake in 1755 whose shockwaves were felt across the continent and for which Seville gave thanks for being spared.

The ghosts of that ancient disruption were still visible in the spidery lines across the walls. I thought about the paintings and wondered about the people in them. Ahead the couple with the small child held his hand. They formed a silhouette like a paper chain.

A sparrow landed in the fountain and drew a few short sips of water. I watched its gullet increase and decrease as it drank. It looked in both directions as if contemplating crossing a road, then flew up into the vines and leaves that wrapped the pillars.

Sometimes I sit here and imagine it's my garden; the reverse *loggias*, that look like the outside of a Renaissance house, but here face the courtyard, like an inside-out house. 'Are you a happy sparrow,' I called gently up to the leaves. There was an approving, shy rustle.

The boy ran across the courtyard, waving his arms, singing random notes to himself. Freed from the dusty inside, with its bloody carpet and boring objects, he was in heaven. He ran to a stop and looked at me curiously. For a moment I thought he was going to dart forward and hug me again. He wound a curl of hair in his finger, then trotted back to his parents. They smiled. 'You have the same hair,' his mother said. 'He looks just like you.'

'He looks like my baby brother,' I said.

I don't have a baby brother. I always wanted brothers and sisters, but the more I heard the continual refrain from my parents about how expensive I was to keep, the more I knew they would never come into being. The boy ran behind the fountain, pretending to hide.

There's an old photo of me in a garden somewhere, looking just the same. Wavy hair, thoughtful, adult expression. If it wasn't for me, they would have had the money to go on holidays and enjoy themselves. It was a good job there was only one of me to put up with. This doesn't come across in the photo, where I smile, and stand where I was told to stand, and look happy.

Through the lanes a girl in black, urgently pretty, pushed a motorbike. A man with blue tattoos steered a bath on a trestle trolley, making his own 'beep' noises, sounding surprisingly car-like. A young man with long hair held a pig under his arm, stroking its ear affectionately. It oinked as I walked by. I tried not to think about where they were going. One of the beggars on the corner tried to put heather in my shirt, and to my surprise I let her. She chattered away and I gave her a euro.

Later I went to Eduardo's. I sat on the far side of the bar under my favourite poster, the girl with the white horse, who's dressed like a man, and Eduardo brought me amontillado. He stood square in front of me with his arms folded.

'How are you?'

I nodded.

'Busy day today,' Eduardo said.

I nodded. And there she was, the girl from the strike. I had just about forgotten her. Marina saw me and hesitated, then when she realised I'd seen her, came over. Eduardo, discreet as a sliding door, held my gaze for a moment like an invisible wink, then disappeared.

'I thought you said you were still at school?' she said grumpily, sitting down.

'I am,' I said, glancing at my new watch. 'What would you like to drink?' I tried to work out where the catch on the wallet was, opened it and found a satisfying number of euros inside. Marina opened her eyes wide.

'Did you find your dad?' I asked.

'Oh yes. He was where he said he'd be all along, actually. I just didn't notice him the first time.'

I nodded, absorbing this. Eduardo, seeing the open wallet, came over and whistled when he saw what was inside. 'Someone's had a good day!' he said.

I smiled modestly. At school my arse, Marina's

expression said. 'I'll have a very large glass of wine, please,' her voice said.

Eduardo nodded. 'And who's this young man?' he said, putting his hands on his knees and smiling.

'This is my baby brother,' I said. Beside me, the boy with curly hair sat swinging his legs. He asked for lemonade and Eduardo nodded solemnly, backing away until he disappeared behind the bar. Marina, picking up the camera, took a picture of us. 'Keep smiling,' she said. 'That's right. Keep smiling.'

4: The engagement

'Delivery of mayonnaise?' I said in a loud voice.

Marble pillars. A counter of polished chrome. I don't normally get to see the lobby, so decided to enjoy it.

A thousand miles away from me on the other side of the counter, an expression of steely disinterest that would put a statue in the museum to shame. 'Why are you in here?' His lips did not move, and he was as stiff as a... well, a stiff, I suppose. I rotated the waist of my trousers and put the invoices down.

'Back's closed up, isn't it?'

'Don't be absurd.'

I placed both hands on the counter. Against the chrome, when I took my hands away they left two perfect black handprints. He was right: it did look absurd. Comforting though. Two decades dropped away and I was doing handprints in poster paint at infant school.

'Have a look yourself,' I said, but he was already on the phone. A few 'why', 'when', 'but' and 'sort it out' type statements, then he glared at me.

'I need to get going,' I said airily, 'you're not the only hotel that needs mayonnaise today you know.'

'I'm sure.' He told me to bring it through and be inconspicuous.

I inconspicuously carried in the ten gallon tub. 'That way,' he pointed, and I walked bow-legged towards the staircase. Past the threshold of the kitchen the doors became narrower, the chrome and marble disappeared and the rough whitewashed paint made me feel more at home. The sous-chef glanced at me. 'Down there will do.'

'Here?'

'Anywhere.'

Back in the lobby a woman of about seventy sat on a central sofa, surrounded by purple rugs. A poodle sat on one of the rugs, which resembled a flattened, de-limbed and dyed version of the dog. There was more space surrounding her than I live in.

'Boy,' she said imperiously (I am twenty-nine), 'come over here.' I sidled towards her inconspicuously. 'Yes?'

'I am Luisa Emilia Gonzalez de Castillo Delgado Sanchez Lopez.'

'I'm Juan.'

She held her hand out and I went to shake it but she positioned it like a duck's bill and I sort of tugged at it.

'I need a handyman.'

'I am gainfully employed,' I said proudly.

'You are not. You carry vats of mayonnaise around.'

I walked away. The concierge signed the invoice and leant over the bar. 'Now. Fuck off,' he said in a voice so low that the poodle's ears pricked up.

'Hard day?'

'Fuck… the fucking fuck… off.'

'Nice to do business with you.' I saluted Luisa Emilia as I walked to the glass doors, which slid open with a sneer and closed with relief once I was through. The van wouldn't start. Some raging and swearing and screaming got it going again.

'There's a message for you.'

It was from Luisa Emilia blah blah de whatever. It gave her address and instructed me to wear clean clothes. The building was ordinary enough but as the buzzer sounded the door released to reveal a pristine white courtyard, fountains bubbling in the centre and extravagant ferns draped round the edges. The buzz and whirr of bikes and cars outside evaporated as the heavy door closed with a muted click.

I waited and imagined it was the sixteenth century and I was being received at the court of Ferdinand II. I laid an arm along the white cane chair and felt it creak discreetly beneath me and wondered if there was still the need for inconspicuousness. I decided that, as I was not dressed in white, this would be impossible in any case. Luisa Emilia swept in after fifteen minutes, the double doors opening in front of her and closing again once her silk dress had followed her through.

'Thank you for being on time,' she said. I stood and bowed. The cane chair, which had got used to my presence, creaked and groaned in surprise. 'And thank you for wearing clean clothes.' I bowed again, tipping my head to one side. She was not to know that my pants were on inside out. 'If I may be so impolite,' I said, 'how did you get my number?'

She walked to the chair opposite and lowered herself into it, after gathering her silks. They rustled, as if she had a few poodles in there. 'I called your workplace.' She held her head high, like it was on a pole.

'I understand that, according to data privacy… privacies, one is not supposed to give out a private employee's private personal details.'

'I know,' she said. 'Now, I have a few jobs for you. You can fit them in above and beyond your mayonnaise-carrying duties if you insist on staying in that employment. You will find me a fair employer and I pay well.'

I bowed my head once more and wondered if the payment would be in doubloons. The poodle, as if irritated that Luisa Emilia's silks were doing all the rustling around her legs for it, rushed in and barked, ran around a few times and stuck its tongue out at the fountains' regular spits of water.

An old man stood on the threshold of the door, holding a tray which wobbled in his grip. 'Do you like Rioja?' Luisa Emilia asked.

'I don't know him,' I replied. She grinned, a mouth of perfectly yellow teeth. 'You and I are going to get on famously.'

I was late for Karolina and she was cross. 'I'm sorry,' I said. 'It's work.'

'Work my bollocks,' she said. Karolina is from Ukraine, and her grasp of idiom is sometimes shaky. When we first met I made the mistake of referring to 'the Ukraine' and she threw a fit. Apparently 'the Ukraine' is a dismissive expression designed to belittle the country that should be called 'Ukraine'. I thought I'd blown my chances, but the first time we were in bed she said, 'Tell me I am from the Ukraine again.' I had to say it over and over until she squealed and bit my hand.

We went dancing. 'I think I am going to leave you,' she said.

'Why? Is there someone else?'

She looked at me in horror and flicked a hand at my face. 'No! No one else! You are bastard, you think I have been unfaithful.'

I felt hapless. 'I just... wondered what the reason was. For you leaving me.'

'Because you're such a bastard, you think I am sleeping with other men!'

I kissed her and told her she was beautiful and we did not split up that night. I was still a bastard though, which I accepted with humility. 'I am going on top, you fucking bastard,' she told me with no uncertainty when we got home, and I accepted this disgrace with as much dignity as I could.

I took a paint-covered tape deck to work by and Luisa Emilia did not seem to mind. 'This is all rather hi-tech,' she said, examining the Michael Jackson tapes and slotting them back into the decks.

I mended her fridge door, put new ceiling lights in in the second living room, ripped out the old boiler housing and put together a new one, and fixed new gold handles to her taps. Her morose elderly servant stood around most of the day, watching me. He was becoming familiar with *Thriller* and even beginning to sway vaguely to some of the tracks by late afternoon. 'Pay attention, Giraldo,' Luisa Emilia told him, smoking a long, thin cigarette. 'You might learn something.' Giraldo nodded, his hands big and uselessly paw-like by his sides.

She poured Rioja into a glass as big as my head and handed it to me. 'Thank you,' I said, swirling it and seeing my startled expression reflected in the planet-sized circle of wine, 'but I must go soon. Karolina is waiting for me.'

Luisa Emilia draped herself across the sofa. 'She loves you, this Karolina?'

I knew this was coming, and she knew I knew, and she knew I knew she knew, and I knew she knew I knew she knew I knew. Giraldo, who had perhaps seen it occur previously over forty years or so, absented himself.

'You're a very attractive man,' she said. I wiped my sweaty palms on my dungarees. 'You're too kind.'

She stretched back and the cane sofa creaked and groaned in protest. 'Come over here,' she commanded. I walked over, all last attempts at inconspicuousness erased.

'My husband died thirty years ago.'

'I'm sorry,' I said sympathetically.

'Since then I have been alone, with my memories and Giraldo.' I nodded.

'In that order,' she clarified. She pulled me towards her and the red cave of her mouth with its yellow stalactites opened up in front of me. 'I am still a woman,' she said.

'I'm sure.' I had known this was going to happen, and she knew I knew she knew I – well, you get the point. But it was still something of a shock. 'I should tell you,' I said, pulling myself up with some authority, 'that I am engaged.'

This was a lie. Last night Karolina had told me she never wanted to see me again, and stalked off into the night with a firm instruction never to come near her ever, until I was dead. This afternoon, she texted and asked if I fancied the cinema.

Luisa Emilia nodded thoughtfully. 'I understand,' she said. 'I understand.'

The restaurant was a vast ship, its few inhabitants at sea, wondering if they would ever again see land. Ferns as big as pianos loomed above us. Luisa Emilia and I were intimately positioned across a table so large we could have fitted in an extra nine or ten people if the restaurant found itself full, a position it gracefully decided not to be caught in. I said that this was just for one drink, because I had to go to see Karolina, and Luisa Emilia agreed with a confident series of 'of course'.

A menu hovered in the air with Luisa Emilia's crushed-green-silked torso beneath it. 'The soup looks good.'

It looked like impenetrable French to me, but I chose to say nothing.

'I think I will have the lamb,' said the menu, bobbing up and down, 'and,' it added, dancing in a rather vulgar way now, 'we must have the '69.'

I covered my laugh. Fortunately the bobbing menu did not notice.

'Yes,' Luisa Emilia said imperiously, the menu instantly inert on the table in front of her, 'the Castilio Fernandez '69 and the soup and the lamb. For both of us.'

'Ah,' I said, picking my menu up and immediately putting it down again. There was no waiter visible but somehow as she spoke, one appeared and the order was taken.

She fixed me with a steely expression. 'You may laugh,' she said in an undertone that made my fork dance a fraction on the tablecloth. 'But you will change your mind.'

I nodded politely and the chap behind the white piano played something a bit louder.

'My husband, the late Alfonso Gonzalez de Castillo Delgado Sanchez Lopez, was special ambassador to Chile.'

'I see.'

I felt my phone vibrating. It was Karolina, wondering where the piss hell I was.

'If you marry me,' Luisa Emilia said as the wine arrived, 'you need never work again.'

She sipped her drink thoughtfully, and gave an approving nod to the waiter.

Karolina kissed me when I arrived. 'I thought you would be cross,' I said, glancing at my watch.

'Of course I am not cross. Are you hungry?'

'Not really,' I said, but she didn't notice and we left our bar drinks and she pulled me along the riverbank. 'We're going to Eduardo's,' she said, 'I'm starving.'

'I've left my job,' I announced.

Karolina sat back and stared at me. A bit of spinach draped itself across her chin like a question mark. 'You shitting idiot.'

'It's okay. I'm working full time for the countess.'

'The who?'

'The… Luisa Emilia de… thingy de thingy… you've met her.'

'The dragon?' Karolina's eyes were as big as plates.

'That's the one.'

I kissed Luisa Emilia's breasts. She knew the moment I was in her employment that she could push the stakes higher. It's a mistake and I accept that, and I should have thought it through, but it's too late now.

She grinned, that yellow incisive diamond cutter smile, and I saw the blackish reddish ominous hole of her mouth and I was a sailor, stranded on the rocks and pulled down by those sirens who breathe oxygen into your lungs and then turn into old wizened hags.

'*Caro…*' she said, '*mi caro.*' I think it's Italian but it's not my place to ask; I just got on with the nipple sucking.

Afterwards we bathed in the gigantic marble pool and I thought, this isn't so bad, even if a decrepit foot did appear from time to time and it was my role to gnaw at the green toenail. It's surprising how quickly you can get used to it.

In bed, however, my concentration finally gave out. 'I'm sorry,' I said. There was a horrible silence between us, which I filled, as one can only fill, with 'it's not you; it's me.'

She nodded and majestically arose from the bed,

scrawny tits poking this way and that like curious mice, and I looked away politely. She rummaged in a drawer and I tried not to look at the diagonal slices of ham thinly papered over her hip bones.

'Here you are,' she said, turning towards me, her blue veined mottled thighs presenting themselves in my face. I pulled my gaze away. It felt like tearing chicken to drop on a pizza.

On the pillow were photos. Black and white images from the 1950s, 1960s. Luisa Emilia, a beautiful, wide smile on her face; journalists behind her, flashbulbs popping enthusiastically. Luisa Emilia looking like Marilyn, a low-lidded, sexy smile for the cameras.

Luisa Emilia like Sophia Loren, a voluminous dress, John F Kennedy swimming in the black swirling pools of her curves. Luisa Emilia with her arms out wide, embracing the world. Marlon Brando studying her with a devilish smile.

As we made love I concentrated on the pictures.

I pulled an orange from the orange tree. It was the most orange orange I'd ever seen. Karolina dumped me, telling me I was a bastard, and that I was disgusting, and I could not agree with her more. I married Luisa Emilia a few months later.

The ceremony was not well attended. Of course I had said no, and of course I walked away and told Karolina I loved her. None of it mattered to Luisa Emilia. I would be inheriting her fortune and her house. She would not take no for an answer. The last time I turned to go she snapped regally at me and I turned, and apologised, and changed my mind, and said yes, all right then.

'Good.' Luisa Emilia nodded graciously.

There's the worry she'll live for another twenty

years. I couldn't help thinking this as we walked up the aisle. But it was too late, and we were blessed, and the six harps started playing and the four photographers photographed. The pictures are in a white album as fat as an illuminated Bible. The other photos, the other Luisa Emilia, I keep in the bedside cabinet. At necessary moments, I pull them out and stare at them.

Luisa Emilia read in the paper about the new metro that was being built. 'I want to go on it!'

I swam a few lengths in the pool, got Giraldo to chill the wine, and thought about my response as I lay on the balcony and looked across the city. 'Very well,' I said eventually.

We ventured downtown the next day. I bought tickets from the machine and she smelt the enclosed air suspiciously. We'd been travelling about a minute when, to the surprise of our tightly-packed fellow rush-hour travellers, she poked her head through my arm and shouted.

'This is dreadful! Why don't these people get taxis?'

With a disappointed glance at those reading books in their elbow or staring into the black nothingness of the tunnel, she waited for the train to slow down and we emerged at the first stop.

'Well I'm not doing that again,' she declared.

I was surprised when she left me.

'The problem,' she said, and it was the first time she had ever spoken to me softly, as if I were an equal, 'is that now you're not working…' Her words tailed off.

'Yes?' I stroked her arm. I liked the perfume I had recently bought her on the platinum card she'd given me.

'Well it's just…' She looked up. 'You're not sweaty any more.'

'No.' My hair had been cut nicely by her beautician's nephew.

'You don't wear dungarees.' She looked at the suit she had chosen for me.

'Well. I could fix that radiator –'

A crease appeared between her eyebrows. 'No, I want Giraldo to do that.'

'He's been trying since November. It's February. We won't need it for –'

'The point is,' she interrupted, and looked towards the sea. 'Ah, well. It doesn't matter what the point is.'

She took the photos from the cabinet. They were crumpled and creased from my thumbs. 'Are these beautiful?' she asked.

'Yes, of course they are, you know they are.'

'Keep them,' she said. She died the next day.

Karolina met me for lunch at Eduardo's. 'You bastard,' she told me and I agreed. We ate sea bass. Luisa Emilia hadn't liked sea bass, she'd said it was like eating a fat uncle. It was the first sea bass I'd had in months.

'Come home with me later,' Karolina said. Her eyebrows raised like kites. 'And,' she added, 'toss-face, this time, stay.'

'I will,' I said sincerely. My pants were back-to-front as well as inside out. I hope she doesn't notice.

When we were tucked up in her single bed Karolina sat up suddenly and the bed caved beneath me and I bounced up and down. 'What? What?' I had been dreaming about Magellan, sailing round the world.

'You stupid penis. Why are we stuffed up in single bed?'

'What?' It was too late, or more accurately too early, for rhetorical philosophy.

'You are rich man. We should be on roof terrace, looking at stars, throwing cigar butts into pool.'

'No, no.' I rolled over. 'She left me, remember. Before she died.'

But Karolina was right. Luisa Emilia had not changed her will. When I married for the second time in six months – and believe me a year ago I would have seen none of this coming – I was a multi-millionaire.

'Get a new shirt,' Karolina said contemptuously before the wedding day.

We ate our honeymoon meal in Eduardo's and did not travel. Karolina was not happy about this. 'I want to go to Hawaii,' she declared.

'Why Hawaii?'

'Because I have heard of it.'

Eduardo wore a red necktie and we had a good party. 'I will miss you,' he said sadly.

'We're not going anywhere,' I said.

'Yes, yes, you will,' he said gravely. At the end of the afternoon he put corks in the half-finished bottles and presented them to us.

I looked at the walls, up to the posters of stylish toreadors, fixed in a resolutely Sixties patina of flared pinkish cloths, high-buttoned jackets, pointed sideburns, and oval-egg spectators. Above them the film stars: the curled glossy photographs of celebrities no one now remembers. And amongst them, there she was. Luisa Emilia, looking down on me regally, as imperiously as when I once kissed the bumps on her calloused hands. She had watched our modest gathering, and in one of the photos I thought I detected less contempt than in all the others.

A few months later we moved out of the white house with the pool. 'I am filthy rich,' I said.

Karolina nodded.

'Can we be filthy poor?'

Karolina thought of Luisa Emilia. She narrowed her eyes. 'Yes, you bastard,' she said.

'Promise?'

She nodded. We fled. We took a bag of clothes and some pictures. Travellers live in the house now. Our golden anniversary is next week.

The Wednesday Ghost

I suppose I shouldn't have killed her, but when do we ever do what we're supposed to do? I went to the park, as often happens when the images become too intense and saw, just for a moment, a red squirrel. It was a flash, a spiral of burnt orange looping itself around a tree branch, which bounced as the squirrel ran along it before vanishing. I hoped it would reappear, but there was just the familiar trickling stream and an occasional brown leaf floating to earth in its own time. Not a care in the world. Bastard leaf.

There's something cleansing about the vein of blue water running the length of the park, absolving my sins, healing the guilt. Six months and two days now and each morning, the fear of the hammering on the door fades a little.

Spat on by rain I found my gloves and diverted to the ornate gateway that leads to the history museum. This is my favourite arch. Can you have a favourite arch? It looks like stone but after walking through and turning back you see that it's actually plain red brick, plastered on the front to look like granite. Now why has it only been decorated on one side? Is it a sign to be wary of the history within, to turn it over and look at it from both sides, before you believe it? Allusion. Illusion.

Graffiti on the brick side. Bricks are fair target. Stone is respected.

Calm, deadening hush inside the museum. Floor polish smell. I glided through corridors. Glid? Sounds wrong, doesn't it, glided. The occasional distant squeak, as an attendant's high heels glissaded – that's better – across the dark wood floor. A cough from someone absent.

A Max Ernst exhibition on the first floor and as the images became increasingly surreal, I felt myself detach from the high-ceilinged rooms and travel past the lead-latticed windows. The engravings were from *Une semaine de bonté*; I needed the leaflet to discover that 'bonté' meant 'kindness'. Each day had its own room. Sunday was bright orange, Tuesday blue, Wednesday yellow. I've always seen Wednesday as a green word. To my surprise, not everyone thinks the same.

One of the captions began with the word 'SO...' in large, Art Nouveau letters, and for a moment I saw this as fifty. A strange age, fifty, and only another few months to go. A decade since I was a young man; a decade until I'll be an old one. And the daily shock of discovering solitude. Sometimes I can squint at this and believe it's healthier, not having to put a shirt on if I don't want to, not having to worry about eating. But if a relationship is a series of compromises, the voluntary adoption of conventions, well. What a price you pay to sidestep convention.

You shouldn't have killed her then, should you, I thought as I reached the third room and saw a man with the head of a bird being devoured by a harpy with angel's wings and chicken's feet. The cough, that I had heard echoing earlier. A woman in her twenties stood at the far end of the room, looking at an engraving of a flamingo with a lion's head, horror-struck as it contemplated a flooded temple. She wore a pale green t-shirt and jeans (the woman, not the lion-flamingo) and had a slender figure, shaped rather like a seven as she leant forward to study the picture.

I kept out of sight. You can't talk to strangers, Stefan, not now you're a murderer. She didn't notice me anyway, but as my shoes squeaked on the way past she looked up and caught my eye. I couldn't help smiling and she held the smile. I paused, suddenly consumed with interest in a locomotive with severed heads emerging from its funnels instead of steam. She smiled a second time; a warm, friendly, nodding smile, almost of recognition.

Have we met before? Surely not. I would remember. I half-opened my mouth and she nodded again, then turned back to her flamingo-lion.

There's only so long you can stare at an engraving of severed-head steam. I squeaked on to the next room. Of course, almost immediately lines now came into my head. 'This place is a bit of a maze, isn't it?' 'What did you think of the room with the giant caterpillars, they're pretty amazing, aren't they?'

The prints in front of me – Thursday I was onto now – swirled and melted into each other. I back-peddled to the previous room – but it was too late, she was gone. A serpent with a headdress like a peacock, breasts curiously apple-like, stared at me. A gargoyle clawed a polite husband. There wasn't enough space between the print and the wall; it was screwed in too tightly, impaling it against the plaster. You have to allow a picture to breathe, to let it rise and fall against its home, or it cannot rest. The gargoyle looked like it might fly out at any moment.

She wasn't in the second or first room either – the woman, not the gargoyle. Where had she gone? I retraced my steps to Thursday. Through the exit to the left to the vivid red of Friday. She wasn't there, nor did she hang around for the weekend.

At the far end the revolving door slowly moved of its own empty volition, the glass panels glittering and flashing as each one in turn caught the light and reflected back upon me.

The museum seemed, and certainly sounded, empty. Why hadn't I spoken to her when I had the chance? And now you'll never see her again. A moment of eternal, existential angst. Ah well. It's your own fault, for being a murderer. Perhaps if you hadn't brutally killed someone in a moment of sudden, scarlet insanity, you'd have been able to speak to her; able to be casual. Like normal people. You just needed to gird your lions – your *loins* – too late now.

I looked at a skeleton welcoming an eagle into its home with exaggerated formality. Next to him, a bowler-hatted fox in a railway carriage looked surprised to have just pulled up next to the Sphinx. Time to go.

On the walk home I felt a nostalgia for earlier decades, stripping themselves like bark from each tree I passed. The beautiful women I knew and courted in my twenties, the velvet-trousered artist, the potential in front of me, and a sexual life opening up like a glittering bowl of fruit. Get a grip, Stef. That phrase, 'empty volition', revolved in my head. It doesn't mean anything, and yet it makes perfect sense.

Perhaps I should start going to exhibition openings again – is it more suspicious to disappear, than to carry on as normal? Does it make the knock at the door more likely, or less? On the way through the gates and onto the Reeperbahn, I seriously contemplated it. But on balance – a firework shot across the road in front of me, skimmed by a high teenager – it would only lead to trouble. People would ask, why did you stop painting – it wouldn't take long to crack.

The firework exploded with a clang on a steel bin. A police truck ambled past, seeing nothing. I glanced back to the park and saw the squirrel again, a streak of vermilion through trees like paint bleeding in from someone else's picture. A red squirrel in the heart of the city; who would believe it?

On the way up to the flat I paused to pick up one of the stale *brünchens* the baker gives me if I come in after six, and ate it on the second floor, pausing to watch a mist descend across the wasteland. Half an hour later I realised I was cold and looked for my key.

He thought he saw the woman several times. Twice on the street, she was standing in the mid-distance, or on the other side of the road. He saw her in the corner of his eye, almost illuminated, but when he turned to look, there was nothing but passers-by and street hoardings. Everyone seemed to have purpose: collars turned up, newspapers rolled, steam streaming from nostrils like ponies hurrying.

He saw her once more by the entrance to the S-bahn before deciding with irritation to rid her from his imagination. He was disoriented, as if unsure where he was on the familiar street, even though he'd lived on various roads leading away from it for much of his life. He was as far as the police station before noticing he'd gone a block too far, and retraced his steps.

He thought about her again on Monday when, trying to reinvigorate interest in work, he unlocked the studio and pulled the dustsheet from his current restoration. When Stefan claimed to have left painting behind, perhaps he was being a little melodramatic with you. He does that; it's like his coat with the upturned collar, it's like reminiscing about velvet trousers. It's true that he isn't currently painting, but he hasn't even put his painting equipment away; it still litters his studio, which is still called a studio, and he now restores paintings for a living. Quite a good living, it has to be said.

Today he's working on a vast, long Venice landscape,

a Canaletto wannabe, and the most interesting thing about it is its frame. Ornate, detailed and humorous, Stefan often finds his attention straying to its curlicues when he's supposed to be working on a flat gondola or a bendy barber's pole. He feels, and this is his artist's posturing again, that he's worthy of better. But his clients recognise his skills, and because of his minor local fame, he's well-known and gets the work.

The tiny figures are the only parts of *Reflection by the Doge's Palace* that interest him; their faces pinkly vague and sketched with two or three brushstrokes, the amorphous features giving space for interpretation, for curiosity. A gondolier stares indulgently, or perhaps patronisingly, or maybe lecherously, at his passengers. A tourist looks with interest at the buildings, or in confusion at where he is, or disapprovingly at the excessive display of wealth. Women on the quay, hands on hips; bored, or curious, or disgusted by the sewers. Or are they flirting with the gilded men opposite?

Whatever they're doing, they've all been coated in a thick sticky varnish sometime in the late nineteenth century, and removing this is the bulk of Stefan's task. Everyone was at it at the time, protecting the paintings for future generations, they thought; but the varnish evolves from transparent to sepia over the decades. The result is countless paintings that now squint on the world through a brown, toffee-wrapping filter. And despite knowing how much difference the restoration process can make, Stefan is still frequently surprised by what emerges from his work. Indiscriminate greys on dresses become bright viridian greens. Dark swarthy gypsies transform into fresh porcelain beauties. Occasionally, brand new figures appear from the murk – a black dog, or a shadowy companion.

There are different restoration techniques for certain colours, because the pigments respond to the cleaning chemicals in different ways; so Stefan addresses a particular block of colour at a time. One process to lift the varnish, another to clean the colour, and only then does he take the opportunity to repair cracks or damage where appropriate. He saves these 'fun bits'. It breaks the day up, keeps him going, and the job briefly becomes more art than science. How much is too much? When does conservation become re-making, when is an invisible line crossed where he's imposing his own creativity on the artist's?

Sometimes the owners of the paintings (it's usually museums, but there are a surprising number of private owners hidden away behind ordinary facades) ask him to do everything he can to improve them; particularly if the artist isn't well-known, or the painting badly damaged. The public-owned galleries, on the other hand, only want the barest minimum done. Remove the varnish; detach dirt; err on the side of caution.

The work is slow, tedious. Punishment for being an unpunished murderer. And by embracing the boredom rather than resisting it, he can reach a level of serenity and calm that might be described as happiness; were it not for the nagging sense that he's not doing what he should be doing in life. You were a highly regarded painter, he tells himself; you could have become a great one. Well tough; being a murderer has changed things. And restoration is a more nurturing career for someone recovering from trauma. This serenity can last hours, before the searing red images flash on his skull again and the head-in-hands screaming leads his neighbours, above below and sideways, to conclude a maniac lives beside them, and/or someone with a very colourful sex life.

A coded knock on the door – always knock with a

pattern, Stefan has told his friends, although he hasn't told them why (they just think he's eccentric). And he is glad of the excuse to pull the dustsheet over the painting and send the harbour into night-time.

'How's it going?' Jan asked.

Stefan shrugged. 'Like the boring bits on a jigsaw. Sky. Water. Too much caramel wedding cake.'

Jan raised his eyebrows at the brown, painty dustsheet. 'Eh?'

'I mean, too much Doge's Palace.'

'Ah.'

'How are you?'

'I'm fine.' Jan munched on a *brünchen*. 'Someone's just given me this, can you believe it?'

'What's it like?'

'Bit stale. Still, it's free.' He ate it valiantly. They went to a bar on the Silbersack.

In the morning he accepted two offers of work and spent a further five or six hours beside the Venice harbour. Around lunchtime an unexpected burst of sun broke through the rain and lit the eagles on pillars, their gold suddenly restored to brightness. Stefan adjusted the blinds and returned to a particularly wonky boat, which when he looked at it kept a figure on the quayside just in the corner of his eye.

Each time he focused on the gondola, the figure resolved itself into the woman from the museum. She smiled quizzically, beckoning him forward. Glancing towards her, however, she assumed her former faceless, plastic gawp. Back to the gondola and there she was again, half-smiling, almost insolent. Look at me, she seemed to say. Look at me.

Just forget about her, he told himself. But she remained, indisputably her, as long as she was on the edge of his vision, resuming her anonymity whenever he looked towards her. Eventually he gave up and went out.

She was in the street too. I pulled my coat collar up and zig-zagged, but she was still there. Everywhere I go, she follows me. She appeared between the eaves of a building and this time I was sure of it; but when I looked there was no one there. Just men in grey coats, walking stiffly and holding umbrellas, despite the fact it was sunny and relatively warm. It's November, so we behave for November, and we shiver in our coats.

I went back to the museum via St Pauli station, one of the two guarding ogres of the Reeperbahn, the other being the S-bahn at the far end of the long street. All stations are ogres, aren't they? They squat and loom and charge a toll if you want to pass. They roar. They echo. In the lost mists of time, there's even a legend that they puffed smoke.

Ornate lobby. Late deco pillars, the narrow strips of stone piercing the roof as much as holding it up. This time I hung around in the twentieth century, hoping to see her between the Beatles buying leather jackets and high-buttoned coats. Air-raid sirens swept me past Hitler's glass stare and then back, back, tumbling towards the other great fire that destroyed much of Hamburg the first time round, centuries ago.

Souvenirs that were a commercial success at the time: remains of wine glasses seared together by the immense heat, looking as though they'd bubbled from the lip of a volcano. Coins fused into each other, their colours green and peacock and violet. Amorphous jet objects. Strangely ominous jagged lumps of matter, the product of a diseased imagination or a late-morning nightmare.

She wasn't there. But I saw her twice on the way home. And she was still in the painting. A gondolier grinned leeringly. I tried to sleep, and I stepped through her dreams.

I finished the painting with less than my usual perfectionism. I just wanted to see the back of it; I hope they still pay me. I made my way to Jan's shop to see if he fancied a few drinks. He looked up from an engraving he was cataloguing and nodded.

'Of course. What's brought this on?' (Usually it's Jan who has to persuade me out.)

'I've got to tell someone,' I said.

'Tell me what?'

I told him. He laughed. 'Ghosts now, is it?'

'I think so. I see her everywhere.'

'Everywhere?' You can always rely on Jan's precise mind. He laid a ruler on the catalogue, leant back on his stool and winced.

'Street corners. Up and down the Reeperbahn. It's as if she knows me. I've only met her once, but she smiled as if she recognised me. She *knew* me.'

'I see. You're working too hard, is all it is. It's happened before.' Jan heard his bell – he must be psychic, I never hear it – and went through the curtain to an overcoated punter browsing through the racks. Pudgy, fifties, grizzly grey, tobacco fingers. His glasses steamed up as the warm air made itself at home on his face.

'Can I help you?'

'Well…' said the man, indicating a seventeenth century engraving of Priapus. Slight American accent, that he tried to disguise. Why? We like Americans here. Assumed guilt on his ample shoulders, perhaps, for – well, take your pick.

'I guess I was wondering where the… good stuff is.'

'This is the good stuff,' said Jan.

Ah well. No customers all day, and then the usual. Jan walked to the counter, enjoying the pitch even though he knew nothing would come of it. 'Many of these come from – you know… the secret museum under the Vatican.' He made his voice inaudible on the last word and just mouthed it. The punter looked at him Americanly.

'And over there – that's the secret wartime stash of you-know-who.'

'No, I don't know who,' said the customer. 'I want tits and cunts.'

'Oh,' Jan said, affecting sadness. 'Well this,' he spread a hand at his empire, 'is much better than tits and… things. This,' he paused grandly, 'is a pornotheka.'

'A whatica?'

'An antique one.'

Silence. The quiet of a traveller, at sea in a land of strangeness.

'Erotica,' Jan explained. 'You saw the sign?'

'Sign? They said any of these shops would sort me out.' He pointed a thumb at the amorphous they, who lived outside.

'Try the shops on either side. Or opposite. Any of them, really.'

'Right. Thanks very much.' The man tipped a finger salute to his head and turned. 'No offence,' he said as he reached the door and held out a palm.

'Not here, no.'

Jan re-materialised through the beaded curtain. 'They have money, don't they, Americans?'

'So I've heard.'

We reminisced about how things weren't as good as the old days, as the rain drummed on the skylight.

'Of course, the internet has screwed everything up.'

'Mmm.'

'Where's the excitement, if you've got it on a plate? You need to go and look for it, that's what makes it compelling. The sense of discovery.'

'I suppose so.'

'No suppose about it. I mean, if a woman just stands in front of you on the bus and takes all her clothes off, there and then... it's not exciting, is it?'

'I'd find it exciting,' I said.

'No, but you know what I mean.'

I nodded and commiserated. You have to support a friend in his hour of need. The rain rattled more fiercely, joining Jan in his annoyance.

'I don't understand why you gave up painting in the first place,' he said.

Being a murderer, I couldn't answer. I just made more sympathetic noises.

The rain drummed erratically, like Ringo. 'Shall we go out then?'

We had a few rums, but neither of us was really in the mood. I drifted back to the 90s, or was it even the 80s. I was in my old studio, six stops out; larger, but not much vibe, no sense of being where the action is. Commissions at one end and what I wanted to do at the other. If I did four hours of commission in the morning, I allowed myself the afternoon to paint what I liked. The discipline; I am nostalgic for it.

But what does it matter now, being a murderer and all that. I had long hair and a moustache; we all thought it was still the 60s, we looked bloody ridiculous actually. I destroyed most of the photos, but apparently people put them up on something called Facebook. I dare not go near it; I couldn't face the horror.

And I can see, as I walk round the flat in my mind, the portraits of Clara that adorn – the word is a cliché now but with Clara they really did adorn, she was adorable – every wall. I painted her from every angle, and stuck the pictures in every available space.

Portraits; full-length, clothed, nude, a bit nude, a bit clothed. Full-length; in a hallway, on a beach, in a hammock, on a boat, jumping from a bed, mirrored. Dancing, joking, laughing, drinking. Kissing her own arms, her legs. I shake now to think of it. Obsession would not do it justice. She overwhelmed. She could construct and destroy me in an evening. Seeing her talk to someone else; it was like being ripped open. Smiling, and it wasn't at me; I couldn't cope.

Not that any of this is an excuse. As a murderer, I can't defend myself. (How would that go? I'm sorry, I won't murder her again.) No – there is no starting point; only endless finishing points, all of them the same.

And as Jan got us another rum (why am I drinking this? Why am I even here? Because I'm a murderer and I can't go home) fast-forward, as one does in one's mind on rum, to the last six months, the giant unfinished canvas of Clara's unbelievable face, dominating the studio. Floor to ceiling, a square of beauty to rival Krakow's Rynek, Trafalgar, that square in Vienna. Two hundred, three hundred hours I spent on it. I never finished it, I even suspected at the time that I would never finish it. I would keep reaching for perfection until one or the other of us died. As, indeed, turned out to be the case.

And she came round, that Wednesday afternoon, it snowed, it hailed, and said she hated it. No sign of encouragement; no forgiveness for it being incomplete. Just, 'I hate it.' Well, you know what happened. I don't need to illustrate – ha ha! Sorry. I gave up my career as a result. No excuses. But those hundreds of hours, circling perfection, trying to land on it like a gnat dizzied by a garden; you can understand, perhaps, even if you can't forgive?

Palette knives everywhere; knives from dinner; even the carving knife was to hand. The perils of the open plan kitchen/diner/studio. Artists should never be allowed artists' flats. They don't think about that in Ikea. But there you go, I'm making excuses again.

There was fumbling, I remember that, the brushes dancing and rattling like snare sticks, the pots of turps bouncing and falling to the floor, the sickly smell enveloping the room. Something about a Stanley knife. Something about Clara saying she didn't want to see me again. Something about the giganticness of the painting. The metallic yellow of the knife contrasting with the purples and whey tones of the portrait, and me lunging towards her, sidestepping the painting. It was a stressful week, I'll admit that, as I go over and over those thirty seconds and probably will do for the rest of my life, or for as long as my mind holds out, whichever is longer. I spent so long on that damned painting that at the moment when the knife ripped into flesh and skin gushed blood, I no longer knew which was the real Clara and which was the portrait.

I look out through my studio window and see steam rise on the wasteland. How lucky I am to have that wasteland there. It was the work of minutes and a few bin liners. If you've visited the Reeperbahn you will know the characters that line its streets. An artist carrying manikin parts in black plastic bin liners and dumping them at dead of night is, if not an everyday occurrence, something most of us have probably seen at some point. So if anyone had seen me, and no one did, there would have been little suspicion.

We're conditioned to think murder is difficult to cover up. It's to stop us doing it, I suppose, and that's not a bad thing, I also suppose. Well. It isn't difficult, if you're a well-regarded local eccentric and your model has disappeared many times before in her life, frequently turning up on a different continent, and who doesn't have the same address six months running, and whose family hold no interest for her, and for whom the feeling is mutual.

'Look at this.' Jan examined a statue of the Venus of Ephesus. She held up two or three of her breasts in one hand, some of the others dangled, and the rest pointed in various directions. 'Remarkable, isn't it? Like an ancient Mona Lisa.'

Jan placed her on the desk. 'Wherever you stand, her breasts follow you round the room.'

'They look rather like eggs.'

'True. In fact there's a theory that –'

'You've got some weird stuff in here.' Stefan picked up a midget with three dicks.

'They were weird people, the ancient Ephesians. It's been here a whole month and no one wants it. Very reasonably priced.'

Stefan nodded.

'I don't suppose you'd like to buy it…?'

He shook his head.

'Discount for friends?'

'Sorry.'

They walked to the bar on the corner. 'Look,' said Jan. 'There's another one. I find this lady disturbingly attractive, I have to say.'

Across the road two men in orange jackets pasted a large advert against a crumbling wall. It showed a full-length image of a woman walking down a street, cleverly designed so it looked like a gap in the wall and she was emerging through it. She held a blue and green orb of perfume as if it were the world.

'Oh…' Stefan murmured.

'Don't tell me you haven't noticed her before,' said Jan. 'She's everywhere. Everywhere, she is. Gorgeous, isn't she?'

'Ah.'

They walked down the street. 'I think,' said Stefan as Jan pointed to a magazine hoarding, the woman from the museum again plastered across it – 'that I need to confess something to you.'

A café by the canal. Tower block windows reflected on the water, spiked by the triangles of churches. And Stefan, seeing guillotine diagonals in them, confessed his crime.

Jan thought carefully before speaking. 'This is why you gave up painting?' He sat upright in his seat; analytical, clinical. What do we do next? Stefan could see his eyes asking.

'Of course.' Stefan breathed on his coffee. It's true, that thing they say about the condemned man – that you notice details more thoroughly. The building opposite had a non-symmetric, cuboid wall of glass. It reflected the reflections, subverting them; questioning reality. What was he doing? Confessing? Why was he doing that? Because he could not not.

'What else do you remember about the evening?' Jan asked. 'What did you do with the body?'

Stefan spread his hands above the coffee and examined the twitch in his fingers. 'In the wasteland. It's handy.'

Jan smiled. 'Sorry.' He adopted a more serious face.

'I see it every day from the window… you don't have to bury things deep, for them to be gone by morning.'

'No one saw you?'

'I wouldn't be here if they had.'

Jan nodded towards the waiter and left some coins on the table. 'Come with me,' he said, pulling the mournful Stefan up by his coat collar.

In the cold air their faces changed from blue, to red, to yellow. Ripples from the canal danced across them, changing their expressions like a newborn baby appears to smile, or appears to frown.

'Stef, I was there,' Jan said. 'Don't you remember?'

He appeared to grimace, appeared to look surprised.

'There was a lot of noise, and I came running up from the shop. Clara was there. She said she was leaving you. You lost the plot.'

'I know, I know. You don't have to remind me.'

'You put the knife through the painting, Stefan. You ripped her face apart.'

'There was blood everywhere…'

'It was paint, Stefan. I helped you clean up.'

They went to the lake and Jan bought Stefan a takeaway brandy. 'It's far too early,' Stefan objected.

'You're very well behaved for a truant murderer,' Jan observed as his friend sipped it reluctantly.

'She drove me crazy…'

'I know.'

'Well if it's true… where did Clara go?' Stefan eventually asked.

'The States, I think. You could probably find her on Facebook.'

Stefan shuddered. 'But I buried her on the wasteland…'

Jan shrugged. 'I don't know where you get that idea from. I put you to bed. You were raving. I think you slept for about two days. Clara was pretty sour about it, I seem to recall. She said she had paint on her coat. Said that we were both complete nutters, and left. I cleared up some of the paint, but…'

'I hallucinated it all? I can see myself doing it, I wake up in the night thinking about it –'

Jan shrugged. 'Too much turps, perhaps. At a time of trauma. Your brain has constructed something you could deal with. You couldn't cope with her leaving you, so your mind killed her for you.'

They looked across the lake. The fountain did its sudden shooting up thing, like it had remembered it was supposed to be a fountain and had better get on with it.

'And it was a bloody good painting,' Jan said. 'Don't you remember?'

'I remember… I don't know,' Stefan said. 'I remember everything disappearing from the flat. I thought you moved it all.'

'I did. The slashed painting. That went on the dump, it's true.'

'What do I do now?'

Jan turned and laid a hand on his friend's shoulder. 'You go back to painting. You're a great painter. Or, you will be. You shouldn't have stopped.'

I returned to the museum. It seemed safe now. There was no ghost. It was true, I had been seeing that beautiful woman everywhere – she was on the posters. Dark-haired, of course, the negative image to Clara's blonde. And the smile she gave me, it wasn't because she recognised me; it was because she thought I recognised her. Her image is all over the city; people must come up to her all the time.

I looked at the paintings that spanned the space above the double staircase. Now I know I'm not being haunted, I miss her. But if you see her again, you can talk to her, now you're not a murderer. Marvellous! It seemed strange, as I moved on to the dark framed portraits, to find oneself not a murderer after all. An ex-murderer; no; not even that.

The paintings present ideas: I develop plans in my head for what I'll do when I get home. A seventeenth-century merchant, fur-lined crags of neck, glistening silver necklace, piles of mouth-watering gold coins on the table and a greyish, unnoticed skull behind. A double portrait, husband and wife, dour, static – look at us, we are important – but the artist evidently too bored even to give their grim expressions any life.

The third is of a family. Gainsborough, or an imitator, the wife in a striking pink dress, dulled to salmon; it could do with a clean. The master in a tricorn hat and hunting breeches, English oaks and elms across their estate in the background, the greens darkened to blue. A springer dog and a small boy, rosy cheeks and pursed mouth, violet eyes cheerful and twinkling. And in the corner of the picture a teenage girl: gawky, nervous and shy but radiant. About seventeen, looking towards the future, wondering what it would hold and quietly excited by the opportunities life might bring. The potential in life; it's dizzying.

It was clearly her. She might have been seven or eight years younger than the woman I saw in the museum, who I saw immortalised in the posters across the city, but there was no doubt about her identity. 'It's her,' I said out loud, and felt myself blush.

The inviting half-smile, looking out to the observer as if in recognition. Who was she? Did she live a long and full life? Did she love? Marry, have children? How old was she when she died? Set me free, she seemed to implore with large hazel eyes. Free me from the claustrophobic, yellowish mist that has fallen upon me over the long, stifling centuries.

'I will,' I murmur.

'I hope you became old and happy,' I add.

I step backwards, and have to steady myself against the banister. *Josef Esterhazy and his Family*, the painting was called. Time to go, Stefan.

Jan poured the champagne. My first exhibition in five years was of portraits: modern faces, in clothes through history. I painted Jan as a Greek philosopher, holding one of his beloved Venus of Ephesus statues. (Tits everywhere. The *Morgenpost* called it 'sublime'.)

Across the room, a full-length canvas based on one of the figures in *Josef Esterhazy and his Family* dominated the archway, positioned so it looked like the woman was about to step into the room.

Which, after everyone had left and I had drunk too much champagne, she did. She took large lungfuls of air, then kicked the windfall pears that were painted at her feet into brown mush.

'Of course,' she explained as we sat on the scarlet sofa, 'Jan was just suggesting that you hadn't murdered Clara, because he wanted you to start painting again.'

'Really?'

She nodded.

'So… I did murder her?'

'Of course. You slaughtered her, the poor woman. It was all over the papers.'

'But… what? Eh?' I can't think of anything coherent to say, so decide not to try.

She drew a calm, rich person's breath. 'Do you know Caravaggio?'

'Not personally, no. Do you?'

'Do you think he should have been locked up for murder… or should he have spent the next thirty, forty years painting?'

'Well…'

'Imagine the works we would have, if he lived to be an old man.'

'Well… it's… not the point, is it…?' I hazard.

She looked at me questioningly.

'Isn't it?'

She put a finger over my lips. I'll worry about it later, I decided. Being a murderer, I felt cautious about kissing her; but she, being unreal, didn't mind.

The Roll of the Sea

The heat dropped rapidly: in seconds it became winter, and the brown leaves turned white but did not fall. The lights went out briefly, Ella stepped forward and a circle of light formed around her.

Two whiskies, also in a pool of light, as she slipped backstage.

'How did it go?'

'Tiring.'

'It didn't show.'

A flicker of surprise. 'Were you there?'

He nodded, a rare flash of smile. 'I crept in at the back. One of the girls on the door turns a blind eye; I think she likes me.'

She smiled glassily, cut the whisky with most of a glass of water and drank a large mouthful. 'You shouldn't give me whisky... I'm always thirsty.'

William drank his neat, and she felt a tug of impatience in her stomach as she glimpsed the dark hairs folding invitingly beneath his shirt cuff, the cufflink a bold, inquisitive oblong of silver.

Maria cooked asparagus then lamb, its rump pink, glistening, sagging on the plate temptingly. Simply served, with a few onions and grilled courgettes, as if they had been rummaged as the meat was being cooked and tossed in to add colour.

They said grace, although neither had any faith. We are so fortunate, Ella would say, and I want to give thanks.

'Even if there is no one to give thanks to?' he once teased.

She nodded. 'Even if.' He met her request head-on, because he loved her, and now it was usually William who said grace. 'For what we have been given,' he said sincerely, his head bowed over the plate, 'we give you thanks.'

The 'you' was all-encompassing and represented, however faint it might be, that brief, beleaguered spark of belief; not an old man in a white beard, Ella would hastily explain, but some something, the difference between being and not-being, the benevolent influence that pushes the planets round the suns and the suns round each other.

Saturn and Mercury weaved between their legs. William nudged them away when they became persistent, but Ella liked the feel of them by her naked feet and would drop small pieces of meat when William wasn't looking, which the cats picked up gratefully.

Maria tidied away the plates, glancing at Ella and William for their approval; when it was eventually, briefly, noddingly given she journeyed down the spiral staircases contentedly. The smell of lamb and rosemary lingered in the air as she washed up in the expansive sinks. Absently she pulled slivers of meat from the carcass, washing the threads of meal down with apple juice.

Ella ran through her lines in the bath, even though she knew them well. It was a ritual, as much as always turning the cold tap on before the hot one, or flexing her toes before she allowed herself to fall asleep. She wondered where these fetishes came from. She could not remember, for instance, a time when she did not turn the cold tap on first; it had seemingly never been, even in childhood, a random choice between the two. The concept was alien to her. As she neared the end of the libretto, William padded along the marble tiles, plunged his hands into the water and massaged her feet. Later, with Mercury and Saturn purring on the sheepskin rugs she read Chinese T'Ang poetry; it put her in the right mood to become Madama Butterfly each evening, in spirit as well as body.

'There is no spirit,' William would murmur as he stepped from his linen trousers and slipped into the huge bath with her, the water rising and lapping around her neck. 'How can you say that,' she would tease, and neither paid attention to his reply – something along the lines of, you are nothing but a mass of billions of neurons, interacting with each other in trillions of ways. They knew this could not be true in a sudden moment of understanding as they sank into each other; if that were true, who is conscious? The thought slipped from their minds and was lost, and they thought nothing of it as it lay sleeping for another few months, until the next time they drank a whisky too many and started to explore, argue, the unknowable with each other.

There were three performances that week and she was satisfied with the middle one. It was only after the final night that real life intruded again. What would she do next; there was no work on the horizon; she would be forty in a few weeks' time and it could only thin out from here. William would tell her not to worry; his job was secure, he had enough for both of them, she must do what she wanted to do, and if the work didn't appear, she could keep trying; she mustn't feel she needed to earn money doing something else. 'Povera Butterfly,' she murmured, whispering *Un bel di vedremo* to herself. A pear rotted in the garden, a brown leaf fell, and there was a scuffle in the bushes as Saturn chased something. Madama Butterfly waited for Pinkerton, not listening to the maid telling her that he had abandoned her, and wasn't coming back.

The cold grey lines of the office. Ella tried to brighten it up with flowers and colourful lamp shades but he always moved them out of his way. Often she removed bouquets from the bin that were not yet dead. There was one solitary decoration, a naked white marble woman who was beautiful but looked unhappy and her eyes were dead.

Because Ella loved him she left him to depersonalise the office as much as he liked. There are plenty of other rooms, she told herself, resisting instincts to nurture and beautify. In autumn she brought dried fruits and flowers, to which he paid no attention but didn't seem to mind; eventually around January she would find them on the floor behind the desk, where they had been swept aside. She made a mental note to admonish Maria about the cleaning; then remembered that Maria too had been banished for cleaning under some files and replacing them in a way that prevented William finding what he wanted.

Poor Maria. Ella looked at her now, eating crusts from a plate and looking up guiltily when she realised Ella was there. A pay rise at Christmas, Ella decided. They already paid her far more than the going rate, and William had said, not too assertively, that she was not to have any more money. He was so used to saying things at work and them being done, that it did not occur to him that Ella might not do as he said. I shan't tell him, she decided. Maria sat squarely, digesting the bread slowly. Ella watched her throat contract and her eyes water as she ate. She needs to lose weight. How long will she live;

not much into her sixties, Ella thought, if she doesn't do something about her size. Puffing up and down those stairs all day, her face scarlet, it can't be good for her.

He was working from home more. She liked reading from the sofa, where she could lean back and see an oblong along the white hallway, then a narrower oblong into his office and just observe him in profile, under the lamp, usually frowning. You cannot escape your destiny, her mother used to say, telling her that she would end up marrying a banker as she had, and scoffing when Ella told her as a teenager that she wanted to be an opera singer. Well, William isn't a banker; although, and she could see her mother's arched eyebrow, he does work for a bank. He runs new product development which, she half-remembered, means he decides how the bank should compete against its rivals. How do we do things differently? Financial services are boring, how can we be interesting? William introduced new ideas to the stuffy organisation, where employees still wore suits with waistcoats and smoked in the office, ignoring small details like it being against the law. Today the stone and the formal hush in reception remained but the bank was finally, William would mildly say, leaving the nineteenth century behind, if not quite joining the twenty-first.

Ella sank into the cushions, lifting her hair out so it dropped down the back of the sofa. William tapped away on the keyboard, a pencil between his teeth; a habit he'd inherited from his grandfather, an architect who made his money helping to rebuild the city after the war. As a child William put a pencil in his mouth in imitation, enjoying the woody taste of it, sometimes unable to resist the temptation to sink his teeth into the soft, slightly bitter flesh and spit out flakes of red enamel.

He watched too much pornography but she forgave him this. It did not matter. There would be a glimpse of flesh, a flash of underwear or a gasp or a groan, a tangle of legs and hair and fluid; she did not understand why he watched entranced, as a squirrel pauses to watch insects, its eyes huge yet beady at the same time, its paws suspended from its shoulders. As he heard the boards creak in the hallway, he would switch it off and she would just catch the aftermath perhaps, freezing then disappearing, and the screen going black. Sometimes she wondered as he moved inside her whether he was seeing the illuminated image that had glazed across his eyes earlier; sometimes she tried to pretend for him, to be what he wanted her to be, but because he would never tell her, she could never guess it right.

Her mother also claimed, on a different occasion when Ella was a teenager, that she would end up alone. 'You'll never hold on to anyone,' she declared, pointing her glass at her so that Ella turned away from the sour aroma, 'you're too difficult. Men don't want someone single-minded like you, they want someone compliant who'll do as they're told.' Ella was relieved to have proved her wrong on that prediction too. She picked up her book and tried to concentrate. Religion is a pre-cultural phenomenon, the poem seemed to imply. Did that make it more likely to be essentially true, or less? Ella rested the book on her lap and glanced again towards the office.

None of it mattered. He was a generous man: she remembered when they first met, how shy he was. 'I'd like children,' he said tentatively after they had agreed to get married, as if concerned that she might not. She could not remember a proposal; in fact, it may have been she who proposed to him. She suggested they wait while she built her career. We can have children after I'm thirty, she said, and he agreed.

The child watched as Madama Butterfly killed herself. The blood bag didn't explode as it should do; Ella stabbed herself several times before she felt it puncture. The stench of stale egg yolk, cochineal and gelatine made her gag as she fainted and died. They made the blood up each morning. Once they had accidentally used the previous day's and she had vomited down her dress as the lights faded.

The child pulled at his teddy bear's ears; fearing the blood, looking round for someone, his fingers burrowing into the bear's fur, its face contorting and grimacing as it was tugged this way and that.

She gave the boy biscuits in her dressing room as he was always hungry after the show. He watched her solemnly as she washed the caked blood from her neck and arms. 'It's a difficult part for you,' she said to him in the mirror. 'No lines, you don't even have a name, but lots of emotion to express. You do it extremely well,' she added, washing her hands. 'You could have a great career in front of you.' He was still holding the teddy bear, its eyes squinting and its pout of a mouth twisted under his firm grip.

After the chaperone took him away Ella undressed and threw the bloodied costume into the laundry basket. Depression must be difficult to live with, she found herself thinking as she looked at the dress, its arms holding on to the side of the basket as if it were trying to haul itself out. Its curves billowed in the middle. As she stood naked in the centre of the room it was like a pupa she had escaped from.

At the end of the run the boy gave her the bear. She couldn't quite hear what he whispered, but she guessed, as she leaned down and her hair fell across his face, that it was something like 'he likes you'.

Saturn died young: cancer. His flesh dropped away from his frame almost visibly, and for the last few nights he slept in the same spot, refusing food, before the vet insisted he be put down. For a while Mercury moped about the house; pausing on the staircases, sitting motionless outside, her ears twitching, watching the depths of the garden, the spring leaves, waiting for Saturn to appear. They buried him by the red maple, William's muscles sweaty and his skin white and raw in the May light. Ella unwound Saturn's collar and gave it to Mercury to sniff, paw over and chew on thoughtfully. After a few days she seemed to understand and after a week she had forgotten him, diving through the garden amongst his ghosts.

She wore her new silk nightdress: dark pink, cut daringly high, further accentuated by a slit that revealed the ridge of her calf muscle. In bed he was insistent, urging. She made herself compliant, and let what he was saying slip over her head; she transported herself to a distant shore, and was happy there if a little lonely. She half-heard snatches of it; that he wanted to watch her with other men, that he wanted to see her being ravished. Afterwards when she curled herself around him, he murmured that he loved her as he fell asleep and this was enough. She looked down on him, seeing his breath rustle the tiny blonde hairs on her neck, caressing his hair where it was beginning to thin at the crown and reveal the secret planes and shapes of his skull. Brushing her hair the next morning she was bright and inquisitive, and ready if not for an argument then certainly to cross swords.

'What you were saying last night, did you mean it?'

He knotted a tie, sending the loops and curves around one another.

'Can we talk about it later?'

'Later, you'll say the same things in the same way, and I won't know if you mean them.'

He opened the mirrored door and the flash of reflections scattered across the room. He selected a dark, blue-ish suit; they are all exactly the same, why does he need to choose one so carefully? He dressed slowly; there was an age before he needed to walk to work. His offices were a few blocks away, in the district that had sprung up almost overnight, like silver mushrooms alongside the ancient canals, the moon observing with faint but knowing surprise the new forest of flats nuzzling against the old warehouses.

Are we leading increasingly separate lives; he lives inside his own mind, and I live in mine. The rectangular view through to his office as unchanging as sky; head bowed over the financial papers which spread out in front of him like a pink, slowly poisoning sea. The squiggles of black fish: sevens with fins, nines with tails, dancing maddeningly across the surface, able to go nowhere. She would come up behind him and stroke his head, the bald patch increasing in size and the hairs spread more thinly across the top, trying to keep their grip, and knowing the battle was a losing one. He would not notice she was there, murmur and sigh from time to time, the deep bass voice of regret and unvoiced fears coming up from the depths of wherever he was. That night she promised herself she would try to enter his world more; she would make the connections. She would let the trillions of leaps between her billions of neurons try to interact with some of the billions of his. When he made love to her silently, she arched her back and said things she had never dreamed of saying. 'A man asked me for a date this afternoon,' she lied. William paused momentarily, then carried on. 'What did you say to him?'

'He saw me drinking coffee, and he saw me looking.'

'You were looking at him? What did you say?'

'I didn't say anything. I was thinking about it.' She let the slabs of silence form around them. Silence isn't an absence, she thought as she watched his expressions change, the frown turn to a narrowing of the eyes and back to a frown again; it has substance, presence. He could visualise her looking, he could see her pursing her lips and glancing down at her coffee, a diagonal of hair falling across her face, and the jealousy stabbed at him.

'I said I was married. Then I asked him if he still wanted a drink.'

She was guessing as she travelled what he might like. It was like being on a beach in winter; you want to go in the water, but know it will make you gasp and you might regret it later. You run in a direct line anyway, shouting and laughing, the freezing water splashing up around you, the horizon bouncing up and down. Afterwards there are no towels, and you shiver, and other people who know better are tucked up in their jumpers, and you wonder, why did I do that?

'What did he say?'

'He said yes, of course.'

He was urgent now. 'Go on.'

'He gave me that look. That look men give women. When they are deciding in their minds whether she will, or she won't; whether they should waste any more of their time or not.'

She felt him shrink away; she leant to the side table and poured more wine for him. 'I'm sorry. I thought it's what you wanted.'

'It is,' he said. 'There's just – a lot to absorb.'

She toyed with telling him she'd made it up. 'So I don't know,' she said, pouring her own wine slowly. 'He might ring. He might not.'

'He'll ring.' In the morning she was half-awake as he made love to her again. Usually she had to persuade him, entice him, distract him; she would cancel the alarm when he wasn't looking then blame the technology when he got dressed in a hurry, concerned about getting behind with work. 'You can't rely on it,' she said as he looked suspiciously at his phone. Today William ignored the alarm as it chirruped away, self-important to begin with, irritated and impatient as it realised it was being ignored; then subdued, lazy, half-hearted; eventually giving up when it realised no one was listening.

Freddy was three now; you'd think he would have learned. If you roll in fox shit, you have to have a bath. They stood in a triangle, Freddy with his tongue hanging out, wondering who he would have to dodge first. William lunged forward, grabbing Freddy by the scruff of his neck. Ella was ready, plastic gloves, the huge bowl of water that erupted and splashed most of its contents over her as the dog detonated its refusal as vociferously as it could. It barked its joy as William lost his grip, slipping over on the tiles, and Freddy weaved expertly through their legs and somehow unlatched the yard door. When they were back inside, giggling and trying to wipe the smiles off their faces, as if Freddy was a child who needed to be chastised seriously, they found him poised nonchalantly in his basket, dripping wet yet pretending to be calmly relaxing, looking round at them with slightly raised eyebrows as if to say, 'What? What are you looking at?'

'Did he call?'

'No, he hasn't called.'

William thought for a moment. 'He's making you wait.' He went back to his diary.

'I'm not making it up.'

He glanced up. 'No, I know you're not,' he said, seeing her truthful expression.

Next day Ella found herself leaving the flat and going to the bar on the corner. From the basement Maria sensed her as the light darkened above, heard boots on the grilles and the wide door slammed. Maria was puzzled and glanced at her watch; then became anxious and tried to think what she might have done, or not done. This anxiety occupied her for most of the evening, and she listened in vain for Ella's return.

Someone spoke to Ella almost immediately, but he was so repellent that she dismissed him quickly. Greasy hair, a tendency to touch his face as he spoke which only drew attention to the reddish spots around his nostrils, and a way of leaning too close to her, round-shouldered, a feral smell of cigarettes and nervous sweat. Does he really think anyone might say yes, she wondered, admiring his impervious confidence, a brief 'your loss' expression as he shambled away. The next hour she spent on her own, the sullen youth behind the bar plunging tea towels into glasses and staring past her as if he didn't quite accept that either of them fully existed. She got anxious; if William discovers it's all fiction, he'll be cross. At ten the bar started to fill and she had glimpses of lives and worlds outside her experience. Later she called William and he told her that, if she did not come back that evening, he would accept it. She felt shocked as she looked at the pot plants sprouting over the bar, the paintings of jazz singers, and was glad he could not see her expression. She was offered a cigarette, which she took.

She floated through thick blue water; it kept her buoyant and she did not need to swim to stay afloat. It was shower gel, or artificial water made of the stuff they used in the blood. Ahead was a circular island of sand and on the other side William, swimming confidently. Unlike their holidays, where he would stay cautiously at the side and watch her.

A yard of sheet between them, its shallow ripples accentuated by the light from the street. 'I can't do this,' she whispered, and was unsure if he heard her. 'I want to be with you.'

'Yes, yes.' He groaned in his sleep, dreaming.

'What's the reason? There must be a reason,' she murmured, but his back was a cliff, ridged and unnavigable.

After breakfast he kissed her. 'No reason,' he said. Ice blue eyes; they had not been looking at her properly for a while, but now they were back.

There was no work for most of the year, but in the autumn the opera house revived the season and for six nights she again became Butterfly, basking in the strong yellow light and the fake leaves that covered the floor. The director was new, a twenty-something fresh from Bayreuth who had not heard of her. He was excited: after the week in Hamburg the production would tour; Belgrade, Dubrovnik, Prague. Koobas introduced her to the orchestra as something of a relic, and she tried to pretend she did not notice.

'Butterfly is a strange title, isn't it,' he said in a pause in the rehearsal. 'It's about a woman who is faithful no matter what; yet a butterfly is a creature who flits. It flutters, it flirts. It glances at one flower then thinks, there are hundreds more; it fritters its time, it is fickle. A prostitute for the flowers. Surely it would be better to name her after a creature that actually is faithful.' He looked around, raising eyebrows at the orchestra as if expecting them to respond. 'Madame Owl, perhaps.'

Polite, ice-breaking laughter.

'Madame Penguin.'

Are butterflies faithful, Ella wondered as she stepped into the light and drew breath. If they are, they can have no understanding of the notion of faithfulness; which makes it all the more remarkable.

She looked down from the high ridge and saw the lights of William's car, driving at high speed along the winding road to meet her. There was a flash of fox on the road ahead of him, the orange and white blur manically dashing into the safe blackness on the far side. The dream transferred to the park where, following the curve of the path, Ella saw the fox again and also a squirrel, cocking its head inquisitively. We can industrialise and concrete as much of the planet as we like, she debated with the squirrel, but animals will still find pockets to colonise, won't you, even in the heart of a dense city. The underground of life carries on, no matter how we change things on the surface.

Past William's office: a grey box, with a narrow vertical window glowing yellow, through which she could see him in front of a flipchart. He was a director now. A hemisphere of suits looked up at him, some rotating their seats, some chewing their pens. 'Emotional connection,' he was saying. 'That's what our adverts need.'

She was back on the ridge holding the boy's teddy bear. William's car sped up the narrow lanes, zig-zagging round the boulders that shielded the road from the precipice. 'Of course,' she said, 'the ridge is the same height as the audience. It becomes high when Butterfly peers down from it, with a hand over her eyes.' William's car spun out of control across the road, hitting the boulders and flipping over, rolling back onto the tarmac. Unable to move, her hands tugged by the teddy bear, Ella watched as people rushed to help William from the wreckage, the car's shiny metal creased and dented, his legs bloody and mangled.

Across the room William studied her perfect form moving in the sheets, pulling and drawing them around her, her arms breaking away from the pillows, her shape shifting and changing, her fists pulling then letting go.

She was singing with a new Pinkerton and their voices did not work well together. It wasn't his fault; he was young, and she could see he wasn't happy. The problems were not due to her age, but it was the obvious and easy answer for everyone. The reviews were harsh: the production is tired, there is no chemistry between the leads, and Ella Freni is too old to play a fifteen-year-old credibly. William did not seem sympathetic. 'When the reviews are good, you say they're only critics, and what do they know?'

He ran a bath for her then took a conference call, embedding himself in the office for most of the evening. The revival was cancelled after Munich. Sitting on his desk, she drew butterflies on pages of his notepad. The next day they had been torn out.

In the morning silence Maria fretted over breakfast, knowing she had made appalling poached eggs. Sometimes they just don't work, it doesn't matter how many times you try. Later she made a vast ham pie. She had a stroke as she was straightening up from the oven and was probably dead, the doctor told them, before hitting the ground. Ella was entranced by his clean white hands; they were piano-player's hands. As the door closed she looked down at Maria's podgy face, eyes embedded like raisins in cake, hands half-clenching, not quite a fist, and it was like looking at a dead child.

Waiting for the undertaker, William made conversation. 'She was obese, what did she expect?'

'How can you be so cruel about it?'

He raised his shoulders and opened his palms. 'It's not cruel. She was fat. She was disgusting, really.' Ella looked towards the kitchen door, then back to William. 'What would she think, if she could hear you now? After all the years.'

That shrug again, that she used to think was open and honest and now found irritating, inappropriate. The half-smile, that she was unsure was patronising or not. 'She's dead. It's meaningless to ask what she would think. She only thought before she was dead, and I hadn't said it then.'

'William –'

'In fact,' he said, pulling a chunk of ham from the pie and chewing it thoughtfully, 'I didn't *need* to say it then, because she wasn't dead.' He ate most of it that evening, as Ella wasn't hungry. It's too salty, he said as he put the remainder in the fridge, with a lid over it to keep it fresh. Next day a broad beam of November sun shone through the window and a sparkling of dust emerged on the bookcase, where Maria had been polishing and missed bits.

Mercury had cataracts. Her bright blue eyes darted from side to side and she seemed to be constantly trying to see round the side of her own eyes. You're a brave cat, Ella whispered as she stroked her and the cat looked up, mouth slightly open, eyes dashing back and forth like someone scanning words on a screen and not making sense of them. It was faintly comical, and all the more moving for it. The games she used to like with string they could not play any more; it seemed cruel, as if Ella was taunting her, so she stopped; but Mercury missed the games, she wanted to play, and it made Ella cry when she tried to decide what the best thing to do might be. Eventually they settled into their new routines. Mercury liked staying on her lap or in her bed now, which she had never wanted to do when William had been there. She resisted the divorce, thinking that as long as they were technically together, there was a chance of reinvigorating what they had. She asked him to wait, to reconsider; but he said there was no point, they did not understand each other any more. 'I don't know what you mean by that,' she said; he was glassy, and she laughed for him.

'Is there someone else?'

'Of course not.'

'It's time now, though, isn't it?' She looked at him appealingly.

'Time?'

'For children. We said…'

He looked at her in astonishment. 'We're in the middle of splitting up, and you're talking about children?'

'That's what we said we… that's what you wanted. Isn't it?'

The day's silences ended with her asking, 'What have I done?' He slept in the room by the office.

He told her not to do the packing, that he would send someone on to do it, but she found she wanted to. She cleared the office methodically, placing anything he might need in boxes, making up charity shop boxes of old equipment, and throwing pens and thoughtfully chewed pencils into the bin. Emptying the drawers she found her pictures of butterflies, carefully torn from the notepad and stapled together. She looked into Freddy's eyes, understanding and uncomprehending at the same time.

'I don't understand it,' she murmured, but how does anyone understand anyone else? You just have to hope you're going in the right direction. We create people, we shape them to our imaginations. They are what we want them to be, but they're not really, and then we discover we cannot cope anymore. Freddy's hot breath pulsed on her skin, and Ella pushed his head away. 'Smelly dog.' Thinking it was a game, Freddy pushed his muzzle back into Ella's face. William wasn't coping either, she knew. I am not what he wants me to be, so he is not-coping in his own way. When he left she said she loved him, and he nodded. 'I love you too.'

Freddy, now shambling on his paws, found Mercury in the hallway. He nudged the body and pushed it back and forth in confusion, then looked up at Ella for explanation as she stepped down in the early morning light.

Freddy stood guard, tail wagging, as she buried the cat next to Saturn. She sensed some cosmic meaning, perhaps a cruel joke of the gods, in that Saturn the bringer of old age had died young and Mercury, the brief and flighty, had lived to twenty-one. She heard William's voice, indulgent and contemptuous at the same time of such meanings, and wished he was there to help. She made a mess of the earth and thought of William's younger back, the muscles rippling, the skin pale and not so covered in squiggly grey hairs as it was now. Freddy barked. Ella tipped the last of the soil onto Mercury; was she even twenty-two, she wondered; she had lost track. There is still a why, Ella thought, and as long as I hold onto that why, and try to understand him, the door will always be open.

Part of her said to herself, why would you want him back? He left you, and he hasn't explained why; let him fuck off. 'Yes, yes, that's right,' she said, hearing his voice in her intonation. Freddy got excited, the 'yes, yes' implying a walk.

The steel grey lines on the train, towards the border. Later an American flag, distantly visible as ships criss-crossed ahead and behind, and she wondered how none of them struck each other. One of the ferry passengers held a nervous cat, its ears twitching at every sound, large brown eyes making it more like a furry monkey clutching at its owner's arms, and Ella had to look away, the cold making her eyes water. The breeze increased and the squawk of gulls and a scattering of rain drove her inside. The cabin air was thick, warm and comforting despite making her queasy. It blocked her ears and the smell of carpet and old diesel dominated. She ordered a whisky and the young waiter watched her with erotic curiosity as he dried glasses. 'Have you worked this route long?' she asked. He shook his head, unable to form a coherent reply.

'Shame it's only a ferry crossing,' she said, 'long journeys are full of possibilities.'

He nodded and mumbled something about preferring to sleep in his own bed.

'Are you Czech?'

'Slovak.'

'Ah, I worked once with the Slovak Radio Orchestra, they were very good.'

He could think of nothing to say. 'I used to be an opera singer,' she added.

'I've never seen an opera.'

A sense of freedom as she went back up on deck that was almost suffocating. William appeared briefly, a ghost in the sea spray. She breathed a sigh, the mist enveloped him and he vanished. She thought of the boy held captive in the bar below and imagined telling William about him. How silly it all seems now.

Quickly familiar with the studio, and enjoying its conveniences – everything within reach, the kitchen self-cleaning because it was so small – Ella soon lost any desire for the house, for the stuff, for the tall narrow stairs, and felt it would be hard to go back to them. It was regression to student land, or a womb. The phone startled her; she had only heard the sound when she tested it two months ago, or was it longer?

'William?' she said, too quietly for the person at the other end to hear.

'Hello? Is Ella Freni there?' The woman arrived the next day, saying she had got lost and how did Ella cope with the cold? Worried about the last ferry, Ella said she could stay over, and Polly looked around in mild panic. This is how we end up, Polly thought, warming to Ella quickly despite the way her mouth hung open when she wasn't talking. Polly spoke niceties to begin with, finding it difficult to start and expecting Ella to ask what she was doing there, and what she wanted; but Ella waited patiently for Polly to lead.

'I need to speak to William.'

Ella nodded.

'I was hoping you could direct me towards him.'

'I can give you his number,' Ella said, reaching out for her address book but not moving when she didn't find it. 'He doesn't answer to me, but he might to you.'

'Thank you.' Polly expected to defend herself against questions, but when Ella asked none, found herself wanting to give information.

'I need to tell him his brother's died.'

'Ah, right.' That open mouth again; it made Polly squirm. She found herself wondering where all the money had gone. 'I didn't know he had a brother.'

'No, they didn't speak.'

'In... so many years?' Ella tried to remember how

long she had been married.

'You see,' the woman said uncomfortably, 'I used to be engaged to William. Before I married Edmund.'

Polly used the silence to rummage in her bag. 'You were easier to track down,' she said, holding out a CD. 'I wondered,' she added, temporarily shy, 'if you'd mind signing this?'

Ella watched as if it were on a stage. William, the younger, slimmer version with razor cheeks, the man she had fallen in love with, before the weight of money, and of being successful and content. Yellow spring leaves turning to green summer ones, and the spotlight narrowing on him, the teenage love affair between William and Polly unfolded. They lived in the same town, and in fact had been at school together, although were not friends. Polly often came to the house, William's brother blushing and clumsy as he tried to join in with their pretences at adulthood: cooking each other meals, which they frequently burnt and blamed on Edmund.

They were twins, but William seemed younger. Sitting opposite each other on sofas and pretending to enjoy Shakespeare. Listening to operas on his father's CDs, secretly glancing at their watches from time to time. 'You could be an opera singer,' William said, admiring Polly's willowy frame and thinking how sexy her voice was when she occasionally smoked.

Edmund seemed taller than his brother and was physically more impressive; he played rugby and was a vigorous actor at school. 'He's the pretty one,' Polly would tease, and William did not mind. In their early twenties he hesitantly proposed and Polly said yes; but it would have to wait until after his accountancy exams, he said. Edmund got a job presenting pop programmes on TV; he bought a house and didn't know what to do with all the money they paid him. He got his teeth whitened, had his hair laboriously and fashionably cut at the studios every other day, and went through a brief cocaine phase, which lasted longer than he claimed to his bosses after his two 'lesser bollockings'.

Arriving at the family home in a red Mercedes one afternoon, with William on the fifth exam, it was inevitable what the next part of the story would be. Edmund whisked Polly away with promises of parties, shopping trips, champagne, and the vision of not having to work. 'Although if you do want a job,' he added as she wavered, 'I know an agency who could give you some modelling, no probs.'

William, tired from study, looked across the mountain of books and could think of no words: his mind was numbers. He managed to ask why, and to express hurt, which seemed to make Polly contemptuous. 'If you ever earn any money,' she said, 'you can find your angelic opera singer to put up with you.'

'Did you have any children?' Ella asked.

'One,' said Polly, after momentary surprise at the question.

The last act was set in the present: high-rise flats in downturn Hamburg, Edmund smoking and eating too much and ballooning. Dropped by the TV channel before his thirtieth birthday, he got work on radio, doing the night shift and taking a while to adjust to the vast drop in salary. They were in debt when he died, drinking too much in the day because he was home alone with nothing to do. The doctor said it was suicide. Polly dismissed this and by the time of the funeral, he had suffered a heart attack. Their son did not arrive; held up travelling, the postcard said the following week.

'So here I am,' she said apologetically, pushing the creases out of her skirt and feeling unsure what to do with her hands. 'I thought William should know.'

Ella nodded. Polly looked round. 'I also… it's not easy for me to say this. I don't have any money. And I wondered if you could help – as you're kind of my sister-in-law?'

'Yes,' said Ella. She rubbed her eye, and looked through the narrow window at the calming tides crashing in the distance. 'I think the best thing is, if I ring William.'

She taught her kitten new tricks and he looked up in anticipation, shoulders attentively poised, paws twitching and ready to pounce. She hadn't named him yet, resisting Jupiter and other alternatives that came into her head. Maybe he would always just stay kitten; did it matter, does he have to have a proper name? He scratched her, painless red lines that formed magically on her hands and ankles. She felt grateful. Her parents were wrong: you can escape your destiny. She glanced at the old teddy bear, who sat on a high shelf so that kitten would not rip him to pieces. He looked down on her, his squashed face and button mouth inquisitive, urging her onwards.

'You don't see what's in front of you,' she heard her mother saying, and smelt the gin as she rotated it in her glass. 'You don't listen, and you don't think.'

She called William, just to hear the sound of the phone ringing. She knew he would not answer, but wanted to hear his voicemailed explanation of why he couldn't be with her right now and his reassurances that he'd call back soon.

Success has made a failure of our home

Grahame Kennard isn't an unusual name, but neither is it all that common, and so when I met someone who was also called Grahame Kennard at a party, I got quite excited.

Lucy thought I'd been mixing my drinks. 'You're never going to guess who this is,' I said. She raised a quizzical eyebrow then smiled that slightly frosty smile she uses when I'm embarrassing her.

'Grahame Kennard!' She looked at him expectantly, waiting for him to introduce himself. Then back at me. Small eyebrow twitch.

'Grahame Kennard!' I added. Later, when the music got loud, Grahame Kennard and I hunched over the plastic beer kegs, our foreheads practically touching. The coincidences were remarkable. We were the same age, roughly; he was two years older. We'd both grown up in the south-west – he in Bath, me in Taunton. The most amazing coincidence was we're both in finance; I work at the Highmount building society and Grahame Kennard advises multinationals.

'You must come over one evening,' I shouted as Lady Gaga made something sound important. Lucy danced over and grabbed me by the waist. 'That would be great!' he replied, and that was the last I saw of Graham Kennard as I was forced into dancing, albeit only for about fifteen seconds of jigging about uncomfortably in an impression of enjoying myself until Lucy gave me a gentle push and allowed me to skulk back gratefully to the shadows.

The next day we both had hangovers. 'It's because the music was so loud,' I said over breakfast, and Lucy gave me her look. Sometimes she seems to be about to laugh, as if I'm being funny, but I wasn't being funny, I could still hear the thump in my head of Mrs Gaga going on about whatever it was. 'Whatever,' Lucy said, pouring us more rice snaps. She used to buy Rice Krispies, but they're just the same, only cheaper.

Lucy bought a new outfit; I couldn't see what was wrong with my old dinner jacket. 'What's wrong with it,' Lucy said, standing behind me and bashing it the way people do when they think they're smartening things up, 'is it hangs off you.' She kissed me on the neck and walked round me like Bruce Forsyth steering a contestant to the right place.

'There you go.'

She brushed some imaginary specks from my collar. 'Come on then, gorgeous husband.' We even splashed out on a taxi. I looked through the sparkly, rainy orange light as the cab bounced up and down, and felt special.

The hotel appeared through the haze of the windscreen, blue lights glittering and then smearing as the wipers swept at the increasing rain. 'I'll get you right to the door,' said the driver, 'can't have you getting wet. What about this terrible weather, eh? Terrible.' We agreed with him it was terrible. The hotel sign was made out in a dark blue light. That's clever, I thought, you wouldn't think you could get a blue light to be that dark. A man in a top hat held the door open for us and we stepped onto a vast blue carpet that stretched across the lobby. It was like walking on sea, and you couldn't hear your feet as you sailed across. We stood in the middle of this sea, adrift between two naked bronze women holding up lamps shaped like flames, until someone embarked beside us.

'Exparqia dinner?' a lady smiled. 'Yes,' Lucy said, and we were pointed towards the far end of the lobby. There were three identical doors, heavy and wooden with gleaming brass fittings. It was like choosing which path one was going to take in life, and hoping you'd make the right decision. The sea wobbled and blurred as we slid across. 'Look at this,' Lucy said. Between the doors were brass plaques, declaring in bold Roman letters the CHURCHILL ROOM and the EISENHOWER ROOM.

The plaques were polished to a high sheen, and when I touched one to feel the satisfying depth of the lettering, it left a gleaming fingerprint. I wiped it away but doing so left a smear. 'Come on,' Lucy whispered. Opening the door was like entering a cinema; the light disappeared and we were pulled inside by distant flashing strobes.

We were sat at Grahame Kennard's table and he made great play of introducing me to people, all of whom were highly amused. 'So Grahame,' said a large, confident man with a massive red face, 'Marks & Spencer shares; should I buy or sell?' The lady next to him, who had a strangely plastic face and wide green eyes, looked at me. 'Grahame Kennard is the expert,' she said. 'We should do what he says.'

Grahame Kennard, leaning back in his chair, cut a cigar. Under the table, Lucy's foot gently slid up my ankle.

I thought, I can do this. 'Well,' I said, 'economy's a mess, right?' Everyone nodded. 'People need reassurance in difficult times, right?' More nods, even from plastic face woman. 'So Marks & Spencer is familiar, you remember it from childhood; you're more likely to shop there.' Nod.

'So you're saying "buy",' said the big red face. Grahame Kennard smiled broadly at me and laid his cigar on the table. Under the table, Lucy's foot nuzzled my thigh.

The rest of the evening went in a bit of a blur. We had a sort of flan thing for starters, which looked tiny on a gigantic plate and had some messy sauce poured over it. Chicken for the main meal, which seemed a bit dull when I'd been expecting something exciting. Finally a pudding with bits in it. Each time I got near the end of my glass of wine, a girl appeared out of thin air and topped it up, which made me feel that I should be drinking it more quickly. Later when I related this to Lucy she said I was being sexist, but I protested; she was a girl, couldn't have been more than seventeen, and I think it was the same one each time but it was hard to tell because she whisked in and whisked out silently, without allowing time for me to pay attention to what she looked like because I was busy holding my glass out. Lucy kissed me absently on the head and said I was funny, and went to put some washing on.

Anyway, I felt I could hardly move from my seat at the end of the meal but the man with the big red face had got some of those thin chocolate mints from somewhere and dropped them down his throat as he asked more questions, like what should he do about agricultural investments. I said it wasn't really my field, which got a laugh. Then there was dancing, there always has to be dancing doesn't there, and I had a light panic when I went to the bar to get a couple of drinks and realised it was no longer complimentary, and when I signed the slip of paper that was pushed across to me (by another identikit girl in black-and-white, and this time I don't mind if I get accused of being sexist because she gave me such an indifferent look that I wondered if she was technically awake, let alone worried about distinctions between girl and woman) I found I was paying twenty-two pounds for two drinks. 'Has it gone up while I was queuing?' I asked, not expecting the robotic expression to change but feeling that some kind of response was necessary. There was even a little dotted line at the bottom of the piece of paper that I could sign if I wanted to leave a 'gratuity'. In the event, my generosity did not extend to this.

Lucy said not to worry and she didn't want anything more to drink anyway, and she danced quite a lot and we spilled into the wet London night feeling that we were leaving the blue velvety cinema after a long, satisfying film. People going about their evenings moved around us; it felt good to be swept up in it. I felt alive and happy and buzzing. We only live an hour away on the Northern line and yet it seems like a different country; how often do we come out in London properly, like tonight? We looked behind us at the hotel, not wanting to leave, and Lucy took a photo on her phone and the man on the door in the top hat looked back at us impassively.

Taxis canoodled on the pavement, their yellow signs glowing hopefully. 'Tubes are still running,' I said, and Lucy nodded. We'd had the excitement and the rain was easing. 'Be more fun on the tube anyway,' Lucy said. 'People will look at us, and wonder where we've been.' And they did.

It was nice of Grahame Kennard to ask us, but coming back to reality was a bit shit. The next morning at work was so quiet it seemed noisy. I noticed for the first time how bright the strip lights are on the staff side, although this may have just been owing to my headache. Why do people have parties on a work night, I wondered as Howard opened the bolts and four people outside stamped their feet like horses coming in from the cold.

Number one came in to collect a pension; why, I wondered idly, would you queue before we've even opened, you can hardly be in that much of a rush for it, nothing else to do I suppose. Number two complained that we'd charged him for going overdrawn; well don't go overdrawn then.

Number three wanted to speak to someone about arranging a mortgage on a property he was about to buy, and told me about it in such a loud voice that the person he needed to speak to could probably hear him.

No one buys a house any more, they buy 'properties'. The rest of the morning was a bit of a blur, albeit a white neon blur instead of last night's gentle blue one. Albeit's a funny word, isn't it. We don't use words like albeit any more, albeit words like asleep are quite strange as well. To be a-sleep seems such an old-fashioned thing to be, like saying what time it is of the clock, although o'clock is bizarre and we don't notice that either. Maybe we do use a lot of old words after all. Most of this occurred to me as I was apparently listening to an old lady telling me in remarkable detail about her daughter's horse, the long and the short of it being that she'd need some kind of loan. I said I'd make an appointment for her, and even though I rang the bell and looked at the next person, she continued telling me about the horse. Palomino, it was.

The afternoon lasted forever and I noticed how cheap the wood was on the counter. It looks like proper wood, but you can peel away the corner and see it's just a kind of paint; underneath it's chipboard. I dug my nails into it.

When I got home Lucy had tied her hair back because it was wet, and I kissed the top of her head and breathed her in for a moment. 'You're back early.' She nodded. 'Last visit got cancelled.' I waited until dinner to spring the surprise on her. 'Smells good,' I said as she bustled about with pans and tea towels and whatnot. After laying the table I pulled the bottle from my bag like a magician producing a rabbit. 'Ta-da!'

'Lovely. I'll get glasses.'

'No, no. You have to look at it.'

'Look at it?' She looked at it. 'Looks very nice.'

'It's a 2008.'

'Is it.'

I don't know how the argument started, it just seemed to come out of nowhere and then escalate. I was probably a bit too excited about the wine and Lucy asked if it was expensive, and I said yes it was expensive, that was the whole point. And she said it was all right, but didn't taste better than what we got from Tesco for £3.99, albeit after you've left it open for an hour or two. It's funny, because usually it's me who's careful about not spending money, and me who says we can't afford things, so you'd think she'd be happy I'd splashed out for once. In the event she said she'd just had a long day; one of her foster carers had nearly walked out.

'You said she wasn't up to the job anyway,' I pointed out.

'I know,' Lucy said, 'but it makes life harder if she goes.'

I thought, probably best if we sleep on it, and took the remaining third of the bottle to the kitchen. I ran my finger over the label before putting it away. The lettering's embossed and there's a black and white picture of a chateau on the front.

When I turned round, Lucy was watching me from the doorway with her arms folded.

At least it's Friday, I thought on the bus, and concentrated on this as people barged into me. I've never noticed how dull we all look at this time in the morning, and how unwell; pasty faces, eyes with greeny bits of sleep in the corners, spots that stand out like crevices because of the low, harsh early light. Do I look like that too?

The day was another blur. I got off the bus early and walked the last mile. Lucy wasn't back so I put pies and chips on a baking tray and set them off slowly. I made a cup of tea and had half an hour on Facebook. I looked for Graham Kennard but he didn't seem to be there. I didn't have any messages, and no one was doing anything interesting; lots of people getting quite worked up about who was on *X Factor*, and extensive rumination about tomorrow night's *Strictly*. Turn it off, I told myself, remembering Lucy's rather dry, shrugging 'waste of time' expression. Lucy can't see the point of Facebook.

This made me type in 'Lucy Kennard'. There was just one. I added her as a friend and sent a message, 'You've got the same name as my wife!!!' and turned it off.

I checked the pies and chips and turned them up a bit, got the rest of the wine from the cupboard and held it up to the light. 'She won't mind,' I murmured as I poured most of it into a glass. I called Lucy but it rang without going to answerphone; she must be on a visit. I tried to read a book but couldn't concentrate, and wondered if Lucy Kennard had accepted my friend request. We could have both of them round for a party, and I could introduce Graham Kennard to Lucy Kennard, and we could have two Lucy Kennards and two Graham Kennards. Has that ever happened before, I wondered; might it be worth ringing BBC3 up, it's the kind of thing they'd make a programme about.

I googled Grahame Kennard and found a string of articles about him. Presenting awards at ceremonies; giving talks in Dubai and Singapore about global finance; a video of him being interviewed on a plane, discussing how he thought Britain could get through the times of austerity. I know someone famous I thought, and felt proud.

'Sorry, I just forgot about them.'

It didn't matter; I don't know why she made such a fuss. 'They're only pies.'

'I know, I know. It's just been a long day, sorry.'

'I'll get us a takeaway.'

'Don't worry, I can do something from frozen.' She opened the freezer, stared into it like that bloke who went to the Antarctic and said he might be some time, then turned to me. 'All right. Takeaway.'

'Chinese or Indian?'

'Ooh, Chinese. I might just go and lie down for half an hour.'

'All right.' I kissed her and she went upstairs, kicking her shoes off at the top. I knew to wait until later to ask her how the day was. She likes to zone out, forget about it altogether, and then over dinner she looks a little less pale and we can talk. In fact, I thought as I threw the blackened pie shells in the bin – they looked rather like baked turtles, not that I've ever seen a baked turtle I hasten to add – I'm surprised she can do her job without bringing more of it home. If I was doing what she does all day, I'd go on about it a lot more. I wonder what baked turtle would taste like? Horrible, I expect.

I ordered the takeaway – the dog-eared menu is covered in enough biro and star marks for me to know what she'd want – and I also sneaked out to Tesco to get us a bottle of wine. Not quite as exorbitant as last night, but much better than what we'd usually have. What am I saying. We don't usually have anything.

It was a mild evening, I observed as the plastic bag swung by my side. February's odd, isn't it, it can absolutely piss it down all week and then feel like spring the next day. He's a scamp, February. Lucy tipped the takeaway onto the plates, artfully avoiding splashes (they go bright yellow the next day; you wonder what your stomach must look like) and I uncorked the wine. 'You can tell it's a good one,' I said appreciatively.

'How's that?' she asked, taking it from me and sniffing it.

'It doesn't have a screw top.'

Lucy told me about Simon, who was having to move on to his fourth foster parents in three years because he was too hard to handle. 'It's just so unfair on him, because he's never going to get a start in life. He's ten, he needs to be doing better at school, but all his focus is on having to move again. It's no wonder he's distracted all the time.' She stared at her food. 'What are these bits?'

'Crispy beef, I think.'

'Oh. It's nice.' We both ate some and listened to our teeth making a song and dance about crunching into it.

'So how was your day?'

'Oh, the usual. Something funny happened this evening, though.'

A Lucy eyebrow.

'You'll never guess,' I said.

'Go on then.'

'Guess.'

'You said I'll never guess. Tell me.'

'Guess anyway.'

She looked out of the window for a moment. 'We've won the lottery.'

'No.' I don't know why she says that. We don't do the lottery.

'I give up.'

'I found a Lucy Kennard on Facebook, isn't that funny? She lives in Haringey.'

'That is funny.'

We cleared up and watched TV for a bit but neither of us paid much attention. 'Early night?' Lucy suggested. She blew the dust off the champagne glasses and we took the bottle to bed with us. It felt very decadent drinking wine in bed, why have we never done this before?

'Classic FM?' she said, giving me the Classic FM look.

I nodded. I'd hoped it was going to be a Classic FM night, and it was, till we were exhausted.

On the bus I flicked through *Metro*, idly glancing at the excuses made for showing pictures of girls not wearing much. Today's was about a record-breaking attempt to form the longest line of women in bikinis. Deeper into the urban oracle was an article saying that shares in Marks & Spencer had gone up; in hard times, it said, people look to the brands they trust and feel safe with. Lucy texted and asked if I fancied a walk at lunchtime; the weather was clearing and she had no visits to get back for. I walked up to the canal and waited in the usual spot; her Fiesta zipped round the corner and she gave me a cheery wave. The blue light on her face through the windscreen made her look gorgeous.

We got three quarters of the way along the canal and I stopped, pulled her towards me and kissed her. 'What's up with you?' she said, and gave me a low-level Lucy eyebrow.

'I just feel a bit romantic.'

'You're funny.'

After work I got off the bus early again.

Having talked to my boss, who likes being referred to as 'Jamie', I treated myself, and this amused Lucy. 'You always said you hated them.'

'I know.'

'You always said, if I get one, shoot me.'

'I know, but look at what you can do on it.' I scrolled down, enjoying the way my fingers felt smooth on the shiny glass. 'Never get lost again – you can bring up a map because it always knows where you are.'

'You said, why do people ponce about with those things and don't they realise how daft they look?'

'And you can store songs, and it's got a five meg camera as well.'

'What's a meg?'

'I don't know.'

'You used to say, why would I want to sit around in cafes getting thumb-ache on a glorified calculator and not have any friends. Oh, what's this?'

'Games. They're a bit rubbish actually. But you can download new ones.'

'No wine today?' she smiled over dinner. 'You can probably download some,' I said, smoothing the surface of the phone, and she pulled her what a hilarious husband I've got face. Later, though, she tired of it a little. 'Did you have to bring it to bed with you?'

'It's got an alarm on it.'

Classic FM was quite exciting this evening. As we were dozing off, I said why don't we have a dinner party this weekend? I was facing away from her but could detect the eyebrow. It can bore into a man's back at twenty paces, that eyebrow. 'When have we ever had a dinner party?'

'Well, we're all grown up now, I thought we could start.'

'Who would we ask? I suppose there's your mum.'

I mumbled something about Grahame Kennard and Lucy Kennard, and seem to recall mentioning BBC3, but I can't remember her reply because I was asleep.

I was there bang on time for the meeting with Jamie. He ushered me in and waved me towards the coffee machine and indicated a chair, all in one movement, which I thought was quite impressive. This is how you get to manager level, with skills like that. I remember my Latin teacher telling me that successful people are like swans – all calm on the surface, but paddling like mad underneath. My life seems to be the other way round.

Jamie talked for some time about infrastructures and 'dead men's shoes', and I tried to concentrate, but, in a nutshell, the upshot seemed to be, there's nothing doing. He looked at pieces of paper and said they'd come from HR, wherever that was. 'Don't have the qualifications… not the experience we're looking for… happy with where you are at the moment…'

I tried to be positive about this. 'If you're happy with my current performance, that's something to build on isn't it?'

He glanced up. 'I hear we nearly gave someone a fifty thousand pound loan for a horse the other day.'

'I know I typed house. I'm sorry. It was just a typo, I meant to write horse.'

'I guess we can overlook that.'

How generous of you, I thought, sitting there with your shiny tie and your fat pension. I had an urge to say as much, but heard the Latin teacher again. Play the game, Grahame, play the game. I nodded, playing the game.

'There's just not much vertical shift we can do here,' Jamie said.

Vertical what? I nodded away energetically.

'If you'd done some courses perhaps…' He looked at his watch and stood up, motioning me towards the door with his papers. 'Sorry, Kenning, I have to see the regional director now.'

I shuffled through the door, the blade of light from the window looming diagonally on me. If I had an accent as posh as his, I thought, I'd have my own office and my own shiny tie and my own dinky coffee machine, purring contentedly to itself.

I cheered myself up by sitting outside on the step where everyone smokes and playing Angry Birds. I can see why people find it addictive. Lorraine stepped over me and lit up. 'Shouldn't you go back in?' she said.

'I've got fourteen years' worth of cigarette breaks that I haven't taken,' I said. Lorraine nodded and wheezed on her fag. 'Fair – cough – enough.'

At home, Lucy was vigorously cleaning the kitchen. 'I'll do that,' I said, taking my coat off.

'It's okay,' she said, 'if we're having guests at the weekend, I want it to look nice.'

It does look nice. I uncorked the wine.

'You're not starting already?'

I looked at her in surprise. 'No,' I said, 'it's so it can breathe.'

'Oh. Breathe.' She squirted Mr Muscle on the hobs and glared at them as if they were offensive and belligerent hobs. Mr Muscle never has to go through this grief, no matter how weedy he looks on TV. A thick curl of hair hung over her face and she looked absolutely edible, despite the rubber gloves, or perhaps because of them. As she was about to say something I stepped forward and snogged her by the cooker, in full view of the window. 'Come on,' I said, 'I want to take you upstairs.'

'All right,' she said, looking flustered. 'Let me just…'

I pulled her hand and she followed. We hardly ever listen to Classic FM in the afternoons. It felt like bunking off.

When Lucy Kennard arrived, it was a bit like that programme where people who don't know each other cook dinner all week and then give really horrible marks in the taxi. She arrived with an exaggerated 'Hiya!' and a broad, brilliant smile, and thrust a bottle at me.

'Chablis, lovely.' There was a ribbon tied in a sassy bow round the neck. A woman who knows about wine, I said later to Lucy, who seemed unimpressed. Dave from the Coach and Horses made up the four. He seemed rather at sea all evening, at one point asking in confusion if it was all right to go to the toilet, and I felt embarrassed for him in front of Lucy Kennard.

I half expected Grahame Kennard all evening; but I reasoned, as I poured the last of Lucy Kennard's Chablis into the flutes and helped Lucy with the starters, that I was thinking too much about how the TV programme might turn out, and not real life. From the look on Dave's face as the plates were put in front of him one after another, he'd have been giving straight nines when he was in the taxi home (although Dave wouldn't need a taxi home, as he lives round the corner. I expect they'd drive him round the block a few times). So it's a shame it wasn't on TV really.

Lucy didn't look at me as she served up the rack of lamb (a clear nine from Dave once more) and Lucy Kennard chatted away about how funny it was that I'd got in touch with her on Facebook and isn't it amazing, the way you can get in touch with people from your dark past, especially those people from school who hated you but now want to be your friend. 'I've got eight hundred and twenty-five friends,' said Lucy Kennard in wide-eyed wonder, 'you wouldn't believe it would you?'

Lucy gave her a look that indicated 'no you wouldn't,' and stuck her knife deep into the lamb. Lucy Kennard explained, lowering her voice and leaning into me, that she didn't have many friends at school. 'I've had a lot of work since then,' she said, straightening up and blinking.

'Well done,' I said, 'it's good to be in full employment in these difficult days. Oh, I see what you mean,' I added when she stared at me.

'What do you do?' Lucy asked.

'A little bit of modelling, but mainly the champagne bar on Spearing Road.'

'Oh.' Dave flushed. Yes we'd heard of it, we assured her. Lucy took the dishes, scraping our remains onto one plate.

Over pudding – I smiled as I saw that Lucy had done a fair impression of what we'd had at Grahame Kennard's dinner, a sort of squidgy thing with a circular drizzle of reddish sauce around it – Lucy Kennard asked everyone else what line of trade they might be in. Dave talked about fixing toilets, and I wondered why doesn't he just say he's a plumber; much more salubrious at the dinner table, and anyway he doesn't fix them, Lucy won't use him because he leaves a mess everywhere and things drip more after he's gone than they did before he arrived.

I alluded to the building society and then about the dinner we'd had with Grahame Kennard, and how remarkable it was that he travels round the world advising people, living the high life, planes, meetings, five-star hotels, offices with palm trees in pots. 'I mean,' I said, 'I could do that. Couldn't I?'

They all looked at me, and Dave nodded. 'I was telling them how they should buy M&S shares because people go back to things they feel comfortable with, and guess what, M&S shares have gone up. I read it in *Metro*.'

Dave pursed his lips and Lucy Kennard gave me a wide-eyed look. 'Then Jamie at the bank was telling me about qualifications and experience and all that,' I said, encouraged by their expressions, 'and I thought, it's all bollocks, isn't it, it's not about whether you've got ideas or not, it's about whether you went to the right school and whether daddy got you a job because he's the boss, and then the promotions start and before you know it you're in Dubai, telling people what to do. It could have been me. It should have been me, I've got ideas.'

'Yeah,' said Lucy Kennard. 'Ideas.' Lucy asked everyone if they'd like a glass of port. Port? We haven't got any port. Where would we get port from? But she produced the port, and port glasses too. I love that woman with all my heart.

Lucy smudged away the bright-lipsticked kiss that Lucy Kennard had left next to my mouth. 'Shame Grahame Kennard wasn't here,' I said as we went to bed.

'I know what you mean,' said Lucy.

It was too late for Classic FM. The next day I woke early, showered and dressed before Lucy got up, and chose the interview tie. I suppose signing up for three evening courses is a bit much, but I'm forty-one; I'm a man in a hurry and I want to do it properly. One of them is at the Bishopsgate, which means trekking into town, but the other two are a bit nearer. As I said to Lucy, it's a good investment. 'I want to be someone you can be proud of,' I said as I opened the Chablis and felt the bottle to check it was cold enough. I've become rather fond of Chablis since Lucy Kennard came round.

'I am proud of you,' she said.

'I'll be back by ten.' I zipped the laptop into its bag. I never thought I'd be a man with a laptop, let alone one with a zip-up bag. Things are looking up.

I got my first certificate easily and have almost enough units for the second one now. Then I'm going to ask Jamie about going on an internal management course. Five years, he said with a smile at the corner of his mouth, and I might have my own office. I looked round at the faces on the bus and thought – you could all do it you know; you could be like me one day. No one caught my eye; they all stared dolefully at their Metros. Someone off Big Brother had a massive lingerie contract.

Thursday night I wasn't really looking forward to the course. The excitement had worn off and it was a pisser of an evening. In the event there was a sign pinned to room D91 saying it was cancelled because the lecturer was ill, so I wasn't too disappointed. I went back on the bus, not being able to face the Northern Line again so quickly. I looked at my face reflecting blue and yellow, with occasional flashes of orange across it as the bus turned corners.

When I got in I thought Lucy had gone out, but I found her in bed with Grahame Kennard. They looked at me in surprise, and Grahame said wasn't I supposed to be doing an evening course? They looked irritated when I said the lecturer was ill. Lucy turned Classic FM down to a murmur.

So I'm doing really well now, and today was my Level Three Qualification ceremony. To my surprise, Grahame Kennard came along, with Lucy too. She seemed keen to see me. 'Grahame's going to Singapore next week,' she said, 'and then Australia for a month.'

I nodded. 'Will you miss him?'

She paused, then nodded. 'The thing is, all I ever wanted was Grahame Kennard. All I want now is the old Grahame Kennard back. I want the Grahame Kennard who comes home in the evenings and brings pizza.'

I nodded, albeit briefly, because they were handing out certificates. 'You must excuse me,' I said, 'I need to go and sit at the front now.'

She nodded. I nodded back.

I went and sat at the front. It felt different at the front. The front's the place to be, I decided, as the applause began.

The Woman in the Caves

She was naked in church. That's when we were called in.

The villagers demanded the police, of course. At the time there was a great deal of suspicion if not downright hostility to my husband Malcolm's profession. Freud had only recently published his *Interpretation of Dreams* and the concept of the subconscious was widely unknown to most people; or if they were aware of it, they denied it even to themselves.

We live on the edge of the village and took the car on a rare excursion. A good old-fashioned family outing, as my father would say, although as far as I recall we didn't go on many family outings to see nude women causing scenes in churches. By the time we arrived there was plenty of commotion outside St Agatha's. Even a man from the BBC was there, scratching his beard and saying this is why Television will never catch on. Imagine it – you'd just have to film lots of exteriors.

Inside she was covered with a blanket, but on seeing us she broke free and strode down the centre of the church, cloth-waving villagers ineffectually pursuing her. I was impressed by Malcolm's calm; I was more alarmed than he was by the voluminous breasts leaping from left to right like over-ripe watermelons escaping from a grocer's stall, and the folds of flesh that reminded me of old calfskin bibles I'd once seen stacked up in an antiquarian bookshop.

She was about the same age as me. When devoid of clothes, ladies of our age are best seen, in my view, horizontally, surrounded by drapes, and ideally, minimally lit, by candles, or even, candle. Malcolm didn't even pause to take the pipe out of his mouth, but feigned to one side as if deflecting a rugby tackle and then assisted the villagers in covering her up. 'We'll take over from here,' I said assertively, but the crowd did not dispel.

'Wants locking up, she does,' said one man who was red-faced from gout, or possibly from looking at her.

'Call the police!' said an elderly lady, praying ferociously at the back.

'The police are already here,' said the constable, the inflection in his voice suggesting that it was not the first time he had had to point this out. It has to be said, he'd not been very effective, although his helmet on the floor nearby indicated he'd tried.

'This is Muriel Limmidge,' the vicar said, as if introducing us at a cocktail party. Malcolm nodded and massaged the woman's shoulders until she relaxed.

In the side chapel she was calmer. 'It's all right,' she said, voluntarily getting back into her clothes. 'They've gone.'

'Who have?' Malcolm asked.

Mrs Limmidge looked at him as if he were an idiot. 'My husband, of course,' she said. 'And – and… *that woman*.'

'What woman?'

She looked away as if about to be sick, then closed her eyes and nodded forward. We propped her in a chair and let her sleep. 'She'll be all right,' Malcolm assured the concerned vicar.

Between us, we interviewed all the others who'd been present. Patterson, the butcher, was in no doubt that she was, as he saw it, 'nuts'. Quite often seen in the street shouting, she was. 'I mean, we all shout from time to time, don't we?' he said. 'After we've had a few light ales at the Square and Compass, for example, after a tough day's work. But this is in the daytime.'

'Has she always been like this?' we asked. Owen the grocer shook his head. 'She's always been a bit funny,' he said, 'but not this much.' He was a quiet, thoughtful man; you could imagine him turning tomatoes over slowly and being patient with elderly customers.

I asked him about the woman's husband. 'Mrs Limmidge seems to think he might be having an affair. Do you think there's any truth in that?'

Owen paused thoughtfully, perhaps mentally rearranging a display of bananas, apples, tangerines. 'Mrs Limmidge's husband,' he said, 'has been dead for years.'

While I talked to the men, Malcolm interviewed the women. We find that you get better information from the opposite sex. It feels more formal, and they're on their best behaviour. Gladys Seagrove, a pale and withdrawn woman who seemed nervous of her own shadow, said that Mrs Limmidge had once been 'the life and soul of the party' but had lately seemed 'away in her own little world'.

Had she suffered from any physical ailments, Malcolm asked? He gets this in early, because if the answers are positive he gets me to take over. He's a good psychiatrist but anything requiring a GP is my department. Gladys thought for a moment then shook her head, fiddling with her hair as she did so, as if fearful a wrong answer would be sinful.

Having established that Mrs Limmidge was a widow, Malcolm asked about her late husband. He'd been the postmaster and ill with cancer for the last couple of years of his life; Muriel had looked after him. They'd had to sell the house, and now she was renting a little cottage.

Malcolm and I agreed that Mrs Limmidge should be allowed to go home and rest, which caused more consternation as we helped her away from the church. The BBC chappie was still hanging around, instructing his pimply assistant to dangle the microphone as we escorted Mrs Limmidge, now looking fragile and distracted.

He asked a few questions but Malcolm chewed his pipe and gave resolute, sturdy answers. 'My patient needs rest,' he said, 'and I'm not going to add to her trauma by interrogating her.' He held a hand up to the microphone, which bounced away like a swatted fly.

Some irrelevant, inane questions about religious symbolism and the Fall – goodness these wireless types do ask the most bizarre nonsense – but Malcolm, never one to be starstruck, kept his nerve. 'We'll be speaking to her tomorrow,' he said, 'now let her by, please.'

The constable trotted behind, saying how he didn't think it appropriate to arrest her, as he could do, for disturbing the peace, and nor was it worth arresting her for indecent exposure, as he also could do. No one paid him much attention.

Next day Malcolm had a full casebook and I said I would go to check on Mrs Limmidge. 'I'd like to see her,' he murmured as he cooked breakfast, his pipe twisted sideways so that there was no risk of ash dripping into the bacon and eggs. 'Still, can't be helped.'

He is an immensely relaxed man. The most flustered I've ever seen him was when we heard about Hitler's invasion of Czechoslovakia last year. He gave his pipe three long draws and as he put his hat on, murmured 'that won't make him very popular.'

I cycled down. Mrs Limmidge lived in the favoured end of town, where it slopes towards the sea. Her cottage was tiny, but immaculately kept; roses and wisteria twining round a latticed porch, globe thistles and snapdragons on the path, and even sunflowers, beginning to smell sickly. I had a moment of embarrassment about our rather untidy town house, tucked away on the modern side of the village. Don't be hard on yourself, I thought as I leant the bicycle against the stone wall.

She did not respond to the door knocker and looking through the windows I couldn't see anyone. I could tell she was in, because there was opera playing – Caruso, if I'm not mistaken, chewing his way through *Rigoletto*. About to turn away, I noticed the door was ajar.

'Hello? Mrs Limmidge?' The hallway was as immaculate as the exterior and smelt of lemon. A gorgeous mahogany grandmother clock ticked loudly; to begin with, it seemed to be in beat with Caruso, then after a few moments they separated and went their own melodic ways.

'Mrs Limmidge?' The living room was even tinier than the outside of the cottage suggested, with barely room for a Chesterfield chair and a circular wooden table, covered in books and magazines. *The Journal of Contemporary Magic* caught my eye, as it had a striking portrait of Tutankhamen's mask on the front.

'Not sure what Tutankhamen has to do with magic,' I said to myself, picking it up and flicking through. The books were well-thumbed and peppered with little slips of paper to help her find particular pages again. One of them seemed to be a handbook, full of symbols and incantations. A passage was underlined. 'It is by turning round quickly that we can see what remains in the corner of our eye; we must, however, move fast.'

'Mrs Limmidge?' I found her in the garden, staring at the sea. I didn't want to creep up on her so I coughed, and when she didn't hear, thought of something to say.

'How beautiful,' I declared, 'that you have a sea view.' I raised my voice as she still didn't turn. 'I wouldn't have thought that these cottage gardens stretched this far. And what a beautiful summer it's been, the roses are very...'

I stood parallel to her and smiled. 'Mrs Limmidge?'

She turned and came out of her trance, or whatever it was. 'How lovely to see you,' she said. 'Would you like a cup of tea?'

I followed her back to the house, relieved she hadn't accused me of breaking in. 'Did you know your front door was open?'

'Oh, no one locks their doors around here,' she smiled. 'Sit down, and I'll, er…'

I sat. 'Tea,' I prompted.

She clicked her fingers. 'Ah yes.' As she pottered to the kitchen I sat back in the chair, which creaked pleasantly behind me. The telephone rang, which she ignored, or didn't hear, and Caruso eventually gave up the ghost and his voice petered out into a crackling Morse code as the gramophone needle reached the centre.

'Here we are, I've only got brown sugar I'm afraid.' She chattered away, her voice competing with the clinking and rattling of china. 'Do you like cheese?' She handed me a plate of offcuts.

'So this is just a visit to see how you are,' I said, picking up the cup and smiling. She looked at me gamely enough, if a little quizzically, and said nothing.

'Because you were rather upset the other day, weren't you?' I took a long mouthful of tea to give her time to respond.

'Oh that,' she said after a while. She leant forward. 'It's because he's devious, you see.'

I made a mental note to emphasise to Malcolm that this was, definitely, a job for him and not me.

'You mean your husband?'

She nodded.

'When did he die?'

'Oh...' she sat back. 'Four or five years ago.'

'And you saw him in the church?'

She nodded again.

I glanced at the books on the coffee table. 'How long have you been a medium?' I asked.

'All my life, naturally. It's strange – I used to think that everyone saw them. Then I realised we are in a minority.'

'We?'

She leaned forward, a conspiratorial twinkle in her eye. 'You do too, don't you?'

'Er, no...' I said. I don't believe in any of that, I wanted to say; I don't believe in ghosts, magic, spiritualism, or seeing the re-incarnation of Christ on one's toast. I didn't say anything though. The last thing I needed was her stripping off and dancing some pagan libation in front of me.

'So I'll come to see you from time to time,' I said, 'if that's okay.' I finished the tea.

'That would be lovely, dear.'

'And we need to make sure we don't have any incidents like the other day, don't we,' I said as I stood to go. I hate the way doctors say 'we', don't you? 'And how are we today.' As if you're having some kind of identity crisis, the sentence structure implying you're two people. But, it's the kind of thing we do, people almost expect it of us.

'I think that was a one-off,' she said, almost ominously. She escorted me through to the hallway, where the chiming grandmother clock signed me off the premises.

Just after six Malcolm walked up the drive with a brace of pheasant over his shoulder. 'Got chatting at a farm,' he said. 'Knocked a few shillings off my fee, and look what he gave me.'

We decided they were too good to rush, and that we'd pot roast them overnight and make do with what we had for the evening. One of the things I like about Malcolm is the way he insists on doing all the cooking – says he likes it, it's good thinking time.

We talked about Malcolm's other cases, none of which were as interesting as Mrs Limmidge. A man who thought he was a horse; a woman who shuddered physically every time she heard the word 'plinth'. A man convinced he was the reincarnation of Pope Pius IX. The usual stuff. 'When I suggested that he might actually be Pius X,' Malcolm said, 'he considered this carefully and then said "I think that would lack credibility." '

So we talked more about Mrs Limmidge. I thought she was faking it, to be honest. Malcolm can be taken in by a performance like that; it must be really hard for him, wanting to make his diagnoses, trying to separate what's going on in people's minds from what they want him to think.

It's like that survey they were doing in the high street the other day. 'Do you like Bosun's Potted Mackerel,' a very polite lady with a clipboard asked us. Trying to be helpful, Malcolm said 'Yes'.

I nudged him; we've never eaten Bosun's Potted Mackerel. But the lady was asking another question. 'Would you be willing to pay five shillings and sixpence a pound?' the lady asked. 'Yes,' said Malcolm.

She went away happy. 'No you wouldn't,' I said after she'd gone. Malcolm looked uncomfortable. 'I suppose not,' he said, 'but she was so nice.'

And this is a man who deals with psychology all his working life. What chance do the rest of us have? But that's what it's like in Malcolm's line of work. You can lose touch with reality.

I went for a long walk on the Purbecks and tried to clear my head. I looked across the land that rolled like green waves of ocean. Malcolm doesn't think there will be a conflict; we can contain Hitler if we're patient enough. He'll over-stretch himself, Malcolm reckons; he'll invade one place too many and then we can smoke him out like a badger from a hole. I don't think he really believes this, but it's cheering to hear. He tries to convince himself, but forgets that not everyone thinks as rationally as he does. Malcolm tries to think of a positive outcome and then imagines how it might be achieved. I admire that in him.

Later I walked along the cliffs. I got the slight giddiness I always feel when I reflect that beneath me are caves; the apparently solid rock is actually hollow. *It's only like being upstairs*, I told myself, but still felt nervous. Inside the caves, it's rumoured, is a weapons store; a secret stock in preparation for the possible invasion. Every man, woman and boy in the village is believed to know about it, but never breathes a word.

The caves themselves are alluring, but I don't go down the narrow path towards them without reason. I imagine the cool exterior as I breathe in and look at the horizon. There's a strange smell, like rotten eggs. It's faint, so it's not actually unpleasant. It's just unusual.

That night, I walked upstairs and felt uncomfortable. You know you're in a solid room, but there's absolutely nothing just a few inches below you. Why had this never concerned me before? I lay on the bed carefully, as if my movements might make it suddenly plunge to the ground below.

I had a morning of surgery so Malcolm suggested we meet up at Mrs Limmidge's in the afternoon. On his way down, he told me later, he'd popped into the pub for a quiet pint and a smoke and got chatting to the barman. 'Hear what happened the other day?' the barman said. Malcolm chewed his pipe and nodded. It was the talk of the village, evidently. 'Old Muriel, finally losing it in church?'

Malcolm counted out a few coins and nodded towards the Plump Duck pump. 'Half.'

The barman heaved on the pump. 'My wife always says, you could write a book about the people in this village.'

Malcolm took his glass and raised it an inch to the barman before taking a sip.

The garden was surprisingly full. The Square and Compass has the most gorgeous views, a sliver of sea visible in the distance, and as Malcolm once admitted in a rare moment of self-reflection, it's very hard to go past the pub without dropping in.

When I got to Mrs Limmidge's, Malcolm was already there. The door was ajar again and I closed it behind me. Something was wrong; I couldn't work out what. There was a different atmosphere; if I believed any of it, I could imagine that one of Mrs Limmidge's ghosts had recently vacated the building.

The feeling stayed with me as I entered the living room and Mrs Limmidge looked up mid-sentence and smiled.

'...as we know that Saturn is the planet of reality, and this influences us when we can be distracted by Neptune.'

Malcolm sat in the armchair by the fire, lapping it all up. Nodding enthusiastically, he waved his pipe at Mrs Limmidge to encourage her to continue.

'Of course,' she said, 'Jupiter is a bit of a tempter; it seems to offer things we like, but it's frivolous, we have to remember that.'

I watched this performance until I had to stifle a yawn. Malcolm's patience is extraordinary, but as she droned on I began to think that it was a little unfair. Surely he should have been gently suggesting to her that it might all be imaginary, that it might not be real? Two little pink dots had appeared on her cheeks and you could see she loved having a willing audience; especially an intelligent-looking man in brown tweeds, with the title 'doctor'.

'It's so pleasing to see that your husband is interested in the secrets of the other side,' she said, when she finally ran out of steam. 'That he's not as cynical as some folk.' Malcolm nodded and scratched his beard. 'Do you see people more in the day, or at night?'

Mrs Limmidge thought about this carefully. 'At night, certainly…' she said, 'particularly when I've just woken up, or when I'm about to go to sleep.'

'Is it always people you know, or strangers? Or a mix of the two?'

She played with her beads as she considered this. 'Generally people I know,' she said slowly. 'I do sometimes see strangers, of course.'

'If they're strangers,' Malcolm tapped his pipe out in the grate, 'how do you know they're ghosts, and not just people?'

'It's different,' she said. 'They're slightly transparent – it's not obvious, but when you know what to look for, you can detect it. The next time you walk down the street, you try looking for it.'

Malcolm rifled around in his pockets until he found his tobacco. 'You think there are ghosts walking around amongst us all the time?' He pulled some strands of Golden Virginia from the packet.

'Mm-hmm.' She sat back, playing with the beads again. It was clear she wasn't sure if he believed her or not.

'It's the clock,' I said.

They both looked at me.

'That's what's different about the hallway. I've just realised. Your clock's gone.'

'Ah yes.'

Malcolm raised an enquiring eyebrow, waiting for either of us to fill him in.

Mrs Limmidge worried her beads. 'Colonel Protheroe came round to pick it up.'

'Protheroe?'

'Mmm.' Mrs Limmidge's face puckered up like an unimpressed cat. 'I owe him some rent, you see. He used to let me off, what with him being my husband's brother…'

'Oh?'

'…but I don't know how I'm going to get money now, what with one thing and another.'

'Perhaps you could read people's tea leaves for them,' I suggested.

She looked vague for a moment, then smiled. 'Do you know, that's not a bad idea. Now, who's for tea? What about… er…' she looked at me, trying to remember my name. 'Or…' she looked a little desperately at Malcolm. 'Perhaps I'll just go and put the kettle on anyway,' she said, pottering out to the kitchen.

'Diagnosis?' I asked quietly.

'Early stage dementia,' Malcolm said crisply. He tapped the pipe on the ledge of the mantelpiece, curious about the strangely hollow sound it made.

'Oh come on,' I said. 'She's barely fifty, she's not much older than me!'

He shrugged. 'That's why I said "early stage". It can happen.'

I gave Malcolm the look he calls my 'stalling pony' and we left shortly after.

'See you soon, Mrs Limmidge,' I said as she waved us off and went back inside, leaving the door ajar. Malcolm had parked not far round the corner and as he revved the car I winced.

'Do you think this colonel character might be able to help?' I suggested.

'Possibly,' Malcolm said, the car lurching forward on the gravel.

I thought we were heading to the pub for a late lunch, but instead of turning off, Malcolm continued driving the coast road. 'Where are we going?' I asked.

'Eh?' he said, turning his head too quickly and knocking his pipe into the head rest. For someone so authoritative about spotting mental conditions in others, he can be remarkably vague.

'Lunch?' I said.

'No, no,' he replied, 'this is urgent.'

'What is?'

'We've got to go and see the squire.'

'The squire?'

'Colonel Protheroe. The man she rents her house from.'

'Why?'

He slowed down to take his pipe out of his mouth. To my surprise, he put it in his jacket pocket, and even lifted the little flap over the pocket and tapped it. Things must be serious.

'Because,' he said, as we drove through large iron gates and over a long gravel drive, 'I think she's on the verge of becoming violent.'

We drove past the sheep on either side of the gravel track and followed the avenue of trees before we reached the somewhat dilapidated Georgian house at the end. 'Shouldn't you tell the police?' I asked.

Malcolm shrugged, which took his hands off the wheel so the car swerved alarmingly. 'She hasn't done anything yet. You can't arrest someone for something they haven't done. We have to wait until she does do something – and then try to be there when it happens.'

We parked beside the ornate fountain, the gravel crunching satisfyingly as we drew up. The doorbell echoed through the house and Malcolm was surprised at how quickly a maid opened the door.

'Do you have an appointment?'

'I'm afraid not.'

'Wait here please.'

It was some time before she came back, but eventually we were shown along various long corridors until we reached what was described as the lounge: a gigantic room covered in heavy silk wallpaper and stuffed with furniture. Malcolm took it all in with a practised eye. Hoarder, I could see him thinking; when one has plenty of money, hoarding can easily become a problem.

None of the furniture was ordinary; all of it was antique and some of it looked exquisite. Certain pieces were eighteenth century, some of them even Chippendale. There were at least seven clocks, all ticking away to themselves and occasionally faintly chiming. I looked around for Mrs Limmidge's grandmother clock but did not see it; there were so many of them though, it could easily be hidden in there.

Protheroe appeared, genial enough. 'How can I help you?'

'Ah…' said Malcolm, hands in his pockets. We were still standing, and the squire did not ask us to sit. 'My wife and I wondered if we could talk to you.'

He loses his authority a little when he's not holding his pipe. It's as if he doesn't know what to do with his hands.

The squire looked at him blankly. 'I'm Colonel Protheroe,' he said, in that sweepingly confident way that some people are just born with; or if they're not born with it, I thought, looking round, they buy it.

'It's about Muriel Limmidge,' Malcolm said eventually.

Protheroe brightened. 'Ah, one of my tenants.' He motioned towards the chairs.

'I see you like clocks,' Malcolm said as we settled.

'Hm-hmm.'

'How long has Mrs Limmidge been your tenant?'

'Oh… well now… that would be since my brother died. A good few years.'

The memory seemed to disturb him. He got out of the chair and walked over to a sideboard cluttered with photographs. Mostly, they were pictures of himself – that mix of confidence and arrogance that good breeding cannot help but generate. There were more hanging on the wall next to me. Protheroe at the races, on a yacht, in tennis whites, and, most startlingly of all, on a golf course with the Duke of Windsor.

Malcolm joined the squire and pointed to one of the pictures of him. 'This one's your brother.'

'Yes, that's right.'

Malcolm's hand moved to the right. 'This one's you.'

'Yes.'

A little further to the right. 'This one's your brother again.'

Protheroe smiled. 'I congratulate you. Not many people can do that.'

I walked up to them, a frown on my face. 'They're identical twins,' Malcolm explained.

'I thought all the pictures were of you!' I exclaimed.

He laughed. 'That would be rather monomaniacal, my dear.' I felt he was watching me as I returned to my seat. I smoothed my skirt behind me as I turned and sat. 'How can you tell?' I asked Malcolm.

He lifted a photo from the back of the collection. 'Here's one of them together.'

'Yes,' said Protheroe, taking the photo. 'That's us at Cambridge.' He studied the photo for a moment then buried it again at the back. 'It was very sad. Cancer. Turned out he didn't have a pension.'

'Was he old?' I asked, and felt myself blush as Protheroe and Malcolm looked at me. My mind must have been elsewhere. I tried to think about Mrs Limmidge. *Saturn is the planet of reality.*

They sat down again. Malcolm asked his usual rally of questions, as if playing tennis: question, answer, question, answer, and eventually he sends a spinner that elicits an answer the speaker didn't expect to give, and he wins the point, and gets the insight.

'She seems to think that your brother is having an affair in the afterlife,' Malcolm said.

'Ah, well…' Protheroe appeared to take the suggestion seriously. 'Edward always did have an eye for the ladies.'

'Were they married a long time?'

'Thirty years.'

'And you socialised, with the other villagers?'

'Yes, of course.'

'Who did she particularly like amongst the other people?'

'Well…'

I got the impression he didn't much want to talk about her but was grateful for the company. For all his gentrified behaviour, he was essentially a lonely man in a gigantic house. Even the walk to the shops, I thought, visualising the various corridors and reception rooms, means an isolating half-hour trek past several flocks of sheep before you see any humanity.

But of course, he doesn't walk, he sends a servant. Which just makes him even more isolated.

'Do you know any of Mrs Limmidge's relatives?' I asked. 'So we could talk to them about her past.'

'Her past?'

'Yes,' I said. It may explain some of her current behaviour.'

'Oh well...' He stood, with an aristocratic wave of the hand that suggested, these new-fangled ways of doctoring may be alien to me, but no matter. He moved to the mantelpiece and lifted a notepad from underneath a Louis XV bust. 'Here's a couple of people you can speak to.' He scribbled on the notepad, tore the sheet off and handed me the folded paper.

The telephone rang. He has one of those huge objects that you can hear from six rooms away. Protheroe waited as it rang three times and we heard the muffled echo of the maid answering it. There were footsteps. A tap at the door. 'Excuse me, sir.'

'What is it?'

The maid kept her face blank; if she had any sense of being mocked, she disguised it.

'It's the telephone, sir.'

'Ah, right.' He didn't move. The maid walked up to him, trailing an exceptionally long cable. When she was parallel with him, she handed the receiver over; he took it without moving his head.

'Protheroe.'

There was an excited chatter at the other end.

'I see.' He breathed deeply, a cigar and port-formed sigh. The maid took the receiver and was dismissed with a nod. 'You'd better get back to the village,' he said, 'if you don't want your Mrs Limmidge arrested.'

'Oh?' Malcolm was on his feet.

'What's happened?' I asked.

'A disturbance. I'm coming too,' Protheroe announced.

'We'll give you a lift,' Malcolm offered.

He stared at us. 'Don't be ridiculous. I shall take one of the Bentleys.'

Before we left I went over to the Louis XV bust. 'I'll give you our number,' I said. 'In case you think of any more names.'

I tore the paper off and handed it to him, then replaced the pad next to the bust, which rather high-handedly ignored me.

'Right, come on then.' Malcolm headed towards the door.

'Dr. James,' Protheroe said. Malcolm turned questioningly.

'It's this way.' We followed Protheroe through a different door.

Fortunately she wasn't naked, but verbal abuse of vicars and policemen is rarely tolerated in today's civilised society. Mrs Limmidge held a finger out in front of her, jabbing it in the air the way a schoolmaster might do after finally losing patience. The villagers stood in a circle, like you might gather around an escaped zoo animal.

On the floor in front of her was a large map, unfolded and concertinaing at the edges. The map was covered with different coloured pins; red, purple, orange, blue and yellow; probably about twelve different colours in all, scattered in different places.

'My husband is having an affair with another woman beyond the grave,' said Mrs Limmidge, her face a contorted leer. 'And I want to know what you –' she pointed at Constable Stokes, and then at the Reverend Hurds, 'are going to do about it.'

Helplessly, the policeman and the vicar held their hands out. 'There's nothing we can do,' Hurds said.

'Your husband has been dead for years,' said the policeman, 'he's outside our jurisdiction now.' He even glanced at his watch, as if to confirm as much.

'It's all right,' said Malcolm, 'I'll handle this.' But the circle did not open to accommodate him. Everyone seemed fascinated by Mrs Limmidge. Rather as mice will stare at a cobra as it sways back and forth above it, they did not seem to be put off by her sense of impending violence. If anything, they were mesmerised by it.

I studied the map. The coloured pins seemed to be making a pattern. 'These are the people you've been seeing?'

Mrs Limmidge glanced down at me. 'Yes,' she said, squatting down, pleased that someone was taking her seriously. Her mouth was puffy, with streaks of foundation in the cracks on her face; it was like she wore a mask. She smelt of lavender and beads rattled at her wrinkly throat.

'That's Gloria Wishart,' she said, pointing to the scattering of yellow dots. 'She was a lovely lady. Used to run the library. Chatted to everyone. The queues were shocking.'

'Who's this?' I said, pointing to the purple dot.

'That's Michael Horncase.' Murmurs of respect from the crowd. Evidently a popular and well-known individual.

I looked up. The hemisphere was motionless; the crowd looked down, patiently watching, waiting for what would happen next. I could see them breathing under waistcoats, twitching fingers beneath woollen cuffs. The light was behind them and the scene was like an old photograph.

'Where's your late husband?'

She pointed to the red pins. 'The sightings seem to converge here,' I said, tapping the map near the bottom.

She leant in and turned her head. 'The caves?'

I nodded. 'An out of the way place, wouldn't you say?'
She looked up at me, realisation dawning in her eyes.
'You know it's a weapons store, don't you?' I said.

Mrs Limmidge nodded. 'Right,' she said, standing up
with resolve. She pulled her cardigan about her and marched
down the path, sturdy brown shoes clicking sensibly on the
crazed paving.

The residents followed her in a well-behaved line. Do
people in villages really have so little to do, I wondered
as the crowd trooped off.

'Close the gate behind you,' Mrs Limmidge shouted as
she walked to the coast road, and the constable, bringing
up the rear, touched his forehead in a brief salute as he
responsibly ensured it was on its latch. I could see that the
front door was still ajar, but she was well down the road
now. Gates must be closed; but doors can be left open.

Malcolm, behind clouds of pipe smoke, came forward
and held me round the waist. 'Nice bit of deduction,' he
said, squeezing me. 'What do you think will happen?'

'I don't know,' I said. 'But I think we should follow them.'

We walked by the sea, hanging a little distance back from
the crowd. It was one of those glorious September days
when the sky suddenly decides to be a bit Mediterranean
and the sea joins in, becoming a sparkly, rolling glitterball.
There was a breezy feel to the day that made everyone
swan along jauntily; it was like being on a school outing.

Malcolm looked around. 'I thought Protheroe said he
was following us?'

I shrugged. 'Perhaps he changed his mind.'

'Perhaps.' He nibbled merrily at his pipe.

I watched the party ahead. 'Are you sure this is safe?'
I ask.

The beauty of the day had affected Malcolm too.
'Yes, I think so.' He looked out to sea. 'I'm just curious

to see what happens now. Be good for the casebook one day, I expect.' He gave me a sly look that I didn't quite understand.

The caves created a kind of collective hush as we arrived. They have a particularly distinct beauty that invokes quiet in any onlooker. The blueish light makes you think of a church, and the arch as you enter forms a theatre. The walls sparkle with some kind of quartz. It appears almost man-made, but its natural grandeur and ruggedness makes it far more impressive than anything humanly designed. The caves are full of strange noises; they creak, they groan. Water drips. Walk there on your own and you will hear the cry of ghosts.

We paused on the threshold. What were we doing here? What did we expect to happen?

Mrs Limmidge strode forward. Perhaps, I thought, this was the moment she'd always waited for. Is there, in all our lives, a key turning point that we're all leading up to, and we don't realise it until the second we get there, then discover we are not surprised, and were expecting it all along?

'Edward,' she declared, and then repeated, more loudly so that her voice echoed, 'Edward!' She was Lady Macbeth; here was the moment then; we must screw our courage to the sticking point, I could see her thinking, and we'll not fail.

There is a clattering sound and we all fall silent; we hold our breath. Lady Macbeth stands expectantly, waiting; and sure enough, Colonel Protheroe emerges from behind the rocks. He stares at us in astonishment. It is like magic: she could not have planned it better than if she really had been in contact with three wizened old hags, promising her the world.

She steps forward, then turns to us. 'The oncoming storm rumbles louder and louder,' she says. 'Hitler's forces are massing on the continent. It may only be a matter of time before we are invaded.'

The villagers watch, agog. Some of us have even sat on the ground, legs out in front of us, watching like it's a performance of the Harpham Players. It's about as well acted, I think a little unfairly, watching Mrs Limmidge's outstretched hands, her somewhat stagey performance.

I suppose if you are a medium, you have to build it up a bit; make a drama of it. She walks forward. Colonel Protheroe looks uncertainly at the crowd, and at Malcolm, and then directly at me.

The old woman stares with venom at what she thinks is her husband. 'But what Hitler hasn't realised,' she says, 'is that we are prepared.'

She kicks at the dirt in front of her. Her feet resonate on the earth, as if she is walking on a stage. The ground, we realise, is hollow. Mrs Limmidge reaches down and pulls at a handle, tugging several times before it opens. From the compartment inside the earth, she produces a rifle and points it at Colonel Protheroe.

Malcolm, unnoticed, has stepped behind her. 'All right,' he says softly. He's a foot or two behind her elbow; we can just make out his profile in the reduced light.

'You've been sleeping with other women, haven't you?' she demands.

Protheroe looks startled. 'How do you know that?' he asks, backing away, but there's nowhere for him to go.

Mrs Limmidge pulls the catch and shoots. In the echo chamber of the cave, the sound is deafening. It ricochets, it rips its way through our ears like thunder. She is an appalling shot. The bullet whizzes a couple of feet past Colonel Protheroe. But the audience are parallel to Mrs

Limmidge. From their perspective, the bullet seems to head straight towards him. He ducks, and falls, to get out of the way of any further bullets. The villagers gasp. Mrs Limmidge fires again, another bullet that goes a good few feet above his head.

But the villagers have seen what they think they have seen. Protheroe lies on the floor, shoulders hunched, hands over his head. I run to his side to see if he's all right. Later, Malcolm tells me how brave this was, as Mrs Limmidge was still waving the gun around.

Gathering their wits, Stokes and the Reverend Hurds rush forward and restrain her. Dear me, these people. They are being terribly brave about it, making lots of noise and shouting, 'right, right, that's enough!' But I notice they waited until both barrels of the rifle had been fired. The remaining villagers step back. It's better than Television.

The entertainment has not ended. Kneeling down, while all the attention is on Mrs Limmidge, it's easy for me to hold my hand over the Colonel's neck as if tending him, light a match and drop it to the ground.

The ammunition catches light almost immediately. I step back, urging everyone to get out of the way. The smell of gunpowder in the air reminds me of the funfair; a deep feeling in my gut and for a moment I am six years old, looking up at the horses whizzing round in a colourful blur, and the sickly stink of candy floss, its pink fuzziness somehow ominous rather than enticing.

We have about fifteen seconds. I shoo everyone out of the caves and pause at the edge to watch the show. Colonel Protheroe explodes like a firework. He turns bright green. The force of it, in such a confined space, decapitates him. It's surprising how quickly the stench of singeing hair spreads across the space.

He burned for hours. It was decided not to send the fire brigade in. The caves, a natural defence, dampened it eventually, although it has left the walls and roof blackened. The shape of the cave made a kind of wind tunnel and this generated a huge inferno, we were later told; the heat must have been immense. There was no trace left of the Colonel.

In the pub I put an order in for two roast lamb lunches. 'Let's hope we can still get them, eh,' said the landlord, somewhat cryptically. I looked across the Purbecks. The most beautiful, the most peaceful of mornings.

Inside, the radio was on. In the snug most of the village men were gathered round. 'I have to tell you now,' the voice of the Prime Minister was saying, 'that no such undertaking has been received and that consequently – ' here the radio crackled and whined, and Jim Burrows thumped it viciously – 'this country is at war with Germany.'

In the distance we heard an air raid siren. We all looked at each other in confusion. It was as if the war needed to be announced – as if it needs a signal, like the chimes of a clock tell you it's time to get up, time for lunch, time for dinner, time for bed.

I went for a walk before coming back for lunch. A good walk sharpens the mind, I always think. Even though everyone had been saying there would be a war, I could still scarcely credit that it was actually happening. It barely seems credible that one man can manipulate an entire country; that he can lead them in a mass delusion to the brink of war and even then, no one steps in to prevent it happening.

Still, if he can do it, it shouldn't be difficult for me to manipulate one batty old woman and a few eccentric villagers. Next week the Mayor wants to give me the Town Award for Bravery, as it was me who stepped forward to help the Colonel after he had supposedly been shot.

I stood at the mouth of the caves. There was nothing left, but you could still feel the heat. I walked over to where he died, and there were a few charred marks on the floor where I dropped the piece of paper where Protheroe had supposedly written the names of some relatives who would speak to us. On it was written, 'Another £50 or I tell him.'

I kicked the ashes. Well, if you get a message like that, you realise you have to act. The cheek of it; I'd paid him £100 already. How long would it go on for? I turn and leave the cave.

We are at war, I thought as I looked at the peaceful sea. I glanced back as I walked away; they'll need to restore the ammunitions. For a moment I seem to see his ghost in the air, sparkling in the light from the entrance. Then I shake my head and turn away.

I cycled to the pub. Malcolm wasn't there but he turned up just as the plates of lamb arrived. The wireless was repeating Chamberlain's announcement and his words echoed in our ears.

We'd all wondered why Mrs Limmidge thought that her late husband, across the misty veil, was having an affair. I thought there were two possibilities. One, was that if he was anything like his brother, he was having affairs left right and centre – whether in the afterlife, or before it. When I met the colonel I liked him – he seemed charming, and of course he was fabulously rich. I didn't intend anything to happen, but he was persuasive.

And life with Malcolm was becoming just a little bit boring. I love my husband, but there are only so many crosswords you can listen to him ticking off in bed before you begin to long for a little more glamour. And it isn't difficult, being a doctor, to come home late from emergency call-outs.

The last thing I expected was the threat of being bribed, but I suppose, having seen his house, he has to get all his money from somewhere. I once asked if I could call Malcolm from the telephone in his bedroom, and he asked me to keep the call brief and leave a penny on the bedside table. To this day I don't know if he was joking or not.

We ordered ginger pudding and spread the Sunday papers out over the table. They were full of what was likely to happen – the tightening of resolve and the formation of Chamberlain's war cabinet. Malcolm frowned at the headlines. 'What's that silly little man done now?' It wasn't clear if he was referring to Hitler or Chamberlain.

After lunch I went to the Colonel's house, to pay my respects. The house auction is next week, the maid tells me. 'Everything is for sale,' she said, distraught. Her eyes were red. 'Can I see the clocks?' I asked. 'I might buy one.'

'Of course.' She led me to the enormous room that he called a lounge. She had a little weep, listening to the clocks all ticking away to themselves. I subtly removed the piece of paper on which I'd supposedly written our telephone number, with its scribbled 'Meet me in the usual place'.

It was his favourite spot; bizarre, what excites some people. He liked to pin me down against the stone floor.

I put new sheets on the bed. Malcolm reads *Crime and Punishment*, laughing occasionally. I give him a quizzical look. 'I didn't know Dostoyevsky was renowned as a comedian.'

'Oh he is, he is.'

The power of suggestion is so strong. When I first met Mrs Limmidge I had a kind of 'bookmark' moment; this person will be useful, I thought. It just seemed to fit into place. And how simple it is to manipulate someone; to look at her pathetic collection of random coloured dots, and all I needed to do was tap the caves' location and say, 'They seem to be converging here,' and be sincere. It was a bonus that she picked up on the idea of the weapons; all I'd expected was for her to be a diversion. The fact she plunged in wholeheartedly and went for it with the gun was pure synchronicity. I almost thought for a moment that she would actually kill him.

Malcolm laughs again, then closes the book. 'I saw you earlier,' he says, 'I went for a walk along the cliffs. You were by the caves. I called, but you didn't hear me.'

'It was a nice lunch, wasn't it?' I say. He nods thoughtfully, and turns the light out.

Poor Mrs Limmidge. She'll be looked after well enough at the sanatorium. In fact she's probably safer there; if there's an invasion, being down here on the south coast is not the best place to be.

I am surprised that I don't feel any guilt. Perhaps this will emerge later. In the night there is a late summer storm. Malcolm turns to me in his sleep, opens his eyes briefly, and says he loves me.

Ferry, moon, child.

Our marriage is a comet, she thought, or is it a meteor? They married in a hurry, six weeks after meeting. The honeymoon was a golden blaze in Tunisia; thinking back now, she couldn't believe how many times they'd made love each day, and still managed to pack in a full itinerary of lazing on the beach, lazing by the pool and lazing by the bar. Tiring, though.

It was three years ago, and the first two months were happy. They had a spare room that they'd kept empty, in readiness; they had a little money saved for emergencies; and they knew that, when the time came, Owen would be able to stop working if necessary, at least for six months or so.

Friday was a non-teaching day and Sara always enjoyed the strange quiet of the flat. She closed her eyes for a moment, then opened them as she heard the excited chatter in the alleyway of children going home. She listened to the squealing, the 'noooo's, the 'shut *up*'s, the '*whatever*'s. The sound of the future. In twenty years' time, when I've left the school and Owen is being squeezed out of work, those kids outside who don't have a care in the world apart from *X Factor* and who snogged who up a tree, and what Kate and Jack did in the park, trying cider for the first time from bottles of cheap plastic that made it spill when you gripped it hard enough to lift it – they will be the people in suits, telling him it's time to go.

'Will that really happen?' she'd asked him as they lay on the beach, looking at the line of coconut umbrellas, and work and reality seemed a very long way away. 'No one,' he'd said, 'wants a fifty-something IT guy, and it will only get worse.' Back in the real world, over the next couple of years she would occasionally remind him of this, and make noises about putting more into the pension, but he wouldn't listen, and maybe he was right anyway, who could trust pension schemes these days?

And when it happens, a voice from somewhere said, our child – our children? – will have grown up and left home. She opened her eyes and closed them again.

There were three or four moments in the day when she heard noises from outside. 'Warning – this vehicle is reversing,' and its equivalent in Welsh, as the man who drove a small van backed it out of his drive each morning. A particular car she always heard starting around two pm and driving away; someone finishing work at the café, maybe? And those children laughing and shouting at quarter to nine, and again at four. Sara liked the sounds, they were comforting and created a sense of order, however meaningless or trivial they might be in themselves.

The door slammed and Sara jumped off the bed and went to the kitchen. Surely she had only closed her eyes for a few moments? She glanced up at the clock; five thirty.

'Coffee?'

'Please. Horrible day.'

'Oh yes?' She stirred the coffees slowly.

'We're doing this staff questionnaire at the moment, and you've never seen such funny answers in your life. "What business are we in?" You'd think that was a fairly straightforward question. But the stuff people come out with, it's no wonder the place is so chaotic.

'Well – '

'Or, "Who has the most power in the organisation?" Someone's put, "we are all empowered to make decisions." I don't know who employs these people. Thanks,' he said, taking the coffee and dropping into the sofa.

Sara flicked through a magazine and he read it over her shoulder when he thought she couldn't see him looking. 'Then one of the questions was, "what would help you do your job better?" And someone's written, "United Nations negotiating skills." '

'Good job you're there to sort them out, isn't it?' she murmured.

'They've got a point I suppose,' he said. 'I'm just worried that we've missed the boat; we're going to get swallowed up by someone else if we're not careful. Nobody thinks strategically.'

'It was a bit like with me and the kids yesterday,' she said. 'It's pointless giving them maths in the afternoon, they can't concentrate.' He nodded, looking at the adverts before she turned the page.

On Saturday she picked up the ferry tickets in town. When she came back Owen was unwrapping a print he'd got on eBay. 'I thought the wall in the living room looked a bit bare,' he said, looking up at her from a pile of polystyrene and brown tape, 'so I bought us a Degas.'

'Looks like a picture to me.'

He held it up against the wall. 'What do you think?'

'She's a bit naked. She's a bit pretty. She doesn't even look real.'

'Eh?' He studied it.

'She's pale, she looks like a dummy.'

'It's *Degas*. It's one of the finest artists in the world.'

She shrugged. 'She's too unreal. No, that's not right. Just "not real".'

'Is there anything you do like?'

'The borders are good.'

He stuffed the bubble wrap into a plastic bag. 'I'll drill some holes this afternoon.'

She studied him curiously. 'There's something different about you.'

'I wondered when you'd notice.'

'They suit you.'

He took the new glasses off and rubbed them on the lens cleaner he'd been given in the shop.

She smiled. 'How long will it take you to lose that and go back to tissues?'

'About an hour.' He put the lens cleaner in the case. 'Well, they gave me a voucher at work, so I thought, why not.'

'They're good. I like them. I wish I was blind too,' she said, putting her arms round him.

Sara packed a small case and left it by the door. She marked some books, glancing at her watch from time to time. She looked at the wall opposite. The Degas stared back insolently. 'I'm nineteen. I don't have a care in the world. I've had a long, lazy bath, I'm drying my hair and it doesn't bother me if you look at me, because I don't have a spare inch of fat, I don't have bags under my eyes, my face is vacant because there aren't any lines. My legs are long, my toes are pretty, my whole life stretches in front of me.'

The gentle curve of her hip; the nipples, delicately and blushingly coloured. 'I hate you,' Sara said. The expression did not change. Sara waited for her to blush, to become embarrassed by her nakedness, but she refused.

'Bitch,' she said when Owen was at work.

Sara sat in the passenger seat, patient as Owen brought the cases to the car. He put them in the boot and glanced over to her.

'Have we got enough Marmite?' she asked.

'Eh?'

'I'm just wondering how much we should take.'

'They have Marmite in Ireland, don't they?'

'Are you sure? Can you guarantee they have Marmite in Ireland?'

'I can't guarantee it, no.'

'You've been to Ireland before, haven't you?'

'I didn't go shopping for Marmite.'

'There's no need to be... oh, never mind.' She got out of the car and went back to the flat. 'I won't be two minutes.' Owen turned the car round and left it idling as he waited for her. He studied the map of the route to Pembroke. 'Seems pretty simple,' he murmured.

'Bitch,' said Sara as she walked past the Degas and got some Marmite from the kitchen. 'Bitch,' she said on the way back. How long will this joke last she wondered, locking the door. Forever, probably.

She got back in the car and wielded two small jars. 'Found these.'

'That's a relief. Glove compartment? You don't want to leave them on display, someone might steal them.'

M4, M4, M4. If you keep saying it, it loses any meaning. The vacuous blue signs tell you you're going somewhere, but you know you're not really. Sara looked with distant interest as the steelworks passed by, puffing smoke and steam into the blue air.

'That painting,' she said, could you put it in the spare room?'

'You don't think it goes in the lounge?'

'Not really.'

'I'll move it. I was going to put up, you know, different pictures, in the other bedroom.'

'When the time comes, we can always move it again.'

After an hour of driving Sara disappeared from the seat next to him. It was the new glasses; the stems were thick and when he looked straight ahead he couldn't see her. He enjoyed this sensation for a few moments; staring through the windscreen and pretending she wasn't there; then it began to alarm him. If she wasn't there, what was the point in going? Would he travel on his own? He would enjoy the freedom, he told himself. He would be able to do whatever he wanted; he could sit in the pub all day.

Behind him, the ghost of a voice seemed to ask if they were nearly there. He closed his hands more firmly on the steering wheel. He glanced across at Sara; the reflections from the windscreen made light blue and grey lines across her face, highlighting the shadows beneath her eyes, and a slight double chin that was only visible when she was in exact profile. He looked ahead and pushed his glasses back on his nose, and she reassuringly reappeared beside him.

Past Carmarthen they came off the motorway and the roads got progressively narrower. The A road was okay, and from the map they only had a few miles to go; but soon they were following a long queue of traffic which got slower and slower. Sara craned her head to try to see round the corner.

'Plenty of time,' he said, 'it's only two o'clock.' The sea was ahead, a narrow ribbon of blue in the distance.

The traffic crawled to walking pace. 'I guess it's because it's August,' Sara said. 'These roads grind to a halt. School holidays and all that.'

'Bloody kids eh,' he said as she wound the window down. They breathed in the scent of cowslips and listened to the buzz of insects and distant farm machinery. As they reached the brow of a hill they looked down to see a long convoy of trucks and cars with trailers or roof racks or boots full of luggage. 'I think we should have allowed more time.'

Bit late now, he thought. 'We'll be all right,' he

murmured. 'It doesn't go till three.'

The traffic stopped completely and for the next half an hour only moved in stops and starts. At quarter to three it started moving quickly, and they came over another steep hill, and saw the ferry in the harbour, with a trail of cars entering it.

'It might be running late,' he said optimistically.

'Of course it's not running late.'

It was two minutes to three as they reached the barriers. 'It hasn't actually gone yet, has it?' said Owen, handing their tickets over. 'Can we still get on?'

The guard shook his head. 'Look down here on the small print, you were supposed to be here at quarter past two.'

'Cosmic,' Sara said. The guard gave the tickets back to Owen. 'Don't worry,' he said, 'you don't lose any money. You can get the next boat.'

'Oh, okay,' said Sara. Perhaps we'll even have time to pop into Pembroke and have a look round the shops, she thought. 'What time does the next one go?'

'Three AM,' said the man, disappearing into his booth.

They watched the ship leave harbour.

'See you at three AM then,' Sara said brightly to the metal box.

'Just be here by two-fifteen,' said the disembodied voice.

Owen followed a battered sign, its condition a memory of trucks and vans turning round in the narrow confines of the harbour.

'Why didn't you look, why didn't you make sure?'

'It's no more my fault than it is yours. Why didn't you look? Why didn't you make sure?'

They parked overlooking the town and walked down the steep path by the side of the castle.

'Don't worry about it.'

'I'm not worrying about it.'

'Do you want to buy another pot of Marmite?'

'Shut up.'

'It'll be all right,' he said, 'we can find a nice pub for the evening, then wait in the car till they let us on board. I guarantee it.'

'We're supposed to be in *Ireland*,' she said.

'I know.' He looked at her blankly.

'Having our holiday.'

'I know.'

She held a hand to her face and he saw the blue veins pulsing; her wrist was fragile, the creases on it beautiful, and her fingernails chipped, which made him want to hug her and protect her.

'I don't want to go to a pub in the town,' she said. There was a brief shower of hot, gritty rain. 'Let's drive somewhere and find a nice country pub.'

'Okay.'

A few miles inland, a brown sign directed them to the Rising Sun. She adjusted her make up in the mirror before they went in. 'Do I look thirty-seven?' she said, looking up at him.

'No.'

'Do I look thirty-five?'

He paused and she thumped him.

Relief, that it wasn't one of those pubs where everyone stares at you when you walk in. Couples scattered round, pondering their mini-universes; old men sat at tables with hands on pints, staring into space; an extremely unattractive specimen at the bar, long greasy hair and a slouched, rounded back, given a wide berth by the barmaid each time she had to cross in front of him.

'Your usual?' Owen asked.

She shook her head. 'Let's try one of the ales.'

'Okay.'

'Two pints of...' they scanned the pumps. 'Night Watchmen, please.'

'Miss the boat?' the barman asked.

A wry smile. 'How can you tell?' Owen asked.

'You can tell.' The barman pulled the second pint.

'We only missed it by that much,' said Sara, holding her index finger and thumb an inch apart. 'Are the roads always that slow?'

'Yes,' said the man, placing the pints in front of them, 'although it'll have been worse today. People coming over for the eclipse, you know.'

'Eclipse?'

'Of course.'

The barman gave Owen change from a fiver. 'I like it here,' he murmured, examining the silver coin in his hand.

One table free. There was a third chair and Sara pushed it aside before sitting next to Owen. The huge brown clock above the bar read eight o'clock. This might be a long evening, she thought as she cast her eye round the room. Curiously lumpy, whitewashed walls that looked as if someone was pushing from the other side. The usual horse brasses. Banknotes from locations which owed their exoticism more to time than geography – Aden, Ceylon. Several darkened pictures, in cobwebbed brown frames, none of them hanging quite vertically. One, a picture of a woman kneeling in a tub, reminded her of the Degas hanging at home. Look at me, said the Degas, look at me. Bitch.

'I remember the last eclipse,' Owen said. 'It was cloudy and a bit of a damp squib really. Like Halley's Comet,' he added, and Sara found herself looking towards the dark space behind Owen's head.

At the next table, four young men in thick black glasses were hunched over laptops. Sara nudged Owen's leg. 'I bet they're some of them,' she whispered.

'Some of what?'

'You know. Astrologers.'

'Astronomers.'

Whatever, Sara thought. Why does he have to be so picky about everything, why can't we just have a conversation?

'I don't know why we haven't heard about tomorrow's though,' Owen said. 'I mean there was such a song and dance about the last one, they couldn't stop going on about it on the telly.'

One of the laptop boys, his glasses perking upwards as if picking up Owen's words by radar, looked across. 'It's because it's only partial,' he said, 'and it's not visible from much of the country. Just this band of West Wales, and over the Irish Sea.'

'So you're what... tracking its progress? Sara asked, trying to crane round to see the screens.

The others looked up in surprise. 'No, we're playing Galaxy Ownership.'

'Oh.'

'I've just bought Orion,' one of the others said, 'and he's just conquered the Acteon galaxy.' He nodded towards the third boy, who had the same glasses and white trainers as the others.

'Excellent,' said Sara, raising her pint. 'Cheers.'

In the toilets, long mirrors that reached from floor to ceiling, reflecting multiple images of herself, stretching into infinity and becoming greener as they did so, as if commenting on her mortality. Sara washed her hands and noticed a child's handprint on the mirror about two feet from the floor. She looked at the fingers, the ghostly outline, and could make out the shape of the fingerprints. She stood up sharply as someone else came in.

'It'll be all right,' a voice said as she emerged and saw Owen sitting in the corner, lifting his pint delicately so as not to spill any of it. The voice was clear and distinct, but she wondered why it was still so insistent that everything would be all right. When is that time going to come, she wondered; and as the days, and the months, and the years went past, would the voice grow fainter? Where did it come from, and where did it get its confidence?

'Do you think I should try Guinness in Ireland?'

'Maybe,' she considered, slipping a hand under his shirt. 'Don't drink too much though, or this will start to fatten up.'

'Ha ha. Maybe.'

They were hopeful at eleven that the pub, tucked away in its grass-covered, dark corner of the country, might close the curtains and stay open; there were enough people sitting around, or playing darts. Even the laptop boys didn't seem to realise it was past their bedtime. Yet the barman called time on the dot of eleven and the customers obediently downed their pints and left. Laptops snapped shut. 'Good luck with tomorrow,' Sara said, and they smiled shyly. 'Thank you,' they answered, one after the other, as if no one outside their circle had ever voluntarily spoken to them before. Perhaps no one had.

'Well,' she said, 'what do we do now for... four hours?'

Owen smiled and finished his long-savoured driver's pint. 'We'll be okay.' Sara pushed the third chair back in its place as they left.

The pub sign light snapped out, shortly followed by the naked light bulbs on the building itself. They crunched across the gravel, holding hands in the unfamiliar darkness. Driving towards the port, they were distracted by something yellow and glowing to their right. It was a castle – not Pembroke castle, Owen decided, because it was on its own in the middle of fields – and on a whim, he took a right branch and followed it.

'Is this a good idea?' Sara wondered as the road narrowed to a single track.

'Of course it is.'

Hedgehogs ventured out curiously, and voles dashed across the road like clockwork mice. In the hedgerows Sara thought she saw a badger, but wasn't sure. Driving past a lake, Owen saw a brown sign with a castellated square, and drove across gravel to see the castle appear boldly in front of them. It was a proper, fairytale castle: a moat, a drawbridge, narrow windows inside bulging turrets, and gargoyles adorning the crenellations.

Owen took blankets, found some packets of biscuits nestling by the Marmite, and they tramped across the wet grass until they found a comfortable position to lie in. They ate the biscuits and listened to the alien night sounds: owls calling forlornly, burrowing and nestling behind them; flapping sounds in the trees, which Sara guessed to be bats.

She snuggled closer and rested her head in the hollow of her husband's shoulder. My husband; how I still love saying that. The shoulder; it seemed to have evolved for the eventual purpose of her lying in the crook of it.

On the stroke of midnight the yellow lights on the castle snapped off and it vanished, not even leaving a trace of its presence on the deep indigo water beneath it.

'Oh,' said Sara, feeling cheated of their night's entertainment. She felt for Owen's arm but her eyes got used to the sudden darkness. Uncountable stars appeared, as if turned on gradually by a dimmer switch. The Plough and Cassiopeia and the usual, familiar constellations had been there before; but the total blackness on the ground, as thick as oil, made the patterns embed so thickly with new stars that the recognisable shapes disappeared.

They kissed and she slipped her hand under his shirt. They rolled over, giggling occasionally. She bit his neck and as he moved underneath her, the stars blurred and zoomed across the sky. He held her stomach as they made love. She cried for a moment, but it was dark and the grass was noisy and he didn't notice.

She saw, in the stillness with him breathing heavily on top of her, a tiny star appear from the horizon. As she watched, it moved upwards, almost imperceptibly, and for a while she thought it was her imagination, until she saw it was a good few inches clear of the horizon.

'Look at this,' she murmured, pushing him gently until he moved away. She pointed to the faintly moving star, but he couldn't see it against the mass of light. 'Just stay still,' she said, 'and you'll see.'

He looked in the direction she indicated. 'Oh yes.' It moved in an unflinching vertical line and now appeared nine or ten inches above the horizon.

'What is it?'

'A satellite, I guess.' It was so small that as you looked, it seemed to wink out of existence; then as you shifted your vision slightly, it reappeared. They watched its ascent, slowly but inevitably moving directly above them. They lay side by side, listening to each other breathing, then watched the satellite pass the zenith and descend on the other side. They rotated on the blanket, brushing lazily against each other's bodies as they moved round, until they were facing the other way and the satellite crawled down the other half of sky.

They must have dozed, because the next thing Sara knew Owen was rubbing her shoulder. 'Come on,' he whispered. 'Time to go.'

She stood and her joints creaked and tingled. She smiled as he reached his hand out to her. With their eyes better used to the dark, she saw a faint outline of the castle.

'I've never seen so many stars,' Sara said as they crossed the gravel. 'And look – I guess that's the Milky Way,' she said, pointing to the paler ribbon of sky that weaved like flung paint. 'I always thought that was a – well, a myth, I suppose. Like the Man in the Moon. I've never been able to see it before.'

'We should get out of town more often.'

In the queue for the ferry they felt like children, the anticipation heightened by the sense of illicit, night-time activity. The mundane surroundings became interesting: a petrol station; a hedgehog scurrying across the road; a dog, scratching a fence. She reached across and put her hand in his lap.

On the boat, the heady mixture of diesel and night air. They took pillows from the back seat and went to the bar, stepping over people failing to sleep and past men in their twenties, valiantly trying to chat up the waitress. Who gets the night crossing, she wondered, apart from people like us who missed the daytime one?

On deck a seeming doze must have been an hour or two because dawn came up. 'There's plenty of time,' she found herself saying, as the last line of a dream that had already disappeared.

Her husband smiled. 'I told you we'd be all right,' he murmured.

Ireland, green and new, formed slowly, impossibly out of nothingness, from the swirling water and mist in front of them. They felt a strange sympathy to the moon, white and virginal, higher in the sky than seemed normal, seemingly still, nervously expecting its encounter with the sun later that morning. A sympathy? Sara wondered. The kind you feel for small animals, that do not know their fate.

'I can't believe we missed the boat,' she said, grinning in the half-light.

He stood silhouetted, like a magician in swirling smoke. 'But we didn't, did we?' he murmured. 'Here we are.'

She nodded. 'Do you really think we'll be all right?'

He touched her stomach. 'Yes,' he said. 'Yes, I do.'

'And you're really my husband, aren't you? You're not going to disappear?'

'I promise,' he said.

And then they saw her – it was definitely a her – running across the deck, golden curls, turning and smiling a cute, milk-toothed smile. They both saw her, but said nothing to each other. The holiday passed in a green blur. They found a renewed confidence in each other, a comfortableness they hadn't had for a while. When they got home, they started redecorating the spare room.

Quietly, Sara got rid of the Degas print one spring afternoon. Owen didn't notice it had gone.

Death and the Maiden

A red void. The void turns yellow, blue: the air ripples in front of me, hazes then cools. Hammering, fluid in my ears, flushing from my skin. The sense of travelling upwards, emerging through a surface of water, chest rising and falling. Limbs solidify, and for a moment I fear I'll be paralysed. I flex my toes. Large, wide, golden.

Three people watching me: two in boiler suits with dark goggles, hands by their sides like manikins. In the middle a young man studies me anxiously. I rise a couple more feet, someone flicks a button on a panel and the red light disappears. The platform shudders to a halt.

I drip wet, the sparks flying from me but muted. My nakedness is admired.

I jump down and the sound echoes. The foundry is bare, chilly. A mouse emerges cautiously from a corner, thinks better of it and reverses into safe darkness. The chatter of air in the radiators. Pipes wind round themselves in corners as if for warmth. My shadow looms on frosted glass as I approach a doorway. Catching sight of myself for the first time in the door's metal I see a slim, lithe figure. Maybe the eyebrows are too high; the nose long and thin, but it's a distinctive, well-shaped face.

I thought I was travelling randomly as I raced across the bridge, my silhouette showing up in strobe flashes as I briefly appeared under each sodium lamp. Cars flash past, their headlights not trained on me. Autumn frost makes the trees look like ghosts.

By an industrial estate, the cloud of smoke dispersing idly, I find a short cut by squeezing under the metal fence. There are six inches spare between the bottom strut and the uneven earth and when I concentrate, I can stretch myself to scrape my way through. Along a plain-looking street I know the house when I get there. I go round the back, past oil cans and ominous objects covered in tarpaulins. The back door is locked but it's not difficult to knock the small pane of glass out, weak in its old putty, and pull the catch. There's a stale smell in the house, cats maybe, or the windows haven't been opened for a week.

An old woman is embedded in a chair too large for her. The television flickers blue and yellow on her face, and a miniature TV is reflected in each eye. She smiles, fattish jowls lifting at the dancing, singing glitziness on the screen. She looks up at me with an amused expression.

'Oh,' she says sadly, 'it's a dream… I didn't expect to dream about sitting in my chair, why can't it be a more exciting dream!' I reach towards her neck and the veins pulse, the blue highlighted in the reflections from the screen. She sprawls in the outsize chair. Curiosity – as at so many things – at her limbs now more doll-like than before.

Her bones crack like a small bird. Afterwards I turn and look at the TV. Surreal images. A singer walks through smoke, to tumultuous applause. He sings a song. Three judges look on, wielding pens like the pins of hand grenades. They criticise the singing and the crowd boos; they say something positive, and the crowd cheers. I turn the TV off and tidy up. I tip the remains of her tea down the sink and turn the lights off. There is an empty birdcage covered in dust and I wonder why she has kept it.

'That's okay. Leave it over there.' Fay stacks the cigarette butts in a pyramid, standing back from time to time to consider it. I feel a crackling in my chest as the young man I saw yesterday walks through the door.

Fay steps back from the pile of cigarettes. 'Oh, hi Adi.'

'Blimey. What on earth is that?'

'Oh, you know. Now that smoking is banned in public, it's become an art form.'

'Has it?'

'Well the more we can't smoke, the more the act of smoking is dismissed, hidden away to corners, is rejected and demonised, the remains of it become something to be celebrated.'

'I see.'

'I had to do it again this morning.'

'Really? They were supposed to install it yesterday.'

'They did. One of the cleaners binned it.'

'Okay. Well….' he glances up at me. 'What I do becomes more and more antiquated.'

'Oh no.' Fay tugs at his arm. 'It's beautiful.'

'Beautiful, yes. But is that where it's at any more?'

She touches his arm again. 'There's room for different types of thing. Is it for sale?'

'Of course.' He walks up to me and notices some grass on my foot. The blades are frozen, crushed as if welded on. He scrapes them away. 'I don't know what those foundry guys are playing at.' He runs a hand across my ankle and I move my leg so he can reach my shin. He looks up.

Fay examines a head floating in a tank, its eyes closed and its mouth turned down.

'Made with the artist's own body fat.' She reads from the label, her own head turned to one side. 'Someone called Hawker.'

'Ideal Christmas present,' Adi says.

'These are good.' Puppets with two heads, looking at each other as if deep in argument. One puppet with no head at all, but where the head should be, a second pair of legs. Another puppet whose body is an elongated head, ending in four limb-like heads.

'Who made these,' Adi says, 'I don't think I've met him.'

Fay shakes her head. 'You won't. He says he can't deal with people if he can't control what they're going to say.'

Adi nods, looks at the puppets suspiciously. There is something ghost-like, resentful about their expressions. Fury at being a puppet, perhaps, and not only that, a deformed puppet that everyone stares at. 'Who was it who said you should go beyond good and evil in your art,' Adi murmurs.

'Nietzsche.'

'Bless you.'

Fay pulls a face. Adi looks at the heads. 'Head, head, head.'

'It's one of those words that if you keep saying it, it doesn't mean anything any more.'

'Aren't all words like that?'

'So er... do you fancy dinner after the party?' she asks.

Adi has turned back to me. 'Mm?'

'Dinner? Later?'

He smiles, and shakes his head. 'Sorry. Too much work.'

She shrugs, and pouts. 'Oh well.' She flicks her hair. 'I suppose I need to be putting finishing touches to the TG installation anyway.'

'Oh yes,' Adi says with more animation, 'how is that going?'

'Well, it's going to be the opening of the gallery in miniature...'

They go through the large swing doors and leave me in the draughty room. I hear, in the distance, gathering people: corks opening, brochures rustling, boots thumping on grilles. Lots of exclamations about the unseasonal weather.

Opening. Red and blue lights, giving visitors curious, cartoon-like features. Silver trays flash, glittering champagne flutes disappear from them quickly. Hostesses dressed as Daliesque flames; licks of orange and red silk snake up and down their mostly naked bodies.

Fay proudly shows visitors her installation: an old-fashioned toilet, the cistern high at the top, the pipes gunmetal grey. It's surrounded by a cuboid wooden frame, the struts appearing to go one way and then the other, like those pictures of boxes that change perspective as you watch.

'It's to promote the Toilet Gallery,' she says to a polite little bald-headed man who nods at everything she says. 'The first gallery anywhere in the world – I think I can say this with confidence – ever to open in an ex-public toilet.'

He nods. 'Is it for sale?'

'Er … well yes I suppose so. Why, do you want to buy it?'

He nods. 'No, of course not. Why would I want to buy an old toilet?' He wanders away, nodding disdainfully.

Adi is centre of attention for much of the evening. Women crowd round him, giggling at his jokes and sipping champagne quickly when he's not speaking to them. Backless cocktail dresses make their inhabitants appear to be made of water: shoulders shimmer and slip; hair is sculpted like waves. Adi gets obscured in the maelstrom, a tall ship disappearing into the storm, sirens luring him. I am impassive as people tap me, nudge each other, flick through their brochures, make comments. 'The middle's not very good.'

'The middle? What do you mean?'

'It's too long.'

'It's okay. It's how the artist sees her. She's stylised.'

'Too skinny for me.'

They continue in a careful clockwise circuit, giving each exhibit the same amount of time. A Russian doll, which looks like a fat, smiling Margaret Thatcher. A visitor twists Thatcher's head off to reveal Tony Blair, grinning like the Joker. Inside Tony Blair is a callow, nervous David Cameron. Inside Cameron is an emaciated Nick Clegg, his face squashed by how small the doll is. Inside Nick Clegg is a shapeless egg of a doll; unformed, unpainted.

The CD player plays 80s pop, its sounds muffled and distorted and amplified in equal measure by the size of the room. Rather like body fat artist Hawker and his velvet jacket, his moustache dyed yellow and his jazzy shirt, the music is ironic. So far I feel that I've been getting the hang of things pretty well (apart from the murder, obviously). I understand most things, but irony is the hardest. I know what it is, but I can't say what it means. Earlier, as the guests entered for the opening, someone shivered in their upturned collar and thick gloves, and said 'it's a bit tropical out there.' Why would you say that? I understand, and yet... I don't understand.

The last hangers-on leave. The free drink is drunk so there's no reason to stay. Fay waits in the hallway, silhouetted by bright corridor light; she puts her coat on, ruffles her hair, gets a mirror out and applies lipstick. Eventually, when Adi nods goodbye to her, she shrugs and goes. Hawker systematically examines abandoned glasses and pours dregs of drinks into a bucket.

'What are you doing?' Adi asks.

'Might come in handy one day.' Hawker leaves, to the relief of a callow, spotty cleaner who does his best. He's about to tidy away a pile of plastic cups littering the floor, then thinks better of it. Adi, hiding a glass of whisky from him, presses buttons on the CD player until the energetic, bouncy sounds cease. He turns the switch for the radio and scrolls through fragments of voices, snips of guitar, keyboard, brief laughter, eventually settling on Schubert. He looks up at me. 'That's more like it.' The cleaner, seeing a man talking to a sculpture, leaves.

The music echoes in the room; the acoustics are suited for it. Violins swoop, decline, fall. Adi studies me, swirling the whisky absently. 'I am definitely giving this up,' he says as I step down from the plinth. I take the glass and place it near the Russian dolls, who look at it keenly. Thatcher smacks her lips. We dance slowly and he says nothing. I can feel his breath on my chest.

The lights go off in cubes. They vanish too regularly to be operated by anyone; it must be automatic. Just me, and the head in a tank, and the dolls and the puppets and the toilet. The last square of white disappears. This, perhaps, is my punishment. To stand, like a school child who has pushed pencil shavings down their neighbour's shirt, until someone says I can get down.

Through the night my mind wanders; an expression new to me, and it seems wonderfully evocative. Wonderfully evocative.

This is guilt then: the constant, repeating waves of fear, lack of understanding, all set against a curious power; a feeling of control. All I can do is experience contrition, hope that one day I will make sense of it – the fear is that there is no why – and promise I will not do it again. And think of Adi. Dancing with me, holding me, bringing me to life.

Towards the end of the night I can't bear it any longer. I know where to go. There are a few flakes of snow in the air and as I rush through streets, the snow appears a luminous blue against the darkness. I slip my hand through the letterbox and unlatch the door. Pictures on the walls. It's plush, well-appointed, spacious, calm. Pink and green and red; a woman lives here. It takes a while to find her. She's in the attic, a converted loft accessed by a vast steel staircase. A huge desk, papers spread out on it. Numbers, dizzying numbers, scattered across pages, down pages. Yellow notes on the edges like bat droppings. A screen, glowing behind her, updating itself with new figures every few moments.

Her expression is impassive. I cannot complain about this as I have been told much the same thing. 'Can I help you?' she eventually says, looking, for some reason, at her watch. As with the elderly woman, she seems to think she's asleep. Emails ping behind her.

'If you don't mind, I'm busy.' She smiles. What a strange thing to be doing at midnight. She is lithe, she escapes when I reach a hand out towards her. I trap her in a corner and she screams. She still thinks it's a dream but at the same time knows it isn't. She swears at me, and at herself, and tells herself to wake up. She tries to dive through my legs to reach the hatchway, where the warm, red light glows from below, but isn't fast enough and I pin her down. The numbers chatter away across the screen without her, oblivious, able to carry on without her.

It's the first proper day of the exhibition and the place is buzzing. Thirty or forty people hold well-thumbed catalogues. The head in the tank, bizarrely, has sold. Hawker turns up drunk and celebratory before being escorted out by gallery attendants. They look like chauffeurs in their peaked caps as they take an arm each and haul Hawker away, legs cycling in air between them.

Lots of talk about the murders. Speculation on why there is a random killer on the loose; the Random Ripper, they are already calling him (they assume it's a him). All day, people look up and admire me. I'm masking a secret, my beauty is wafer-thin. It's eased a fraction by observing that most people are not upset by the deaths, but instead find them rather exciting. The conversations move on with equal interest as to whether the snow is going to settle and whether we will have a white Christmas.

Late in the day Adi arrives and stands at the back. He speaks to a gallery attendant who nods and leaves the room briefly, returning with an upright trolley, the kind you might stack boxes on. 'Give me a hand,' Adi says, and they manhandle me onto the trolley. The attendant pats me on the bottom. 'Nice figure you've got here,' he says, showing crooked teeth to Adi.

'That's enough of that,' says Adi primly, and together they take me out to the car park. 'I can manage now, thanks.' The attendant wheels his trolley away. Adi lays me down in the back of the car; I move my head and knees to help him.

He backs the car up to the studio and unlocks the double doors. There's no one around so when he opens the boot I spring out and follow him into the building. I recognise it all. The Chinese screen in the corner, frogs and ducks eternally caught crossing rivers, streams of water eddying around rocks. Leopards watching from behind trees. The chaise-longue, piled with old cushions, contents bursting. One wall is covered with huge paintings in ornate frames, some hanging, some suspended and some stacked from the floor. It surprises me, that I'm familiar with it when I've never been here. Adi goes to the battered, curvy green fridge and takes out a bottle of champagne.

'Someone gave this to me at the opening,' he says,

carrying two glasses between the fingers of his other hand. The cork fires into the ceiling. He pours both glasses and hands me one. His expression changes; he looks ashamed, and even glows red as he realises, what is she going to do with it?

I set the glass down and go to the back of the room where the CD player is. I look through a few cases, all splattered with paint and some of them stuck together. He really needs to sort all this out. A woman would never let it get into such a state. I find the Schubert quartet that was on the radio earlier, and press the play button.

This makes him laugh. He wonders how I knew, but tells himself not to worry about it. I'm probably imagining the whole thing, he says, let's just roll with it. Fay's fault, for bringing round that funny tobacco a few weeks ago. Not doing that again.

I hand him my champagne and he drinks it for me. We dance for a minute or perhaps it's an hour, or maybe it's a day. He seems self-conscious with his arm round my waist; I shift my hips so his hand slips to my bottom. He smiles and declares that whatever's going on, he's going to enjoy it.

Lying face-down I turn to look at him. He sketches me, his legs crossed in a four, the pen flying and blurring over the page. As the sun comes up he looks at his watch. 'We must get you back to the gallery.'

'Must we?' I say.

He drops his notepad. 'I didn't know you could speak.'

'You didn't ask.'

We drive back. I feel like a dog, excitedly looking out of the window as his master takes him on an adventure. I watch people slipping on the ice, walking carefully with their hands outstretched to the railings as they step tentatively through the parks.

Another day on the stand. Is it just me, I wonder. Do the Russian dolls come alive and chat to each other in the dark? Do the frogs and the leopards on Adi's screen hide in the lacquered trees and leap across streams? What about the puppets, do they get together and bitch about their lot? They could. They might. Why wouldn't they?

In the evening he takes me home again. The attendants think he's gone mad. The aroma of tobacco and blankets and strange outside smells of snow and ice make me close my eyes.

He finishes work late. Commissions, quick oil daubs of coastline, estuaries, bay views. Colours that he doesn't bother to mix, straight from the tube onto the canvas, form the shapes and patterns of the scenery, mostly from his imagination rather than from reality. 'Boring,' he says.

They are beautiful, they glitter, they change shape as the light alters.

He yawns and I follow him upstairs. His bedroom is in the loft; the walls are diagonal with alcove windows. Candles in dusty corners; I find some matches. 'These haven't been lit for ages,' he murmurs. I give him a glass of whisky.

'I've been steering clear of whisky.'

'Why?'

He laughs. 'Because I thought I was making you up.'

'But here I am.' I tap my thigh and it clangs.

'Yes... well. I thought I was hallucinating you.'

'Perhaps you are.'

He nods. Perhaps he is. The thought frightens me. I lean over and try to kiss him. He pulls away. I watch his features dance and flicker in the candle light. 'There is something at work in my soul,' he says, swirling the whisky and looking at the yellow reflections on the wall that move like waves, 'that I do not understand.'

I nod. 'Let's not worry about it too much.' I go to the bed and lie down. The sheets smell of him. 'Draw me again.'

I watch him as he sleeps. I slip through the door and go down to the studio. I push the heavy corrugated doors to one side and slip out. Racing across the fields. A rich luminous moon; in corners where the snow hasn't reached, the trees are purple, the grass blue.

A house with beams, seemingly made of geometric shapes; triangles overhanging the ground floor, more triangles in the roof. Red rectangles of doors contrasting with the blue square of swimming pool. Circular rugs. Vast canvases filling walls, splashed with paint. A cube with half a sheep in it. I cannot find the other half. A large, winding staircase and then long corridors.

My feet silent on the thick carpets. A couple in bed. The woman screams but the man just looks at me in incomprehension. My fingers slide onto his throat and he does not resist; it's as if he hasn't woken up properly. A ceiling fan rotates lazily.

I slip into bed beside Adi and put an arm round him. When he touches my leg there is a tolling sound.

'Sorry. I can't help it.'

'It's all right. It just takes a while to get used to it.'

'You mean you've never taken one of your sculptures to bed before?'

'No,' he says haplessly.

'I wasn't born yesterday,' I say, pressing my hands on the bed. 'Am I really supposed to believe that?'

'Yes, he says, 'yes, you're the first.'

I lean in and rub my nose against his. It squashes attractively against his face. 'You say all the right things.'

I try to kiss him but again he won't return it. 'Why not?' I squeeze his hand and it goes white. Eventually he pulls it away. 'Sorry.' He rubs his hand and brings the life back into it.

He dozes. I watch the sun come up.

His alarm goes off at six and he jumps up. I find it strange, the animal inquisitiveness of people – I say people, this is the only one I have studied in any depth – they think they are not animals and get cross if you suggest they are; after all they build houses and drive cars and some of them compose piano sonatas or discover penicillin – and yet they are the same as the other animals they protect, get sentimental about or eat.

They twitch in their sleep, get irritable when hungry, frown when expelling waste, behave irrationally when they feel the desire to reproduce, show anger disproportionate to the irritation. He dashes about making breakfast and tells me there is something serene and magical about me.

He pours the sour, stale food residue of a cow onto the dried, flaking remains of last year's corn crop and then – you won't believe this bit – eats it.

'I'm glad you stayed. Right,' he adds, putting the rest of the cow stuff back in the fridge to prevent it decomposing further, 'need to get you back.'

I hold on to him, try to kiss him and he shies away. Stubbornly, I refuse to leave and fold my arms. 'Is there someone else?' I say.

He orders me outside and eventually I follow him. He starts the car and I climb into the back. I curl round in the roomy boot so I can see him, and he looks at me in the mirror. 'There was,' he says. 'It ended.'

'Why?'

He drives down the road, muttering as the clutch refuses to engage and the gears whirr. We bunnyhop onto the road and eventually the car gets going. 'An artist?' I ask.

He shakes his head. 'Child psychologist.' We drive over the bridge that I crossed that first night. It explains how I knew where to go, I suppose. I can understand things if they are already in his head.

It's as if he's gifted me what's in there; and as I think this I can see him six months ago in the workshop, making a small model. A maquette: a voodoo device in reverse. Instead of killing the real version, it has created it. He pushes his fingers into the clay of the model, forming the shape of my body, massaging my head and neck into being, kneading the form of my chest, legs, feet. I see his thumbs, huge and out-of-proportion, like a giant from my point of view as a six-inch doll. The form emerges beneath his hands and he talks of his frustrations and hatreds.

The car bumps and rattles along the uneven back road to the gallery. 'Tell me more about her,' I say as we arrive but he shakes his head. He takes me in and installs me on the plinth. 'Beautiful.'

The gallery attendants, opening up the shutters, nudge each other and tap their heads.

The door flies open. Silhouettes form against the orange morning light. One silhouette kneels and points a gun at Adi; a second walks rapidly forward. The gun is dropped when the second shadow waves at him. 'Adrian Slade?'

'Adi.'

'Mr Slade, I am arresting you for the murders of Jean Phyllis Lambert, Sarah Joanna Johnson and Adam Michael Harris. You do not have to say anything, but...'

He looks at them in astonishment as they continue the litany. I am impassive, wanting to move but unable to.

Behind them, snow falls in the oblong of the doorway. It's stunning, glittering and reflecting against the orange and yellow of the sunrise.

Hours later I shift position and look through the window at the park. The frozen lake confuses ducks and pigeons; they scurry and flutter round the edges, finding breaks in the ice and sticking their beaks in. One duck waddles to the edge and plummets, dropping through the ice and bobbing back to the surface after a few seconds. Frozen water dribbles down his head and neck. Although do I not shiver, I feel the sensation of shivering.

Two swans walk magisterially across the ice, swaying from left to right. They look up at me; even though I know, rationally, they are not looking at me, they are just looking, and it happens to be in my direction. Yet I feel watched. They reach the edge of the lake and, when they see the broken water that the duck fell into, elegantly reach down and sip.

In the distance a second pair of swans makes their way across the ice. Unlike the first two they slide on their bellies, like polar bear cubs might when trying to navigate. They try to swim and skate along, bright orange feet trailing comically behind.

A cramped, darkened room, an old lamp between Adi and his interrogator, face hunched and unshaven, the greys and browns of his clothes echoed by the radiator, the chipped desk, the old wooden sills.

'This is all a bit of a cliché isn't it?' Adi says. There is a black glossy window; he guesses he's being watched through it. It surprises me that I can see this unfold. Perhaps I haven't been trying hard enough so far, but now I concentrate, I can see what's going on. Maybe it was later, and Adi was telling me about it; I only remember it as a blur. It's getting hotter, and my memory is more fluid. What was firmly impressed now seems less so, like circuits melting.

So my memories – if they are memories – are that they question him, circle like birds, set up arguments, lay traps, lead him in directions that are designed to implicate him. The flaw in their arguments, it could be proposed, is that he didn't do it. This technicality, for a while at least, is a detail.

He does not have alibis. With Ms Johnson, thirty-nine, the detective says, you have been on record as saying – here a piece of paper emerges – 'I'll kill her'.

'Yes,' Adi agrees, 'I did once say that.' The detective glances at his notes. 'We say lots of things we don't mean,' Adi continues. 'She was my agent… she dropped me.'

'Miss Lambert, ninety-two, was your primary school teacher. Adi looks stunned. 'Gosh, yes. Yes, you're quite right – I hated her. Silly cow. I often fantasised about pinning her against the wall and throttling her.' He looks pleased. The detective taps his pen on the desk, then upends it and glances at the glass panel. Adi strokes his face, thinking back, remembering.

The detective leans forward. 'Can I take that as a confession,' he says, wielding the pen.

'What? No, because I didn't do it. Don't you know the difference between fantasy and reality?'

'Sometimes one wonders, sir.'

'I'm not surprised, cooped up in here all day. You need some fresh air.' On the desk, a silver gadget flashes red lights importantly. 'What's that?'

'It's a recorder.'

Adi laughs. 'You're joking.' He picks it up and rattles it like a matchbox. 'What does it record, three minutes?'

The detective takes it from him and puts it back on the desk. 'How could you get a tape inside that's small enough?' Adi asks. The detective is silent. Adi stares at the LED counter pulsing.

There is a whiteboard with hundreds of dots on it, three names in red in the centre, lots of names round the edges and lines zig-zagging around. Only Adi's dot connects with all three central dots, and there is a smiley face drawn above it.

After forty-eight hours they let him go. That Adi has a motive for each victim and no one else does, is not enough evidence to hold him. Suits sweep by, paper passes back and forth, cigarettes are smoked from windows, other cases come up and need to be attended to. Wait for the next one, someone shrugs, and maybe he'll be less careful.

'We'll be speaking to you again,' Adi is told, and for the rest of the day he just sees the detective's large, square glasses and a shaving cut on his chin.

Having learnt to concentrate and find what's in his head, I see his ex leaving him· boxes quickly packed, clothes pushed unfolded into bulging travel bags. The obstinacy with which he carries on working, ignoring her. Blonde hair sticking to her face, obscuring it. Her pleas, to give up the work because it was consuming him, and his angry reply that he doesn't want any more ultimatums. For a while I love him a little less; why did he treat her like that?

More snow. Huge scoops of ice cream on the pavements where people have shovelled it from the roads. I slip to begin with but find I can walk if I move in a left and right motion, planting each foot squarely and with equal weight. The wetness of snow on my face makes me change direction and run through the woods. I imagine myself as a bronze arrow shooting through the trees.

The coldness, the freshness, makes me feel alive and more awake than I've been before. When I get back to the studio I pull the heavy doors aside with excitement. I want to tell him about my day.

I go from room to room. In the studio I look through his stuff. Postcards, browning and crumpled. Objects I cannot see any use for; broken things carefully stored in drawers. Maquettes on surfaces. New images, the clay still wet. He has been making these recently. Making them while I have been in the gallery. Other women.

I find the maquette of me. It's a good likeness, if not quite as attractive. I look again at the other figures, and am pleased to see they are not as pretty.

Running through the woods. To begin with, I cannot remember where it is. I only know what is inside Adi's head, and Adi always drives; but I can't go along the roads or I'll be seen. Eventually I work it out; the woods to begin with, then under the bridge, along the far side of the road for a few miles, cutting back beneath the underpass and past the village that the foundry is near. The snow is brown and slushy on the roads.

Few people, but the noise and heat at the foundry is intense. Hammering, clanking, steaming. One or two workers in blue boiler suits wandering like zombies; it's easy to hide from them. I find the main room, its circular shape echoed by the vat in the centre. Glimpses of myself in the window panels and metal trims. Another worker in a transparent visor has flames and sparks mirrored across his face. He rests his oversized gloved hands on the side of the vat then turns to me. He moves like a robot, and as he pulls his visor up I see it's Adi.

I feel a thumping as though he is shaping and denting

my stomach. He looks guilty. The other women. How many are in there; I move forward and peer down into the reddish blackness of the pit. A sense of unreality; how can he do this to me?

'I love you,' I say, then regret it. Has he got bored with me? Well; I know what I've done wrong. 'I'm sorry.' I read the look in his eyes; the flames flicker across them. 'You know, don't you?'

'It couldn't be anyone else.'

'I was doing the right thing – it was what you wanted.'

'Yes, yes.' He steps forward.

The steam rises above the vat. I can be truly sorry. That is enough.

Another boiler suit emerges and for a moment I tense, then relax. It doesn't matter now if anyone sees me. They can go to the police. They can say, as the widow of Adam Michael Harris, forty-six, did: 'It killed him! I saw it!'

I watch this happen. The police don't believe her, and the more insistent and hysterical Sally gets, the more they nod to themselves. They don't write her off as mad; it's subtler than that. Drugs, or delusions, or genuine belief: none mad, but still wrong. Flustered, the immaculately black-clad and high-heeled widow (distracting, but not enough to distract Britain's finest from their duty) declares that she saw a giant gold man (you have to forgive this) and how he killed her husband.

Notes are taken, agreement and encouragement is followed, eyebrows are raised here and there which are not noticed. Sally gives a full statement then goes to her spa for the weekend. It sinks in, as she sinks into the water, how much she will inherit. This rapidly turns to panic as she realises this is a motive. She concentrates on breathing, keeping her nose just above the line of water, the warmth relaxing her, lapping round her body's contours, telling her that everything's going to be all right.

At home the police find traces of ecstasy and coke. An empty bottle of vodka, spinning under the bed when they pull the duvet to one side. 'That was Adam,' Sally says when the plain-clothes officers police arrive at the spa.

During the interview the giant gold man fades away. 'Perhaps it was a dream,' she says to the patient policeman. 'Perhaps, yes, I might have taken a little bit of the drugs, which,' she adds, concentrating on the bleeping, flashing, silver oracle, 'was very much a hundred per cent Adam's idea, and I don't know where he got any of it from.

'But the main thing is, I didn't kill him.' The four million, about to be issued to her by cheque, makes her new friends doubtful. Lack of evidence. It's always lack of evidence that stops you believing in things. Sometimes you have to take that leap of faith and believe what seems most obvious, if least likely.

When they ask her if she knows Adi Slade, she has to think for a moment and then remembers, yes, her husband was going to be his dealer – art dealer, she adds quickly, smiling nervously – but then decided he wasn't good enough. They had a bit of a falling out.

The new boiler suit walks towards me. Lifts the visor. Looking back at me is myself.

'I'm Marion,' she says.

'I didn't expect you to believe me,' Adi says to her, ''till you saw for yourself.'

'She's prettier than me,' Marion says.

Adi shakes his head. 'No, she's not.'

Yes I am, and they both know it. I don't have the vertical line between her eyebrows, I have larger breasts, my thighs are slimmer.

'Why is she here?' I ask.

'Because I can't do it.'

Marion lifts a rifle. I laugh. 'What good will that do?' I

walk round the side of the vat. 'I'm made of metal.'

'Go for the hands,' Adi murmurs.

Marion fires, misses; fires again, and the bullet scrapes my wrist. 'All of this was inside your head,' I say, 'it was what you wanted.' He nods.

'Really?' Marion lowers the rifle a fraction. I reach out to her. Short of her neck, however, I stop. My fingers flex. 'She can't do it,' Adi says. I like the look of entrancement on his face; I want to hold on to it.

I keep reaching, my fingers twitching, but I cannot touch her neck.

'Why not?'

'It's because I don't hate you,' Adi says to Marion, almost apologetically. 'It only seems to work if –'

I turn and grab Adi's neck instead. No problem there, which surprises all three of us.

'Wait… wait…' he says. Under my grip, he leans forward and kisses me. I relax into his arms and return the kiss. His hand is on my back, and I enjoy the feel of it, before two hands reach under my arms and I am swiftly lifted, swinging in air, then dropped into scalding heat.

My eyes thicken with mist. A glow on my body as I scramble against the sides of the tank, but cannot climb out. Adi's thumb hovers over the blackened switch and Marion pushes his hand down. The red light flashes and the platform sinks below me.

I scrabble at the lip but can't heave myself up. I try a different tack, leaning against the wall and propelling myself as if pushing from the side of a swimming pool. My legs slip away into nothingness. The bubbling increases. The clanking sound of the winding gears creates a pitted sensation in my stomach.

Marion and Adi peer down with looks of detachment and also a kind of disgust as I flail around. I am disgusting then, am I? The feebleness with which I resist, the crawling, the knowledge that I am going to cease to exist but fighting it anyway; the repellence of the insect.

There is nothing else in the tank. He was not making another statue after all. The platform descends to my waist. I try to stay calm. This quickly turns to panic and I scrabble at the side of the tank again.

'Please,' I say.

'We can't risk it,' Marion says, and I feel a surge of contempt. Who are "we" all of a sudden? I did what was inside his head; why is it me that's being punished? Their faces are red, as if viewed through a sweet wrapper.

Outside the snow breaks up. The swans flap and panic as the ice disintegrates beneath their feet, then they settle on the water and swim. The exhibition closes. Visitors stamp their feet and put their gloves on, and say how glad they are it's not so cold. Spring on its way, people say, and smile. A shopkeeper scrapes the remaining snow from his doorway. Piles of blackened, turned ice loiter on corners, like ill-formed snowmen, then disappear.

Adi and Marion walk through the park. She pulls him to the edge of the path and points to snowdrops in the grass. They hold each other and kiss. The sound in my head becomes too loud to concentrate. The bubbling water closes over me.

Marion looks up at Adi and her face is mine, tinged with bronze, the new sun making her glow. My face is carved perfectly: the bow of the lips, the line of the nose, the cheeky, dimpled grin. There is sheer happiness carved across her features. The pleasure is etched deep. The sun burns bolder, more confident. It gets hotter.

Dragons

I

The room was huge and Hector did not miss the irony of the double bed. Usually, even when Sally specified a double, you got two singles pushed together.

Eight lamps lit up the room when he put the card in the holder. Sally did know how to get a good deal, he acknowledged, crossing the wooden floors to the window and glancing down to the palm trees and shop fronts five floors below. She'd expressed surprise when he said he was going to go anyway. I'd like my half back, she'd added as he stacked the last of the boxes.

He had doubted he would enjoy himself on his own – but. He scratched his wrist as an old woman emerged from a shop clutching a bright green handbag with tissue paper wrapped round the buckles. Later Hector opened his suitcase and shoes and sun cream fell onto the floor as the clip had come untied in transit.

In the lift, which seemed smaller, boxier and shinier than usual, but maybe that was just his state of mind, a couple with a dog looked past Hector at the mirrored panels. The dog yapped and pricked its ears up as the lift lurched and dropped through the floors, and the man said something and the woman shrugged, their expressions undetectable behind sunglasses.

A thin wall of heat struck Hector as he pushed through

the glass doors of the hotel and had the first shoulder-relaxing, pleasurable moment of being on holiday. Heading roughly in the direction of the old town, the bustle of the city relaxed him and he felt detached as time slowed down enjoyably. Work and Sally and the things in the house that he hadn't done dropped away like stones tipped from shoes.

A look round, a drink in a bar, some slow and lazy tapas somewhere – there would be the comedy of misunderstanding and pointing at things and saying '*uno*' and big smiles, which would thaw the waiter, a few proper beers – why did even cheap lager taste good here, compared to the drain water at home? – then an early night, dreams of beach and sea and echoes.

Why would he not come on his own? A sardonic, blonde-tinged vision appeared in front of him and he ignored it.

He studied the map to see if he was going in the right direction but couldn't make head or tail of it. All the street signs seemed to have different names to their equivalents on the map. Even the hotel's street was different, on the blue crumpled line in front of him, to what the sign above told him. If he lived in an alternate universe where taxis did not exist, he would have failed to reach his room in the first place.

Mind you, Hector had never been much good at finding his way around. As he hesitated Sally, striding ahead, turned to look at him with a raised eyebrow and a thinly contained 'it's this way.' He followed her and she turned out to be right as usual. As she faded, the square with the cathedral opened up in front of him. Children played on the stone steps and dogs barked as the early evening breeze blew sprays of water towards them from the fountain. Elderly men walked with their hands behind their backs, studying the curves and arches of the church and adopting disapproving expressions as teenagers languorously stroked each others' hips. Middle aged couples looked round in confusion, argued briefly then sat at pavement cafes, staring at the menu prices with determined expressions that said they were going to enjoy themselves.

Stone gargoyles lured Hector under an arch and he paused by an ornate window barred with iron grilles. Hidden inside was a jovial picture of St George, his armour and horse draped in what, to Hector, was the English flag, slaughtering an indolent dragon. Joyous soldiers – Crusaders? Hector didn't know – surrounded St George and the painting was housed in a spindly Gothic frame.

Where does the dragon myth come from? Hector asked the faded face of St George. They seem to have crawled out of the caves in Wales, and in parts of China. And here in Spain too. Anywhere else? He didn't know. He hadn't been on the planet long enough to know. But where might they have originated? Someone's fevered imagination?

Perhaps they're based on dinosaurs; that's credible, he thought, they do look like dinosaurs. Then he remembered with a giddy sense of the telescoping of time that dinosaurs were unknown two hundred years ago, and the painting in front of him was, according to the inscription, from the fifteenth century. He turned away, the familiar brief anxiety squeezing his shoulders. Maybe coming alone wasn't such a good idea after all, but – keep moving. Do as you originally planned.

Perhaps it's time for a *cerveza* in a bar. To distract himself he bought some postcards and flicked through his tatty phrasebook for 'stamps'.

Afterwards he idly followed a stunningly beautiful woman into the shop next door. Her face partly masked behind large dark glasses, she browsed through jewellery and elegant, leather-bound notebooks before taking a small bronze pendant – a dragon again – to the counter. That's the kind of woman you could fall in love with, he thought, knowing that he would never dream of speaking to her. He lifted a double-layered wooden bracelet from the stand and pretended to examine it as he admired the line of the woman's shoulders, her narrow back and insolent, high-waisted bottom. She looked up and he studied the bracelet. It was made of fifty or so squat wooden disks, their colour varying from pale brown to black, strung together on elastic. It cost a euro. He took it to the counter.

Now I've got my magic bracelet, he thought, decorating his wrist with it as the woman cast him a disinterested glance and walked briskly away, I can draw a line under things; I can become a different person. It's true, he thought as he caught his reflection in a plate glass window; I don't recognise myself. I am a man who wears wooden bracelets. The kind of man who travels alone, a man of the world – I've probably got a flat with a white carpet and I eat avocados quite often. It feels good, and I am on holiday.

Around the corner was a surprisingly peaceful square with an orange grove. The bustle of the city vanished in the space of a few feet. Across the concrete diamond two women in black ambled along, looking at him with bored interest and circling their hands as if they were speaking, although both were silent. He was now in a sleepy village in the hills that had not changed in centuries. Around him, shutters came down on the windows of antique shops.

He hadn't thought he would do well in the heat, but seemed to be managing well. Sometimes you can convince yourself into believing anything, if you tell yourself it must be so. If you decide it's too hot you will be too hot and want to lie down. Imagine it's hot but you're enjoying it, and you start enjoying it.

The hotel had recommended a restaurant but Hector got lost finding it. He resisted the urge to call Sally as he wandered around the backstreets, his sense of direction vanishing as he passed crumbling buildings, the occasional bold green and red graffiti somehow complementing and supporting the aged buildings rather than defacing them.

Down a side street there was a modest restaurant, unmarked and indistinguishable from surrounding buildings, but the lights and sound of chatter and clinking cutlery drew him towards it.

'*Per una*?' he asked, his spartan Spanish working well as the waitress gave him a wide, friendly smile.

He had been used to saying, '*Per dos*' and '*dos vino blancos*'; it took some adjustment to get used to the lonely '*una*' and the blank seat opposite, gaping back at him like one of van Gogh's personless chairs. Their sense of meaning and potential was increased by the person who should be sitting in it, but wasn't.

For a moment Sally played with the narrow glass in front of her, rotating it in expectation of what would soon be poured. Hector chose to stick to beer and avoid the memories associated with wine; its coldness, taste, colour each triggering different aspects of she who would soon be referred to as his ex-wife. The word felt unwieldy and jagged in his mind; it would sound razor-like in his mouth.

There was a full, abandoned glass at the table next to him. Visibly, Sally was drinking it for a moment, pursing her lips and wishing it was white not red, before the image faded. You only notice the singularity of objects when you are alone, he thought before observing almost immediately that he was not lonely; he felt a kind of detached melancholy that was not, to his surprise, unpleasant.

The room was low ceilinged and beams sagged in the centre, weary of supporting such a plain ceiling for so long. Paintings on the walls, obscure splashes of paint built up thickly on boxy canvases, were shaped to fit the nooks and alcoves; some of them were narrow oblongs, and a couple triangular.

The universe, he decided as a beer and a menu magically appeared in front of him, gives you what you want, if only you have the confidence to ask for it. To begin with he dismissed this thought as indulgent, but increasingly it made sense. In the past he'd plodded along and felt that life was in charge of him, rather than the other way round. Now, if he concentrated on asking for the right things, and didn't overdo it, he got what he wanted.

Not in a selfish or exploitative way, his thought process rushed to add; he would never have left or abandoned Sally, he would never have hurt her; but it is true that he had wished for freedom, and despite it being technically she who left him, he'd asked for freedom in the right way and it materialised, with minimal damage, and she was happy and he rolled with it and now, like a man finding himself the right way up after falling down a hill, he was happy too.

He didn't share this theory with anyone because he recognised how self-absorbed it might sound, crazy even. If there *were* anyone to share it with, he thought with a glance at the unoccupied chair, they would have to test it for themselves; there was no value in taking him on trust.

His first tentative test of the concept had come a couple of months back. He'd been fed up with his job; what he wanted was something with less repetition. The old Hector would have soldiered on, gone in each day determinedly, asked half-heartedly for a new role and taken it on the chin when told, there isn't anything you're qualified for. New Hector focused on asking the universe for change, applied to a couple of adverts in the paper and three months later, was cheerfully handing his notice in.

We influence the universe, he concluded. Or, more

concretely, our post-religious purpose is to reach the point where we accept we exist in a purposeless universe. At that point, the benevolent force that's out there will suddenly pop up. After all, you don't get the answers for an exam until you've laboured over the exam.

Hector believed with conviction that he was right about this but, without being able to offer any evidence for it, he kept his thoughts dormant. How did this sense, this spirit for want of a better word, manifest itself? Not as a white-haired old man living in a cloud; not even something that can be coherently described with the means we have at our disposal – language, and a narrow vision of reality. Yet whatever it is, it's there. You can see it out of the corner of your eye, like a distant star that disappears if you look straight at it, but reappears faintly when you glance slightly away. Just because it's elusive, doesn't mean it's not there.

And it's not what we've supposed in the pre-secular can age, that it controls the universe, or winds it up like a clock and lets it go. It influences, rather than dictates. If you tap into it, as Hector was beginning immodestly to feel that he had, you shape it positively.

This did, he supposed, run the risk of people thinking he was nuts. I need to get this clear in my head, thought Hector as he sipped his beer. Am I influencing the universe, or is the universe influencing me?

Couples slowstepping in and out. A bored waiter, leaning on a counter. A woman emerged from the darkness of the corridor and made the sign of signing a bill to the waiter, continued towards Hector and sat parallel to him, facing the glass of wine that had appeared abandoned. She sipped it and reached for a book from the seat next to her, opening the book magically at the page she had been on. This was a quality Sally possessed and which Hector had always admired.

'What are you reading?' The words came out without him expecting them. Old Hector would have wanted to speak to her, then talked himself out of it. She's on her own, she's reading a book, she doesn't want to be disturbed. New Hector said sod it. If she doesn't want to talk to you, she'll soon let you know. Her bill's about to arrive – in fact as he thought it, it did arrive – and if she wants to escape, she can escape. In the event, she looked up more quickly than someone absorbed in their reading would have done. 'It's about the history of the south. The architecture's very interesting. Christian buildings built on top of Islamic ones.'

'Really?'

She nodded. 'They adapted them to suit themselves. You can look around and see the curves of the mosque transforming into the church's pillars as your eye moves across.'

'Wow.' He tried to think of something intelligent to say. His meal arrived and she drank the last mouthful of wine. She paid the bill.

'Have a glass of wine with me, if you'd like to,' new Hector somehow came out with. He fully expected her to say no but she smiled and sat in the chair opposite him. 'Thanks.'

'Travelling alone?'

He nodded. 'It wasn't the plan, but the plan changed.'

'I wasn't going to come to Valencia at all, but here I am.'

He introduced himself. 'Leah,' she replied. She had been travelling a meandering route and had three more days in the city.

A glass of wine appeared in front of her and she looked up at the waiter. '*Tinto, no blanco,*' she smiled. The waiter was apologetic. 'Ah,' he said, shaking his head as he took the glass away.

'I've been travelling along the south; Granada, Seville, Toledo.' She flicked through some pictures. A giant glass of red wine sailed across the top of Seville's cathedral. 'Thanks Marco,' she said, and the waiter blushed as he slipped away.

'You've been here before?'

'Once I find a good restaurant, I like to stick to it.'

Hector recalled Sally criticising him once for wanting to go to the same place. 'What's the use in doing that,' she said, 'when there are a hundred other places to visit? That's the whole point of going on holiday,' her shoulders creating a mountain range on "whole point". 'Do something different.' He had agreed. The restaurant they went to the next night had poor service and Sally complained about it to him in the darkness hours later, when he was trying to persuade her to make love, and she impatiently sat up in bed, scrabbling for a cigarette and asking why people opened restaurants in the first place if they weren't interested in giving pleasant experiences to people.

'Your first night here?' Leah asked. He erased the inner movie and nodded. 'You stumbled on a good one.'

'I like the triangular pictures.'

Leah glanced round. 'Yes they add to the look, don't they?' She showed him more pictures, pointing out places of interest she'd meant to visit but hadn't had time. 'If you try to do too much,' she said, 'you end up skimming over everything. Or, you get absorbed, and you come away feeling you've missed out.'

Marco asked Hector if he had enjoyed his meal. He nodded, remembering nothing of it. 'It was great.' The waiter went away satisfied. 'Do you fancy another drink here,' Hector asked, 'or would you like to go to a bar?'

'Yes,' she smiled, 'I'll come for a drink with you.'

They got up to leave. You can influence the universe, Hector thought. Old Hector would have asked her for a drink and she would have said no. New Hector made it sound like a choice.

Marco looked at them wistfully. He put the receipts in the till and went through the beaded curtain, looking at the boxes stacked up in the hallway and the tap that was still dripping. That guy came in and sat down, five minutes later he's talking to her, five minutes after that she's sitting at his table, then they leave together. You've either got it or you haven't, he supposed as he heard noises in the main room and went back to see a group of businessmen settling into the chairs, pulling their jacket tails out from under their bottoms and flexing their hands as if about to start playing pianos. This will be fun, Marco thought as fingers started clicking.

'I have no sense of direction,' Hector said, 'so I'm in your hands.' They walked through a narrow gap between the cathedral and buildings that had organically built up around it.

He adjusted his magic bracelet. 'Nice doors in this city.'

'Certainly handy for getting in and out. Have you been in the cathedral?'

'Not yet.'

'Actually I found a way of getting in for free: pretend you're going in for a quick pray and they let you in without paying. If you look like a tourist they get money out of you. I kind of object to giving money to the church, don't you?'

'I haven't really thought about it.'

'Just take off your yarmulke before you go in, will help.' She looked sideways at him, but didn't see his reaction because they turned another sharp corner. 'I discovered this place last night.' The bar had red and blue lights, cushions on the floor, low tables you might eat sushi from. In the corner was a gigantic wooden elephant; possibly even life size, Hector hazarded, his experience of elephants not extensive.

He wasn't sure what they talked about. You never are

when you're in a bar, are you, you talk and you drink too much, too quickly, and you get up and keep going to the bar and buy more drinks, and whatever it is you talk about you do it passionately and with interest, and you let the other person talk, and when they talk you nod and keep eye contact and smile at the right intervals. It seemed to be working; old Hector would have got nowhere, and yet here we are, and she seems interested in me, and it's all going rather well.

He was interesting, although he talked about himself too much. She watched him energetically top up both their glasses and not notice how much more he was drinking than she was. He had been drinking beer in the restaurant, but as soon as she said she wanted wine, he joined her. But, do not let these details put you off. How often does the right man come along; I think we can forgive him a little excess drinking on holiday, and anyway he's probably just nervous.

Did I really describe him as the 'right man' she thought, holding a finger over her lip as he asked her about her family, where her accent came from, and she wondered which slices of life to choose from; how do you get to know someone so quickly; how do you summarise yourself in a few sentences that will appeal to someone you really like?

She introduced her parents in soft focus and told the stories that always went down well about her accident-prone younger brother, the time as a three year old when he dropped his teddy out of the first-floor window and jumped out after it, bouncing on cardboard boxes that had been fortunately put out by the bins. Their mother glanced up from the kitchen to see two legs sailing downwards like autumnal twigs, socks not pulled up as always, laces untied.

A frenzy of window locking and fretting whenever he was upstairs followed, once the unharmed boy had emerged into the kitchen, frowning because he couldn't find his teddy bear amongst all the rubbish; yet as a teenager, his first experience of drinking in a barn was to turn to his knocked-over lager can and follow it through a gap in the struts of the roof, bouncing thirty feet below and landing on a solitary bale of hay outside the building, surrounded by acres of concrete. These days, Leo would now reflect, they don't put hay into bales anymore. If he were ten years younger, he'd be dead.

Hector didn't laugh at the story, as most people did; he found it alarming. Well, she thought, if my instinct tells me he's the right man, then enjoy the instinct; doesn't matter if his sense of humour isn't quite the same.

He topped their glasses up. He was confident, self-assured; she worried that he did this kind of thing all the time. And despite her wanting him to talk to her when she was reading her book, she was still surprised when he did, and found it strange that someone as confident as this had taken any interest in her in the first place.

He played with the bracelet on his wrist as he talked, removing it and rubbing his fingers absently against the beads. She noticed this with surprise, then interrupted him – he was saying something about wanting to go to the new aquarium, because his job was something or other to do with fish – and said she had to go to the bathroom.

Not that there's anything wrong with being Catholic, she told her reflection in the mirror, but it wouldn't work; her mother would never accept it. How was this possible? You meet the right man and… ah well. He's not *right* after all; how could he be, you've only just met him. She studied the mirror until enough time had passed for a credible trip to the bathroom then washed her hands, pumping the soap dispenser several times.

She pushed through the door; he was still playing

with the beads, pushing them over and over on each other; not even noticing he was doing it. How long had he had that bracelet; since birth, perhaps. Since, what do they call it, baptism? His features, though – the long curly hair, the features, surely he's Jewish? I can't believe he's not. When I mentioned the skullcap to him, surely… and she remembered she had not seen his expression. Ah well. What were the chances. She should have known better than to think you could meet someone so randomly, so seemingly perfectly.

'Another drink?'

'Actually,' she said, 'I'm feeling a bit ill.'

'Really?'

'Mmm. I've been feeling a bit headachey all day; I think it's just the amount of travelling.'

Hector nodded. 'Can I walk you back to your hotel?'

'Yes, thank you.' She looked uncertain as they stepped outside. 'It's this way.' She strode forward. For a dizzy moment he thought this might be a pretext to get him back to her hotel; an alleged headache avoided having to sit there having drinks all night that she didn't really want, and speed things up a bit. He shook this thought away as he followed her. Am I obnoxious, he wondered; do I expect too much? Sally sneered at him, telling him he was self-obsessed and the rest of the world didn't really care one way or the other. He followed the curve and rise of Leah's hips and felt horny.

The air was warm and close; you only get a few weeks like this each year back home. Old Hector started to poke and prod inside his skull. What made you think you could win a girl this beautiful anyway; after half an hour of talking to you, she doesn't want to know. Old Hector morphed into Sally, eyes flashing darkly. Ahead, the yellow of the lit stone swam and blurred.

Her hotel was more impressive than his. Palm trees outside, an intricate glass panel with the name of the hotel, the *Reina Victoria*, written in elegant Art Nouveau looping letters. 'Thank you,' she said with one foot on the step.

Ask the universe, he told himself. Why was there that shuddering of fear, the desire to run. 'Would you like to meet up for a drink tomorrow?' She didn't answer. Ask the universe. 'Later in the week?' he added.

'I think I'm going to be busy actually.' A tight but sympathetic smile. 'The itinerary's fairly full.' God, that sounded terrible. It's not his fault. It's just – well.

Hector tried to understand the ambiguous look. If you ask, it will answer. 'What about when you're back in England? We could meet up?'

'Sure.' A sense of relief as he dug in his pockets. England is hundreds, probably thousands of miles away, thousands of days too, and he can't track me down if I don't call him. Hector wrote his number on a piece of paper, leaning against the wall, which crumbled behind the pressure of his pen. He's a nice guy. A shame in a way. Maybe it would be all right? But the values are different. She heard her mother saying the words. The *values*, Leah.

'Bye then.' The glass door slid closed behind her. He won't hear from her again. But ask the universe. If you mean it, it will happen. Or it won't. How will you tell if it's the universe answering, or not answering, or just chance?

He tried not to think about this too much. Did it mess up his theory? Maybe you just didn't ask for it *enough*, he suggested to himself. He turned round in case she was watching him from the doorway. The grand, closed, double doors looked back at him blankly.

Crossing a side street he thought he recognised, Hector was instantly lost. Turning, he couldn't find his way back to where he thought he had been. There were no taxis. With a mild sense of doom he took the map from his pocket. Splitting along the seams, as he held it up it concertinaed in a seeming attempt to form a paper chain.

Concrete and stone as he rounded the corner. Another square, as quiet and sleepy as the one earlier and with orange trees; but not the same one. The geometry was similar, the yellow Baroque buildings could easily have been identical; it was like dreams you have of your childhood home, where the bricks feel right but the layout is wrong.

The oranges glowed bronze from the sodium lamps. The stone of the walls appeared made of wax. He reached up to pick an orange but they were just out of reach.

Before it had all gone wrong, before Sally spoke to him only to be contemptuous, she would smile when he told her about his ambition to pick an orange. A small, insignificant desire maybe; but, when oranges come from plastic trays in supermarkets, meaningful. Sally found this romantic, poetic even. 'Good luck with your orange,' she said when she went with the last of the packing boxes.

He walked under a different tree, stood on tiptoes and reached to his full stretch. Tantalisingly, the twenty or so oranges were all but unobtainable.

'But they look like I can…' he said, stretching. He tried a third tree; all just beyond him.

He jumped onto a concrete balustrade that zig-zagged round the edge of the square. At the corner, the tree was only a few feet away from him and he was parallel with the oranges. He leapt, reached his hand out, made contact with an orange but failed to pull it from the branch, and fell on the tree's concrete base. He rolled over and looked up to see the bough bounce up and down, heavy with oranges, all intact.

Maybe, this way. And the relief when, more by luck than judgement, he stumbled on the right path, recognising the familiar wedge of a high, narrow bank; the curve of the road; a dented lamp post. He thought of Leah. You won't hear from her again. Or, is it that I'm not taking the broader picture into consideration? What is the 'broader picture' anyway?

Hector rounded the corner and saw the squat, ornate exterior of the hotel in front of him. Is it just because I'm drunk that I'm thinking like this? Or is it *in vino veritas*? Sally's sardonic eyebrow raised and he argued with her, feeling himself truculent, but fed up with the soft drone of criticism. The expression applies just as much to beer as it does to wine. It should be called *in alcoholis veritas*. Sally snorted and called him a pedant.

He remembered, as he went up in the lift with its endless mirrors, a statue somewhere, some marble bloke about to pluck a fruit, suspended in perpetuity, about to satisfy his need but never quite able to reach it, the expression on his face a glazed mix of delight and anguish.

II

I have never, I am fairly sure, walked along a river bed. White light from the stone, the haze of heat as Hector stepped from the bridge onto the scrubby tubular floor. His map was now skeletal and split across its seams, so that half the city seemed to be in the active process of disappearing into a void; climate change, perhaps, or just the realisation that the apparent universe was so much wooden props and struts.

The rear of the map carried information in English. The river once ran through the centre of the city, weaving and meandering its way for nine or ten miles, through the centre of the new city to the Mediterranean, at the Gulf of Valencia docks. Half a century earlier the river had flooded disastrously, killing hundreds (thousands? This bit of the map was on a seam). Inventively, if not inevitably, the city authorities diverted the river, away from the population and the built-up river banks, allowing it to journey in its own time to the sea.

As a result, a green sunken spine now curved through the city, looping immediately above the old town and forming a natural upper limit to it, and this ferny space had evolved over those fifty years into a channel for the city to breathe, run, walk dogs, play football, sunbathe. It created a giant question mark: the curve above the city, then the straight stretch towards the docks. And the sea, Hector supposed, was the answer to the question; the full stop at the far end.

A jungle for stray cats, strolling cockily or cautiously through the undergrowth, pushing scraggy limbs forward and shaking heads as they weighed each other up; torn ears, patches of missing fur and weeping eyes not preventing them patrolling their spaces, exploring and guarding their borders. The old stone bridges remained to carry traffic above the ghost river, leaving the runner/walker/cat in peace far below. At least following this path, Hector thought as he passed ornamental gardens and bridges with blocks of flats as their backdrop, I can't get lost. A circular pool was sculpted around the base of one bridge, heavily decorated with graffiti. 'Take me somewhere we can be alone,' some angular writing pleaded. A friendly, wide-looped hand answered 'Oh yes!'

In the sand and mud that had transformed miraculously into soil, trees grew. The bumpy, uneven surface levelled out. More orange trees. Hector played with his bracelet. The fruit still hung just out of reach but he watched the oranges with steadily increasing desire.

To be able to take such beauty for free was dreamlike, idealistic – indecent even. When was the last time you had something this good for nothing, he wondered, watching the nearest of the oranges as if it might leap off the tree and promiscuously offer itself to him.

Opposing dogs bayed and growled and Hector found himself valuing and pricing absent sex, his thought patterns wandering as they did when he was away from work and hadn't eaten enough. Sally's mesmerising, earthy smell conjuring a series of magical then wistful then confused then resentful feelings. There should be a museum for lost sex.

He paused in the shade of a tree. A fat gleaming orange lay just above him, ready to fall. He reached out half-heartedly and it was, to his surprise, within his grasp. He looked around uncomfortably. Were you allowed to pick them? Was it legal; would the fruit police leap out of the bushes and arrest him?

He reached and plucked. It made a snapping sound as it tugged away from the bough, which bounced in freedom afterwards. Hector smelled the orange's bright, waxy scent. Wanting to delay gratification, he put it in his bag.

Alien buildings as the river park evolved into the City of Arts and Sciences. A white globe, looming through the foliage like a crashed spaceship. A domed building with struts and pods like the ship's crouching inhabitant, nothing more than a giant eye on feet, proud to be so foreign to our understanding of what sentient beings should look like. Joggers ran past this new world, their trim bottoms working hard to get away from Hector and reach wherever it was they were going. Further on the park opened up into a haven of landscaped rivers and pools, the water an impossible faint blue, as clear as the Aegean but paler: a watercolour, imaginary blue.

There was a science centre housed in a whale skeleton, an opera house disguised as a sea urchin.

Across a suspended white bridge the park collapsed into dust and heat. Hoardings surrounded a building site that stretched beyond three lanes of zooming traffic. In the centre of the chaos a steep dome erupted from the uneven soil. Men toiled across its surface. Some applied an indigo paint to the silver shell. Others swung along bridges that crawled along the upper surface. Two thin yellow veins ran vertically, rattling and thumping occasionally as debris dropped down. Below, clouds of dust rose from behind the hoardings and there was the steady whine of drilling. It was like a cathedral being constructed.

Did this mean the aquarium had not been finished? Hector tried to remember where he had heard about it. He instinctively reached towards his jacket pocket for the leaflets he had collected from the hotel, before his hand slid against his t-shirt and he remembered the jacket was hanging up in the wardrobe.

He followed people hurrying round the curve of the site and the octopus-like *Oceanographique* appeared in front of him.

A flash and flicker of lights. Beluga whales emerged from the subterranean blueness: serene and vast, flipping and wheeling in the water like birds turning through air. Flash.

A low, deep, occasional rumble, like a jet plane slowed and softened and modified; the sound of the universe, perhaps, the echoing noise from the expansion of the cosmos. Flash.

A lightning bolt against fin, grey expanse of space, mournful eyes. A man grins at his child, moves his arm up and down, trying to provoke reactions from the whales. They are gracefully ignored, the whales familiar with the bursts of light from the ghostly monkeys who eternally peer into the world. Sometimes as they turn, vast genitalia make their presence known: a huge penis lengthens and uncoils like something airbrushed into a bizarre film; or perhaps a corpse, bloated in bright blue acid. The female genitalia is a dark cavern from the same unearthly movie; grimy blue-grey like the negative of its human equivalent.

Flash. Sally's image blinked back at Hector from the reflection in the glass, telling him to pull himself together. Smirking at whale cocks now, is it.

Flash. As his vision cleared Sally flicked her hair and merged into the reflection of a woman standing next to him.

In the next room children, trapped in a bright blue bubble, accessed by crawling through a gap under the tunnel of fish. Ahead was a canopied walkway, fish and skate zooming overhead. It was like voyaging down a time tunnel, back to the dinosaur age. Sharks, looming gormlessly, sailing through existence with their mouths open and swallowing even stupider fish. It's why they've stayed thick, thought Hector. They haven't needed to evolve.

A shark lumbered up to the glass now and looked Hector dimly in the eye. This was surely never the plan, Hector murmurs with an itching uncomfortableness. The plan; is there intent; is there just an indigo void.

In the blueness a fish like a unicorn, complete with bizarre pole on its head, charged towards him. It swam back and forth through the tunnel, searching for something it couldn't find, distressed. Hector had an urge to lie down on the spot and pull thick blankets from somewhere over his head and sleep, and let the sea of people exist without him.

The final tank before the release into sobering, reassuring daylight contained coral. Shells clung to tentacles; green and purple blobby seaweed floated about. Hector wanted to pick it up and feel squishy moistness under his fingers.

Swimming between them, strange, unique creatures. They had long threads like tails trailing from them, and were a greeny-blue colour. They had wings – it wouldn't be fair to call them fins – rippling with a blurring, intricate effect, like a jet's engine blades rotating. *Dragonfish*, the caption said, and looking closely their heads really did look like dragons.

No, Hector thought. Their heads don't look like dragons. Our dragons look like dragonfish. Hector knelt and put his face against the cool glass.

III

The beach silver blonde, the overhead sun piercing white reflections on the sea. Late May, a good time of year to come: hot and renewing, with your skin glowing and smelling of clean air and salt, but not too hot, not so hot you can do nothing other than lie and turn purple.

Toes white and cool on the warm sand. Fragments of blue and even green in the dust if you look closely enough, like ash from a volcanic island. Maybe a planet like Jupiter, Hector supposed as he headed towards the sea, past stone changing huts.

Dots of bright colour on the sand; red and blue and yellow bikinis. Near the water the ground banked steeply as if presaging something important or unexpected; Hector's feet sank in the browner, wetter, thicker sand. He felt a pleasurable burn across his neck. His cold northern climate seemed as distant as – well, as distant as it actually was. Impossible to believe he would ever go back. A great cog or wheel had changed and he now operated at a different speed, a different temperature.

Sally pursed her lips in front of him and told him to get a life. He concentrated; she shimmered in the haze and vanished. He stood at the sea's edge and sensed clamps lifting from his shoulders. Near the horizon, the hulk of a tanker appeared to list. The curve of the earth? Or some more local effect?

The sea was still, ruptureless. It was as if he could pull the blanket of water back and experience what was hidden beneath. It had meaning but he couldn't quite grasp what that meaning was. Perhaps that's the meaning it's trying to communicate. Perhaps it doesn't matter that you can't quite identify what it is, it is enough to know that it's there, that it exists. The suspected randomness is wrong.

Hector turned and zig-zagged past the fluorescent marker buoys of bodies nestled in clumps, sand-burrowed. Couples in late middle age, wiry silver hairs contrasting with deep copper skin, the flesh beaten and hammered like the bottoms of old pots. Statues of young women, one leg bent, an arm across the face, breathing shallowly. Solitary skinny pale men, concave thighs and bellies, large eyes watching hopefully and hopelessly at the same time.

On a bright red mat three girls quickly mutating into women. Eighteen or nineteen, perhaps twenty. One kneeling and pouring water into a plastic cup, one sitting, arms stretched behind her, fingers in the sand, legs crossed, the third rubbing lotion on her shoulders, breasts lifting as her hand slipped behind her neck. All wore nothing but thongs, turquoise, green and orange, matching triangles of bold colour. The girl pouring water sat down awkwardly, one leg under her buttocks, spilling the water as she settled. Hector made himself not look.

Their sunglasses concealing their thoughts, each stared at him trying not to look at them. The second woman rolled over and lay on her front, still looking in his direction. The small of her back rose and fell. The third, in orange, rummaged in her bag then looked up. Hector crossed the beach restlessly, feeling the urge to go somewhere but not knowing where, feeling that if he kept going he might find out. I'll just walk a few hundred years more, he thought. *Yards*.

The sun made him sleepy and the words formed sluggishly and wrongly in his brain. Is the sand real, he wondered, or imported? He didn't know, and does it matter? It's a beach with sky, sea and sand; that's all you need to know. Question the solidity of what you're standing on and you see uncertainty everywhere; not least because we're only sticking to it by gravity.

There's a small, so small as to not worry about, but actual, possibility that on any random day, the universe could just flip out of existence.

A breeze and the smell of ozone sent a ripple of goose bumps across his skin. He sat then lay down, feeling the sand explore his hair and ears and burning the backs of his thighs. He felt he could sink into the sand and go – somewhere else.

A woman of twenty or so in a black bikini lay a few feet ahead of him. He resisted the urge to groan at the vision of unattainable heaven. She slowly applied sun cream to her arms, then lifted her knees up to cover her legs with the same careful attention. She looked round in each direction to see that the cream was spreading evenly. She looked up at Hector with curiosity then continued to cover her stomach and neck. She glanced at him again then lay on her back.

Dreams with no meaning, no narrative; not even images, in the meaningful sense of the word. He was a human-sized grain of sand, looking at the other grains of sand with a mix of envy and curiosity and knowing he would never know what they really thought. He was inside cloisters, aware of how each pillar and arch was formed of millions of individual grains of sand: how did they stand up?

Temples, churches perhaps, forming dizzying towers above him, impossible architecture, about to topple on him. He woke with a sense of loss. The woman in the black bikini was still there, gathering her things together. She folded her towel and brushed sand from it then turned away from Hector to dislodge sand from her back and the insides of her knees. She bent over to take jeans from her bag and climbed into them, jumping up and down until they contained her. She bent over again to pull a t-shirt from the bag, which she put on in one swift movement, both arms through at once, then pulling the top down over her breasts when it caught and remained above them.

In a film, he thought, we know these two people are going to get together, yet this doesn't happen, and I'll never talk to her anyway. Although, if you asked the universe, and the universe said yes? Was it time to test the theory? A proper, scientific test; one that would have an introduction and a method and everything. Sally rolled her eyes. He sat up straighter. He had no confidence; there was no way he was going to get up and talk to her.

She glanced at him again. This is your chance, the alarm bells intoned. You can't do that, a voice in his head said. A different voice pressed, what does it matter – you haven't lost anything. What's the worst that can happen – she tells you to fuck off. Go now, he told himself. I will. He did not move.

Now if she were to talk to me on the other hand... but women do not do that, no matter their confidence. That's the rule. She slowly lifted her bike, its wheels dragging on the sand. Scenes where he had had opportunities and done nothing about them scattered themselves. Valuable seconds slipped away. She turned with a mild shrug, and made to go.

'*Ola,*' he said, the word uncomfortable in his mouth. The wooden discs on the bracelet separated comfortingly and settled reassuringly against his arm.

She stopped the bike and turned. '*Ola.*'

'Do you speak English?'

She shook her head. '*Nada.*'

'Ah… okay. I only know, "*cerveza*" and "*vino blanco*".'

She nodded.

'And "*no entiendo*" is always helpful.' She laughed.

'But… no English at all?'

She shook her head. Ah well. If we can't communicate…

'Okay,' he said, stepping onto his back foot.

Ask for it, he told himself as she turned again and walked her bike to the sea wall. Ask the universe, and the universe will say yes.

'Can I buy you a drink anyway?'

She understood, and smiled as he fell into step alongside. He tried not to watch the rise and fall of her breasts in the tight t-shirt, the triangle of sunned flesh that appeared between jeans and t-shirt on her left hip as her right leg moved forward, and then vice versa.

'What's your name?'

'Bella.'

'I'm Hector.'

'Ector?'

'Hector.'

'Ector?'

'That's right.'

She laughed and said something that he loosely and inaccurately translated as 'I get it wrong'.

'No, not at all.'

By the wall the three women he had seen earlier lay on their fronts parallel to each other, facing down towards the sea, sunglasses presenting identical, anonymous, expressionless masks.

'What would you like?' Hector asked as they walked into the bar and it took a moment for their eyes to adjust to the darkness.

'*Cerveza, gracias.*'

'*Dos cervezas, por favor.*'

They sat in an alcove and he took a large mouthful of beer. Bella sipped at hers.

He wondered what to say. He drank another mouthful. This could be harder than it seemed. She smiled encouragingly, holding her bottle in her lap and pulling at the label, which slid around then fell off; she looked at it in surprise and they both laughed.

'It's that temperature,' he said, knowing she would not follow but feeling the need to speak, 'when it's not too cold, and not too warm, the label peels off.'

She nodded, smiled.

'Can you play pool?'

Bella looked at him uncomprehendingly, and he pointed towards the tables. 'Ah.' She shook her head.

'I'll teach you. Would you like to?' One table was busy: an intent couple prowling around each other, a colour and a stripe left and the black lurking dangerously by the corner. The second table was empty, lit enticingly by the overhead canopy. Hector knelt to push coins into the slot, pressed the button and waited while the innards of the table rattled and growled then vomited the balls into the drawer.

Bella studied curiously the particular order in which Hector put the balls into the triangle, taking some out and dropping others in, placing the black carefully in the centre and pushing the triangle forwards briskly then backwards slowly, repeating a couple of times until he found the right place, and finally, with a flourish, lifting the triangle away carefully like removing a stencil from a freshly painted surface.

Dragons

By a process of miming and speaking in English and hoping she would pick some of it up, Hector showed Bella how to play and she grasped it like a child with a new language, impressing the teacher with the speed of her knowledge, the flexibility of how she adapted. He broke off forcefully and she nodded, logging the information for later as she saw how the balls split to corners and one or two loitered on the pockets, teasing with the possibility of dropping and then changing their minds. Taking her first shot she wildly miscued, the cue an unwieldy stick that prodded the ball and shot into space, leaving the cue ball dribbling nowhere near the colour.

Hector paused behind her and held the end of the cue, nudging it towards her splayed fingers and moving it left and right, then central, to show how to keep the cue still and follow it through smoothly, leaving it pointing in the correct direction after striking the ball. She nodded, made knowing noises and issued small, occasional explosions of excited Spanish that he loved hearing and felt that he understood, sort of, not really, as she grinned in surprise when the white came under her control and she developed a feel for pace and position.

He showed her the angles you needed to hit the ball to go into the pocket. 'This is actually the easy bit,' he said, and she understood and colours to her astonishment quickly dropped into the pockets.

'I love this,' she said in hesitant English. And something he loosely translated as, 'why have I never discovered this before?' She potted two more; there was a scrap between them; he potted two as well, then she got a fluke into the corner.

She laughed as he put his arms round her to help, then pushed him away, indicating she knew how to do it now. A thin cut into the middle; she lined the cue up carefully, screwed her eyes up as she aimed it towards

213

the left edge of the ball, hit it too hard and it rattled in the pocket, but dropped. The white bounced round the cushions, ending in perfect position for an easy black; he winced. She potted it; he still had a stripe on the table. He congratulated her and bought a second round of drinks; she knelt as she had watched him do and pushed coins into the slot, collecting the balls from the drawer like she'd been playing it all her life.

The next game they played properly, without him helping her, and he won, but only just. The third, she won with a couple of his colours left on the table. A whoop and a celebratory dance around the table. She kissed him on the mouth, victorious and happy, and the couple on the next table asked them for a game of doubles, and they lost and didn't mind.

Bella bought drinks. Sitting at a table in the corner, she drew the beach on a napkin and a wavy line alongside it; some houses, with windows, one with an arrow pointing to it; then a blob to represent the city, with the river that wasn't a river snaking alongside, the question mark heading towards a point which she tapped with her finger. She said something that he guessed meant 'where are you staying?' and he tried to point on the blob, with about as much accuracy as he felt when walking around the old city.

'*Me lleve a cabo esta noche,*' she said. He didn't understand. She touched her t-shirt, then his, and made a walking motion towards the blob on the map. She pointed to the amorphous representation that could be a hotel or a bar. '*Si*, that would be great, what's the word, *gracias*.'

She laughed. 'I like your speaking.'

Darkening sky; emptying beach. Sunglasses back on. A white haze rolled across the sand. A minor sandstorm, the waves black and choppy in the distance. People stood, shaking their beach towels out and wrapping themselves in; holding hats tightly as they flapped about, some blowing away towards and above the sea wall. The bikini women departed like three Graces, giggling and arguing with each other as they went, bottoms swaying provocatively. The sun declined, slowly, unwillingly.

'Come,' Bella said, holding Hector's hand and tugging him along an alley where the squall became a roaring, twisting wind tunnel. On the far side of the buildings they were protected from the wind. She crossed the road and he followed her to the deserted metro stop, the end of the new line that had been built for the Americas Cup.

The metro hugged the streets on the overland part of the journey, the houses and shops sliding past. Bella sat contentedly opposite, hands in her lap, looking at him, enjoying the silence. Emerging blinking into the hot light of the main square, he knew the way now and held her hand as they weaved through traffic.

Drinks. There was nothing to say. She was inevitable. They were drunk. An encouraging smile that he couldn't help basking in. Not quite touching her skin.

Bella played with the bracelet on his naked arm. '*Mi caro*,' she said in a repeating, circular way as they moved without him noticing and suddenly she was kneeling across him, cool palms flat on his chest. '*Mi caro*.' She spoke until his head was filled with a chatter he couldn't decipher, all vowels and feminine endings flowing over his face like the tide, then she was silent and closed her eyes and the gulf of communication between them was like the view from the beach, sand contrasting with sea, nuzzling against the shores and never being able to understand each other.

'*Habla conmigo.*' The sheets were cool and damp with sweat, ghostly half-images of their bodies, the coverings pushed into rumpled clouds at the foot. What do I say, he wondered. And does it matter. He told her that Sally was meant to be here with him, but they were always arguing about anything and everything and whatever she said he had to pick holes in, and vice versa, and it was never going to work, so it was best that they'd ended it when they did.

Bella spoke, long and complicated. He nodded and looked confused and she tried phrasing it in different ways, staring towards the window for inspiration. Eventually she wrote on a piece of paper. He looked at her breasts heavy on her knees as she formed the letters carefully in a large looping hand, and it was the following day at breakfast, not noticing the empty chair in front of him, that he laboriously translated it as 'you come to see me again?'

Her number was underneath. For most of the day he saw and did not see the stone and the elegant architecture and the reddish sky, and the smell of coffee and the sound of bells and pigeons, and rang the number in the afternoon, and there was a sound that he assumed was an error in connection. He tried again in the evening and again the next day, and got the same sound. He rotated the bracelet on his arm and looked at it thoughtfully.

IV

The Museum of Intelligence. Having walked round most of the exterior of the concrete box, Hector decided he was in need of its wisdom because he couldn't find the door. Eventually he spotted a raised walkway that led towards a small glass entrance.

A paradoxical sense of moving from inside to outside, as the dry and dusty exterior transformed into a lush, grassed patio. He was surrounded by two-dimensional cows in different colours, bright pinks and greens and blues. They grazed peacefully, ignoring him. Ahead a vast glass wall, stretching so high that the natural light emphasised his sense of being outside; no ceiling was visible unless you craned upwards.

In the centre of this oasis a woman sat stranded behind an information desk. By a Japanese couple intent on vast leaflets, she pointed in different directions before returning to a default position caused by the high stool she was perched on, hands gripping the edge of the desk in case she fell at any moment to the thin layer of grass.

Doors led from the main space but none of them opened or led anywhere. Hector looked at a plan which stated that the exhibitions were on the top floor. There was a glass-fronted lift, ascending slowly into the roof forty feet or so above. A long queue waited at the bottom, so he found a staircase which went up one flight and then stopped at a brick wall.

He went back down the steps and asked the lady balancing on her stool, '*questos los*, er, the… um… *planos*?' Hector asked.

'It's okay, I speak English.'

'Great. I just wondered how I get in?'

'Yes, mostly we take the lift, over there.'

He glanced towards said lift, which at that moment gracefully arrived. The doors opened and four people got out. Four more squeezed in, leaving a queue of ten or so people left. Slowly, the lift moved upwards.

'Are there no stairs?'

'Not really, no. The stairs are owned by other people.'

'Ah.'

'If you're frightened of the lift…' she looked at him sympathetically.

'No it's not that, it's just I thought it might be quicker. Don't worry.'

'You're welcome.'

Hector joined the queue. The lift descended. Four people replaced the four inside. It ascended, came back. Hector drifted into Bella's bed, and stayed there for a few hours. The lift went up. The lift came down. Hector got in with three other people.

The lift juddered upwards, the floor dropping away and taking Hector's stomach with it. He pressed against the glass. The people below were eggs on the grass as Hector watched from twenty, thirty, forty feet. When the lift lurched to a halt it felt like it would tip forwards. The door opened onto a concrete square with a pink mat, and pictures of the top of the Eiffel Tower. Doors led in unknown directions.

Confused individuals milled about, including a couple who Hector initially thought were exhibits. The man wore a large straw hat, gaudy Hawaiian shirt and shorts so baggy they flapped despite there being no breeze. His white, hairy legs ended in beige socks and sandals and he clutched a large open map. His wife wore sunglasses, a billowing, flowery dress and tightly clutched a handbag as if fearing it was about to be snatched. The man gave Hector an encouraging, eyebrow-raising smile as Hector pushed at one of the doors. 'Good luck,' he said in a broad southern American accent. As the door opened a hand reached out and blocked Hector's path.

'Billet.'

'Sorry?'

'You are English?'

'Yes.'

'Ticket.'

'Ticket?'

The man looked at him blankly. It was traumatic for him to go through this so many times per hour, but he was a professional. 'Ticket.' He could say it in nine other languages too.

'But it's free,' Hector said.

'Yes. Ticket.'

'It's free.'

'Museum is free. Special exhibition, ticket.'

'So you pay for the special exhibition…?'

'No. It's free.'

'But if it's free, why do I need a –'

The man pointed to the lift. 'You can get a free ticket from the desk at the bottom.'

By the lift, a queue of five or six people waited, gaping into the blank space behind the glass doors.

'There's a queue for the lift. And there'll be a queue back up again.'

'What?' He frowned uncomprehendingly.

'Can't you just let me in? I mean if it's free, I don't need a –'

The man pressed a button on his radio, and a far door opened to reveal two larger men in uniforms. They walked towards Hector, hips rolling.

In the queue for the lift Hector was joined by the American couple. 'We had the same problem,' the man said. 'Baz.' He held out a large fat hand and Hector's fingers disappeared inside it. 'Teri,' said his wife. 'I can't think why they wouldn't let us in. We even offered them money.'

They got in the lift and Hector tried to avoid the view of the dizzying drop. The lift remained suspended for a moment, as if not sure which direction to go in, if any, then fell. A vivid childhood memory of Charlie after he had left his chocolate factory, and disappeared into the great glass elevator.

A ghostly Hector stepped aside from the real one and pressed all the buttons behind Baz, who resembled a portly Willy Wonka. The lift lurched upwards, smashed through the roof of the museum and twisted and turned in the air above Valencia. They looked down on the city with its green riverbed now clearly visible, and the broken roof of the museum revealed its mysterious secrets of intelligence, and everything made sense. The real Hector stood while the lift travelled and the glass doors slid open.

Six visitors waited, their faces carrying the glazed look of having tramped around an unknown city for the morning, and only half-wondering what they were doing here. 'I hope you've got your tickets,' Hector said, but they looked uncomprehending, shuffling forward as the front four got in the lift.

'I love the architecture of this place,' Baz said. 'It's as if it's been, I don't know, pulled inside out.' They went to the desk, where the woman carefully put a leather bookmark inside her book and laid it on the counter. 'Can we buy tickets?'

'You don't need to buy tickets. It's free.'

'I'm going to get some air,' said Hector. 'Nice to meet you.' The outside heat was full and his skin shivered.

End of siesta time, and the shutters on an antique shop leapt up one after another. Its cool exterior was as tempting as ice cream. A cave of bronze, chrome and mahogany beckoned. He listened to the echo of his feet and the sounds of carts rattling on cobbles, distant bikes revving and occasional church bells.

Rooms branched from each other along oval warrens that linked back onto themselves, like a suburb of Alice's wonderland. From its seemingly modest exterior the building had a palace's depths. The silence and pale smell of dust reassured him. In a particularly dark alcove, clocks ticked in competition with each other; hundreds of them, each more ornate and polished than the last. There were boxes, piled up without a clue to their contents. Hector opened one and found more boxes inside. Elsewhere there were small carved wooden boxes; opening these, he saw tiny sealed boxes.

A stuffed parrot guarded them. 'Nice bit of ormolu,' Hector said to the parrot, nodding towards an elegant French mantel clock. Buried amongst the treasure he fished out a chrome desk calendar; the kind of old-fashioned ornament you see in noir films; a curvy, shining body, like a cigarette case hammered and fashioned to a new purpose. It had three canvas scrolls behind the oval windows, the top one displaying the day in a heavy font, the lower one declaring it was November and the middle one a large, curvy seven. Hector rotated a thick chrome knob on the side and the day moved from Thursday through to Tuesday. He moved the middle screen through eighteen, nineteen and twenty, and finally turned November back through October and September, feeling the leaves leap back onto the trees as he did so, until it reached May. Having corrected the date he returned the calendar to its nest of shining objects. It seemed lost though, so he looked for a more prominent place for it. Taking it through various rooms he wondered if he would ever find his way back to the entrance.

In the next room Baz and Teri examined sculptures of animals. An unlikely coincidence perhaps, but then milling tourists tend to end up in the same places, so Hector resisted the urge to find meaning in the encounter. The friendly expressions of surprise over, Baz showed Hector the monkeys, elephants and giraffes that they were thinking of buying. They seemed to be made of junk; bits of old metal, bicycle parts, disembowelled lamps, silver forks and spoons bent into new shapes to create noses and ears. 'Aren't they fabulous?' Baz said, grinning from ear to ear.

'What do you think,' said Teri, looking doe-eyed at the giraffe, who stuck his silver spoon tongue out and gazed mournfully from behind fork-prong eyelashes.

'They're interesting,' Hector said. There was a sort of ox-like thing, a cow with steel scallop shells for ears, a fish made from bits of fish-slice, and horses galloping on knife-handle legs.

'Definitely the monkey,' Teri said, 'and I think the elephant.'

Baz nodded. 'How will you get them home?' Hector asked.

'Oh, we'll find a way. There's always a way.'

Hector was still holding the calendar. He looked underneath and a faded sticker on the purple baize said it was five euros. The owner, an albino who wore glasses that were like binoculars attached to a wiry frame, nodded as he looked at it sadly, then rang the number up on the old till.

'Thank you,' said Hector, handing over his note. The shop keeper tried to see what colour it was, and Hector told him it was a ten. The man gave him his change. 'Good bye English person, good bye.' Later he found large cardboard boxes for the elephant head and the grinning monkey to be gently lowered into, their faces in the changed light appearing fearful as the lids were closed on them. Teri joked that they should punch some holes in the cardboard, and the old man said he would do whatever they want, whatever they want.

V

He was on a square, but it was not the square he intended to be on, or the square that the map, determinedly, told him it was.

An assertive, golden Baroque building dominated and Hector stared at it for a while, in the hope that studying it for long enough would reveal what its purpose was. A church at the side, also Baroque but deferential and knowing its place, its grey stone modest and understated, its lines simpler, dowdier. Its bells chimed apologetically above its open door. Surprising himself, Hector went in.

He stepped over the pronounced lip into a vestibule with blue and white ceramic on the walls, like his grandmother's kitchen. Black and white tiles on the floor, that turned into diamonds and made you feel dizzy if you looked at them for too long, like those pictures of squares that appear to be facing one way, then as you look at them, magically turn the other.

A narrow door, creaking and groaning in the silence as church doors should, led him to a compact nave. It felt like being in a box within boxes. Each alcove was filled with images painted in sober, muted colours, countering Hector's assumptions about Baroque churches. There was very little glitz. The altar and the side panels and a lick of gold on the banisters, but nothing more.

Nor was there any of that dull, Baroque brown, the insipid cheap chocolate that seemed to coat everything that wasn't gold in the eighteenth century. Instead, olives and pale blues. The frescoes were attractive and engaging without demanding attention. A *Last Supper* over the altar, which Hector's guidebook told him was famous, without saying why.

More frescoes covered the inset panels, the gouges sliced from the walls topped with domes. All the spaces between the domes were frescoed too, God abhorring a vacuum as much as nature does. A dragon, nostrils flaring, expression quizzical.

Dragons again. We all know what dragons should look like, yet no one's ever seen one, so how do we know what it 'should' look like? This dragon was wrong. It didn't have splayed feet, its belly wasn't fat enough and its head wasn't quite the right shape. What are we recognising, and how do we know it's wrong? Where does that collective knowledge about dragons come from?

'I could do with a beer,' Hector told it, and it looked mournfully back at him.

Two elderly women loudly settled themselves in the pew opposite, knocking the echoing wood with their shins and handbags, kicking the prayer mats into touch. Both wore wide, thick-rimmed sunglasses, the shades blacker than black. They laboriously put down large, bright yellow bags made of thin card with cord straps, chattering away all the while, their speed of conversation not altered by whether they were looking at each other or not. The tops of the bags gaped open; inside each container were boxes of chocolate.

Hector turned away to look at men in ruffs, bowing courteously to Mary on a donkey. He listened to the sibilant whispering of the two old women getting louder and louder and wondered, why am I here. Thirty or forty feet up, around the domes and indentations of the walls, was a railing with a narrow ledge, just wide enough to walk along. There were two small, dusty doors, where a brave cleric might venture and circumnavigate the perimeter of the ceiling. Hector wondered how long ago anyone had been there.

Shuffling movements seemingly above and around him, although the acoustics made it hard to tell where the noise was coming from. He glanced up and looked round the railing but no one emerged. As more congregation entered, a voice could be heard singing, mostly intoning on or around one note. It seemed to originate in front of him, but the altar and nave remained empty. Perhaps it literally did come out of the air; maybe it was an angel.

A second voice quickly joined the first, singing at a slightly lower pitch. Hector recognised it as Gregorian chanting; or, at least, with his knowledge of Gregorian chanting from adverts, it sounded like Gregorian chanting and so he assumed it was Gregorian chanting. If you don't make these leaps, you realise that we don't actually know anything. If we don't make the leaps, we get bogged down in what we don't know, and stay in the trees, not eating the berries we don't like the look of.

A third voice joined in, then the harmonies and scales became too complex for Hector to tell how many voices there were. It could be six or ten; it might still have been just three. The empty space in front of him, contrasted with the sound now filling the church, needed to be occupied. There was a sense of something about to happen. Did this preface, or presage, a service, Hector wondered; and if so, should he think about leaving?

Ten minutes more chanting followed and Hector was immersed, swimming in the music with no desire to go. The nave filled with incense and the smell, combined with the smoke clouding the altar, made him look for the magician.

The old ladies to his right still whispered but the chanting made their words inaudible. Unconsciously, Hector took off his bracelet and started playing with it. Another old lady appeared, shuffling on surgical stockinged legs.

'*Buenas dias… buenas dias…*' to each member of the congregation, all of whom recognised her and nodded back politely. She paused to bow almost imperceptibly to the altar and said good morning to the two chattering ladies, who broke off their discourse to offer her chocolate. She took one gratefully and stood next to them, chewing patiently, her eyes releasing moisture when she carefully swallowed, as if she had ingested a razor blade.

A pause in the music. As Hector rotated parts of the bracelet between thumb and forefinger, the elastic snapped and the black and brown discs scattered in all directions. Drawing his knees up as coins of wood rolled along the aisles and beneath the pews, Hector remembered playing marbles in church as a child. Seeing how well they rolled on the flagstone floors, he had been unable to resist.

The fifty or sixty parts of the bracelet went their different ways. Some rested against the altar. Some ended up in corners, where they would remain for two or three centuries. One slowed to a halt at the elderly woman's foot, her sturdy boot with its thick surgical stocking looking like it might trip on it at any moment; but she trod on it without noticing, shuffled forward and sat in the pew in front of the chocolate box women. One rolled back up the aisle, where a short man in a green jumper and leather jacket, despite the heat, found it and held it up as if it were money.

One last old lady stepped over the threshold of the door, noticing a bead rolling towards her. She had nervous skin, knotting its veins and puckering apologetically around her eyes, their intelligent blue made pale by the surrounding reddish skin, and as the eyes darted about she bent down nimbly and surprisingly agilely to pick the bead up.

Some of the discs were played with by children who fought over them for a few moments then took it in turns to roll them, build towers with them and pretend they were currency, quickly developing a scene in which a disgruntled customer demanded his money back for poor quality items. The children were silent, but above the music could be heard the occasional loud 'sssh!' from their father, followed some time later by a loud, 'you're annoying everyone!' which echoed round the church in another pause in the music.

One more was trodden on by a sober man in a grey suit, who came in discreetly, bowed in three directions, and flexed his arms; he had a huge watch, bulging underneath the suit sleeve, and he studied it intently for a moment before sitting on his own near the back.

Behind them all stood the American couple, Baz clutching his splayed map, sandals tapping on the flagstones, and Teri in another hideously swirly dress. I guess it's not that much of a coincidence, Hector supposed as they gaped at each other with wide-eyed nods of recognition, Baz nudging Teri in the ribs and pointing, and Hector mouthing that they should say 'Hi' outside, afterwards.

The city's big but it's not infinitely big, it's actually

possible enough that you're going to bump into each other again sooner or later; especially when they are so instantly recognisable. Baz's shirt featured red Hawaiian trees instead of blue ones, and the shorts were green not pink, but they could not be missed in a crowd.

Sometimes I feel I don't even know what my job is, or how I ended up here. I work in the aquarium, he thought, yes that's it; but there's something wrong about that, or if not wrong, then not-quite-right; is that really what I do? The sense of it all going somehow incorrect, just a prickling on the back of the neck, but not knowing what it was that he was doing to create that feeling, nor what to do about it.

You're on holiday, he told himself, you have no complaints, what's the problem? He saw Sally telling him to pull himself together, and he pulled himself together, but it did not make the problem go away. Grow up, she told him, her hair tossing impatiently. She faded into the blues and greens of a woman riding her horse across the mural.

The chanting continued on the empty stage. Abroad is a different country, Hector thought as his brain wandered elsewhere, most of the frontal and logic-processing parts occupied in listening to the music: they do things differently there.

The man in the green jumper walked up the centre of the aisle, his heavy boots echoing on the stone floor. A lull in the music meant his footsteps were audible. At the top he paused, one foot on the altar, and looked up at the *Last Supper* with an 'ah!' He held his arm out, and pointed it in the same direction as Christ, then turned and stood centrally. The harmonics of the chanting became more complex and wreaths of smoke emerged through the cracks in the side-door.

Casually, the man removed a small, sleek gun from his jacket pocket and held it with arms outstretched, palm outwards, the gun shining in his hand as if frozen or varnished. The chanting continued.

This is the moment to ask, Hector thought as time froze to a slow sludge. It was a pinpoint of time that felt like falling into a black hole; inside, you reach the centre in an instant, but anyone watching from a distance would see you suspended forever.

Please, he thought, reaching towards his wrist to discover the bracelet no longer there; please, he said out loud even though he was silent.

The man lifted the gun up in slow motion. No one else noticed, heads down or absorbed in the music. The man's face became Sally. *This is why I left you*, she said.

What does she mean, Hector wondered, as the man put the gun in his mouth. The echo, when it resounded through the church, made the walls shake. The calm expressions of the fresco pilgrims were briefly startled. One singing voice ceased after another. The body fell diagonally across the steps. That looks uncomfortable, Hector thought.

The congregation had no time to panic or even react; they stood or sat in their pews as they had been, looking up at the altar in a mixture of wonder, confusion, disbelief, fear, uncertainty.

We are still here, Hector thought as he followed them out a few moments later, past angels playing lutes in triangles between the arch ribs, their expressions ambiguous, mocking even. A laugh from somewhere, as if underwater. In the vestibule he blinked in the light coming through the chink in the heavy dark door.

On the wall opposite, for some unfathomable reason, a stuffed alligator, blackened through age, grinned inanely.

'We don't know.'
'But why did he do it?'
'We don't know.'

'Who was he?'

'I expect the police will tell us.'

'And the TV people. Look, TV people here already.'

'How do they know? How do they know so quickly?'

'I reckon they have them on standby.'

'But how can they be on standby in exactly the right place?'

'Standby for what?'

'There's a lot of them.'

'What do they do the rest of the time? Is it adverts pays for it, or taxes?'

'One of them's state owned, I don't know which one though.'

'Which is the one with the adverts?'

Almost drugged with thirst, Hector dropped his bag on the floor and the orange rolled out.

'I'd forgotten about you.'

He sat by the fountain, laid the orange on the stone and split it with his thumb. The taste was miraculous. Sally pulled an unimpressed face.

Hector felt surprised, when he looked down at his clothes, that he was not dressed in khaki, there was no pool of blood at his feet, and no one was trying to arrest him. He ate his orange.

Acknowledgements

'The Murder of Dylan Thomas' was a Seren Short Story of the Month and later published in *The Lampeter Review*. 'Fiesta' was first published in *Wales Arts Review*. 'The Thief' and 'The Roll of the Sea' were first published in *The Lonely Crowd*. 'The Woman in the Caves' was first published in *Tales of the Female Perspective* (ChinBeard Books, 2015). 'The Wednesday Ghost' was first published in *A Flock of Shadows* (Parthian, 2015).

THE MISSING WOMAN
and other stories

Carole Burns

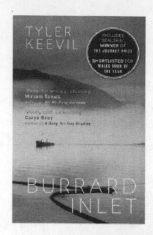

TYLER KEEVIL

INCLUDES 'SEALSKIN', WINNER OF THE JOURNEY PRIZE
SHORTLISTED FOR WALES BOOK OF THE YEAR

Beautiful writing, stunning.
Miriam Toews
Author of *All My Puny Sorrows*

Wisely told, uplifting.
Carys Bray
Author of *A Song for Issy Bradley*

BURRARD INLET

ALL THE PLACES WE LIVED

RICHARD OWAIN ROBERTS

PARTHIAN

Short Stories

SECOND-HAND RAIN

GEORGIA CARYS WILLIAMS

GOLDFISH MEMORY

MONIQUE SCHWITTER

THE SUNDAY TIMES
EFG
SHORT STORY AWARD
shortlisted

Clown's Shoes
STORIES

Rebecca F. John